HONOR Thy THUG

WAHIDA CLARK

CASH MONEY CONTENT

First Trade Paperback Edition: November 2013

Book Layout: Peng Olaguera/ISPN

Cover Design: Nuance Art*

For further information log onto www.CashMoneyContent.com

Library of Congress Control Number: 2012954020

ISBN: 9781936399499 pbk

ISBN: 9781936399390 hardcover

ISBN: 9781936399406 ebook

10 9 8 7 6 5 4 3 2 1

Printed in the United States

HONOR Thy THUG

1

FAHEEM

My heart raced as I stared down at my seven-year-old son's blood-soaked shirt. As his last breath left his body, so did my spirit. I slowly lifted my hand to stroke his little face, and a piercing pain stung my heart. I knew that he was dead. The limpness of his body told me so. But still I refused to believe any different. Warm tears rolled down my cheeks, seeping into my skin. "I can't leave him."

"Fah! Fah! Let's go, man! The hook is on the way! This joint is going to be crawling in a minute, dawg!" I heard my cousin G yell.

His voice shattered off the warehouse walls but hit my ears like a whisper. I couldn't move. I felt my lips moving, but I heard nothing. "My son, man. My son, G." I knew I was saying it over and over.

Thirty-six hours earlier

I dropped my wife, Jaz, and my daughter, Kaeerah, off at the airport. They were headed out to Cali to go visit Tasha. I then

1

scooped up my son's uncle, Wali. I needed him to get the skinny on this nigga, Steele, before my fam from up Jersey arrived. I didn't think I would have to pull my gats back out of retirement because I had considered that chapter of my life closed. But this bitch of a baby mother of mines, Oni, along with her scandalous, crooked-ass, wannabe-gangsta brothers, fucked with the wrong nigga and he in turn fucked with me. Now I had to send for backup.

Oni and her brothers had robbed Steele's people of their coke, meth and a shitload of cash. In retaliation, since Oni and Steele had been fuckin' off and on, this nigga did the unthinkable, he snatched up Lil' Faheem . . . my only son. My seed. So, since I had nothing to do with the caper, my plan was simple: Give Steele his shit back, and get my son; I made Oni and her brothers cough up the bricks and about three hundred grand. They knew if they didn't it would be over for them.

When my fam from up north touched down, I spent a couple of hours filling them in on what all had gone down and what was about to go down. We were holdin' and ready to get to what used to be one of Atlanta's hot spots, an old club called *The Mix*, which was off of Candler Road. At one point in time it was the place to be.

I looked over at my cousins G and Snell and said, "Our main objective is my son's safety. All I want to do is get him outta there. I ain't got no beef with these niggas. So none of that *we go in shootin' ask questions later bullshit*." It sounded good being said, I was just praying that's how it would go down.

"C'mon, nigga. You know we got you, Fah. That's why you got us down here," my cousin G said with his usual air of cockiness.

"Once little man is out the way, then if them niggas look wrong, I'ma push them melons back. Real talk."

I checked my gat one last time. "Time to roll." I had G riding shotgun, Snell and Wali's punk ass was in the back. The *only* reason I allowed the nigga to roll was because Steele wouldn't meet with us unless at least one of them muthafuckas who stole from him was present. Me personally? I wanted all of Oni's brothers to come, because I had planned to dead them all. And this would have been the perfect time and place to do it. But for now, Wali would have to do. Today would be his last day breathing.

After about twenty minutes, we pulled into the parking lot. "This it?" G sounded disappointed. I don't know what he was expecting. "This shit look abandoned."

"It's closed down. Them niggas just use it as a hang out spot and a place to conduct business." Wali told us.

I pulled around the back of the club. Wali had already told me that if something went down, there were only two exits. One in the front and one in the back. So I decided to park in the back, while hoping that my gut instinct was right. I pulled up next to a black Suburban, the only car there. I assumed that our guests were already inside. I deaded the engine. We got out and met at the trunk of my ride, looking around the deserted lot for anything or anybody out of place. Satisfied, I then checked out the three duffels one last time and slammed the trunk shut. I kept the one with the cash and gave Snell the other two with the bricks. One had coke, the other meth. G was the firepower. We headed to the back door, and there was two niggas standing in the cut, obviously waiting on our arrival and clockin' our every move.

"Spyder, what up, nigga?" This nigga had a long neck and was skinny as a bean pole. Wali greeted him as if he was a regular there and we were enjoying an evening out on the town.

Spyder hawked and spit in Wali's face. To my surprise, Wali was cool. He wiped his face with the back of his hand, smiled, and said, "I see somebody ain't get no pussy last night."

Spyder then anxiously grabbed the duffel bags and checked their contents. No one bothered to pat us down. *Red flag.* Gratified, he led the way, while his partner, who looked like a linebacker, took up the rear. My heart was racing. I was anxious to start bustin' niggas right then and there. But I knew I had to be cool until I got my little man out of harm's way.

When we got inside the old club, there was this faggot muthafucka, Steele waiting on us, mugged up. Wali did good with his description. He was tall, thin, with sharp, cold eyes. As soon as he spotted Wali, he stood and swiftly drew a shiny Heckler and Koch, one of my favorites, and shot Wali in the leg. *Fuck.* Everyone drew their weapons. This nigga was precise and I was worried.

Wali stood there screaming, obviously in pain. "Shut up man! You ain't dead." Snell yelled at him.

This nigga Steele then had the nerve to calmly take his seat and was now propped up on a leather sofa like he was a fucking don or some shit. His long black dreads with red tips hung loosely over his shoulders. The image of him toking a cigar vexed me as much as the smoke that clouded the room. *My son.* I had to stay focused. *I was here to get my son*, I reminded myself.

"You can relax your weapons. Just know that I ain't done with that scum." His muscle lowered their weapons, then myself, followed by G and Snell. Wali was still wailing in pain.

"Aiight, we here. I got your shit, now where is my son?" There was no need for formalities.

"Who the fuck is you?" Steele sneered while mean-mugging me as if I gave a fuck. He knew who I was.

"I'm a monster. But today, I come as a father. I just want what belongs to me, my son. And in exchange I'm giving you back what belongs to you," I said as I patted the duffel bag I was holding and nodded to the two Snell had.

"Oh yeah. I heard about you." He looked at me with contempt. "Let me see what y'all working with."

"They already checked the bags at the door. Let me see my son. Your shit is all there."

The nigga took a minute to size up the situation, and then nodded at the linebacker. There was a door behind him, and when he opened it, a chick came out with my son. He was blindfolded, and they had his hands taped together in front of him. It took everything within my power to not lose control.

"Aiight, you see him, now pass over what belongs to me," Steele barked.

My nostrils flared up. I took a deep breath, and then unzipped the bag so that he could see the cash. Snell did the same thing.

"I didn't say show it to me. I said pass what belongs to me over here."

I didn't know who the fuck this nigga thought I was, but I wasn't new to this shit. "Nah, nigga, same time."

"Dad?" Lil' Faheem called out, and my knees got weak.

And just as we were getting ready to make the exchange, with shit already tense, Wali's bitch ass starts to yell. "Y'all niggas are clowns, taking kids and shit!"

Steele rose to his feet, yelling, "Muthafucka, you and that bitch violated me. Do you realize how lucky you are to be breathing right now? You, your sister, and your brothers! You know how much money y'all cost me?"

"Fuck you, nigga!" Wali spat.

This time I pulled out my gat and pressed it against Wali's temple. "You ho ass nigga. Will you shut the fuck up! This nigga got my fucking kid! Are you out of your fucking mind?" I gritted.

"Faheem, fuck that pussy. That's why we took his shit! If it wasn't my nephew, he wouldn't have gotten shit back!"

What did he say that for? The Heckler and Koch reared its ugly head again and this time, Steele shot Wali right in the middle of his forehead. I knew he was dead before his body hit the cold concrete. I jumped back right on time. G was a little late because he got splashed with brains and blood.

"Uncle Wali!" Lil' Faheem yelled out. The broad wouldn't let him go as he squirmed to get away.

Steele and his cronies started laughing.

There was nothing funny to me. And, that was the last straw because that's when my son cried out, "Daddy! Help me! Daddy!" At that point, it was over for me. I lost it.

"Hold the fuck up! Can we finish this business? I am here for my son!" I yelled at the top of my lungs. I must have made the muthafuckin' concrete shake, because niggas got quiet, real quick. "Now, look. I ain't got no beef with you, man. I ain't got shit to do with what they took from you. If you want to kill the whole damn family, you got my blessing. Shit, I was planning on doing them myself. But right now, the only thing I'm concerned with is my son. If it wasn't for him, I wouldn't even be here."

Steele stood there taking in what I was saying. Finally, he asked, "How I know you weren't down with them?"

"I never heard your name until a few days ago. I don't run with them, you know that."

Steele placed his finger up to his lips as he studied me. Then he said, "Dig, if I ever find out that you was with these muthafuckas, I'ma give you what he got." He glared at me. "Now, set my shit on the table." Me and Snell picked up the bags and did what we were told. "And you!" He pointed to the girl. "Release his son."

They took the blindfold off and shoved Lil' Faheem towards me with the force of a professional wrestler. Once I got him in my arms, I breathed a sigh of relief but I was still tense as fuck. Then I heard, "That nigga about to start poppin' shit off!" *Who?* Next thing I knew we were in the middle of a real gun fight. As bullets started flying, I felt a hot slug pierce my shoulder, and I flew backward damn near tumbling over a table. With a burning sensation enflaming my shoulder until it was virtually numb, I managed to muster the strength to squeeze my gat and let off a few rounds. The sound of bullets merged with the rapid fire of loud claps consumed the atmosphere. Then I hit the ground, covering my little man with my body and I could see niggas ducking and sparks flying through clouds of gun smoke.

When the smoke cleared, I rolled off of Lil' Faheem onto my back. The pain in my shoulder wouldn't let me move. My ears were ringing. I stared up at the ceiling for a minute. "You alright, lil' man? Daddy's here for you." I felt for his hand as I looked around to see who was standing and who wasn't.

"Fah, you aiight, nigga?" I heard Snell ask as he made his way over to where I was.

"Who started poppin' off first? And did we dead all of them muthafuckas?" That's what I really wanted to know.

"Spyder is down, but Steele and the bitch got away. They got the bags."

"Fuck them bags! We gotta get out of here. I'm hit in my shoulder. Help me up so I can get little man in the car." When I looked down at my son, my worst fear had surfaced. He was bleeding from a wound in his head, and his body was limp. I started calling him and shaking his arm. "Faheem. Faheem. Get up! Daddy's here, and he's not going to let anyone else take you away from him." I tilted his head back and tried to give him mouth-to-mouth, but deep down, I knew it was too late.

"He gone, Fah. We got to get the fuck outta here," G said as he bent down and gently placed his hand on my shoulder.

"Get the fuck off me!" Tears came to my eyes as I tried one more time to give him mouth to mouth. I grabbed him and lifted his body to mines. I wanted him to hear my heart cry for him.

"Dawg, the hook is on the way. Come on, let's get him in the car. We gotta get the fuck outta here. Let me take him," my cousin tried to convince me once again. I was fucked up, and nothing he said made sense, and I wasn't trying to hear nothing he had to say. My son was dead. No parent should ever have to experience this feeling. I only needed to feel the last of the warmth left in his body. Vomit threatened to spill out of me. I knew right then and there I would never be the same. It was over for Oni and her whole damn family. I couldn't help but wonder if this was the karma coming back to me, from all of the families I made cry during my career in the streets.

"Fah, the hook will be here. What you wanna do?" G asked me.

I didn't give a fuck if he said the police was behind me. At the moment nothing in this world mattered to me. My son, my *only* son lay dead. And for what? His bitch of a mother and her ho ass brothers. I weighed my options as the faint sounds of the sirens whispered at a distance. The warehouse was dark, cold, and filled with the smell of gunfire. It felt as if the walls were closing in on me. I couldn't think straight.

"My son, G. They shot my son." I squeezed him tighter, wishing I could turn back the hands of time. I hadn't even gotten used to the idea of having a son, and now he was dead. Hell, I just met him no more than four months ago, and just like that . . . he was gone. I did a lot of things in my life, but never in a million years would I have thought that the ultimate sacrifice would be the life of my child. My only son, who I didn't even get the chance to know. I hadn't even learned all of his favorite foods or if he had bad dreams in the middle of the night. Did I tell him that I was going to be the best father that I could possibly be? He was just getting used to me being a part of his life. All I could think was I didn't get to tell him how much I loved him. I wouldn't get to teach him how to drive, talk about girls . . . damn, I felt cheated. At that very moment, I wanted to die right with him. But I knew I would never be able to savor the sweet taste of revenge. That was more important to me.

Snell was standing over me, his face wet with sweat and tears, the wrinkle in his brow reflecting the urgency in his voice. He was now begging me to leave. Impatiently, he rushed back and forth from the front door and back to where Lil' Faheem and I were lying. "Believe me, man, I understand how you feel. I swear, I know your pain. You already know I've been there when I lost my daughter. But Fah, the hook is coming and ain't no way we gonna be able to explain all this fire and these dead muthafuckas in here, including lil' Fah. They ain't going to be trying to hear shit!" Snell was trying his best to reason with me.

For real, what he really wanted to say was, "Nigga I ain't trying to go to jail!" I appreciated his loyalty and would remember that.

"Nigga, I got this. Ain't no sense in all of us dealing with this shit. Y'all go ahead and bounce."

"Can't do—"

"Snell! Y'all just go," My voice cracked. I looked him in the eye. "This is my battle. I got it from here. You and G go. Call Jaz and tell her I need her and to get here. Don't tell her shit else but to get here, now."

I looked around at the dead bodies and then back at my son.

"Make sure the strap Wali had is still on him. But grab up ours." I kicked the one I had away from me. "I got this. I know what to tell them. Go!" I scanned the room and there was a lot of bloodshed. Half of the people that were alive an hour ago laid sprawled out on the concrete floor, dead.

They scrambled around collecting our straps and then were out the back door. I had to pull myself together. If they didn't get out now, we all would be fucked. I went back to hugging my son while getting my story together. The pain of having Lil' Faheem's lifeless body in my arms filled my body with sorrow and rage. I swore on everything I loved . . . I was going to make everyone involved suffer before I killed them.

KYRA

I was on pins and needles. The address on the front door matched the one on my driver's license. I peeked through the windows and the house was completely empty. I jotted down the realtor's number off of the *For Sale* sign in the front yard.

I was told that I used to live here. When Nurse Wright at the hospital dug into my background this was my last known address. But seeing it didn't jar my memory at all. Maybe the real estate agent, Jordan Brown, would be able to give me some answers.

"Excuse me, lady. Do you want me to take you somewhere else?" the impatient cabbie asked me.

"Yes. Give me a couple of minutes." I walked around to the backyard, desperate to remember something. Whoever lived here hadn't in a while, according to the height of the weeds. Nothing registered. Nothing looked familiar. I headed up front.

"Are you ready?" the driver asked me. He saw that I was looking over at the neighbor's house.

"I'm ready." Disappointed, I got back into the cab.

He wasted no time pulling off.

We headed for the address that was listed for my emergency contact, Tasha Macklin. I said a quick prayer, asking that if her house was empty and up for sale, I would have the strength to handle it and God would tell me what to do next. Because if no one lived there, or I couldn't get answers, I'd be shit out of luck. And then the only thing left would be to call Nurse Wright. Something I didn't want to do. She was my nurse throughout the months I was in the coma, and had taken a liking to me. She was there with me when I came out of it and all during my rehab. After I completed rehab, I was given a clean bill of health, but she didn't want me to travel back here alone. I insisted. I felt that I had to start somewhere. If I was going to reclaim my life, I had to do it on my own. And I was determined to regain it all back. Stuck in the cab for what felt like an hour, I was hoping that I had the right address. It was taking forever for us to reach my next destination.

"Excuse me." I leaned up and boldly tapped the cabbie on his shoulder. I asked, "Are you going the right way?"

"Yes, ma'am, I am. According to the GPS, we are one and a half miles away."

I was glad to hear that. I sat back in the seat. My stomach swirled as if I was upside down on a rollercoaster. It was threatening to release everything I had eaten for lunch. I peeked up at his GPS and saw that we were now less than a mile away. We made a left turn, and the houses were getting bigger and bigger. Everyone was trying to outdo one another.

"O.J. used to live in this neighborhood." The cab driver stated with pride.

I guess the cabbie decided to turn into a tour guide at the last minute. But I didn't care about O.J. or the fact that all of a sudden he was trying to be friendly. I had my fingers crossed, hoping that a For Sale sign was nowhere to be found. I felt the vehicle slow down, and then it came to a stop. My eyes scanned the property and its surroundings. Thank God, somebody did live here and hopefully it was who I was looking for. Toys were tossed around on the freshly manicured lawn, and it was quiet, except for the faint whisper of an airplane high up in the sky.

"Thank you," I told the cabbie, and paid him his fare.

"Ma'am, would you like for me to wait?" Now all of a sudden he wasn't in a hurry.

"No. I think I'll be all right here."

"Well, just in case, here's my card if you need me to come back."

I took it from him, grabbed my purse, and got out. I was sick of riding. I had that bumpy plane ride from Phoenix. And then the long ride in the cab. I was hungry and ready to unpack and get comfortable. But even more anxious to meet Tasha Macklin. The words on the mailbox read "The Macklins." So . . . this was it. I was at the right place. I waited impatiently as the cabbie took my two bags out of the trunk, jumped back into his ride, and pulled off. He was out of sight before I sucked in a deep breath, picked up my belongings, and trudged up the walkway, forgetting about my hunger pangs but getting more excited with each step I took. A smile spread across my face. I was close and I could feel it. I reached the front door and set my bags down. My stomach was churning. I rang the doorbell. I rang it again and again and again.

No one answered.

RICK

I didn't realize how much I missed California. The pace. The palm trees. The L.A. streets. The weather. I deeply inhaled the L.A. air and reminisced about the days I used to wreak havoc on this city. Denzel Washington, *Training Day* style. Being here had me feeling rejuvenated. I pulled over and called my woman, Nina and told her that I wished I would have brought her with me and that we had to talk about relocating out here.

"I'm having my baby right here in Arizona, Rick. Not California," she snapped.

"Baby, what difference does it make?" I tried to reason with her before I figured out I was wasting my time. "Look, we'll talk about it when I get back." I hung up, thinking, *Arizona? California? What the fuck difference does it make? Women.*

Speaking of which, I had finally pulled up in front of my ex-wife's house. I scanned the area. Being a detective, I know how much people are creatures of habit, and she was no exception to the rule. I rang the bell and knocked, but she didn't answer the door. I went around back for the spare key, and sure enough, it was in the same spot, down in the flower pot.

I went inside and did a walkthrough. Surprisingly, I didn't get nostalgic. Most likely because she'd made sure it never felt like home to me in the first damn place. Everything that I remembered was gone. Everything was new. She had stripped the damn place. Stripped it of anything that had to do with me. Nothing was the same.

When I went upstairs to her bedroom, I went straight to the closet to see what kind of man she had stuck her claws into. Whoever he was, I felt sorry for the muthafucka. But to my surprise, both closets were full of nothing but women's clothes. I looked down at the shoes, and it was the same scenario, all women's stuff.

I walked over to the dresser, and she still had the picture of me and her at her sister's wedding. The rest of the pictures were of her and a dark-skinned sister with a mole on her chin. In some of the pictures, they were hugged up; in others, they were out to dinner or in the backyard. Wait a minute! She must be gay with all of these pics with the same broad. I gots to be one hell of a nigga, if I can make a bitch switch sides. But then I thought, what if she was gay while we were together? Then the joke was on me. *Ain't that some shit!*

Hell, I needed a drink. I left her bedroom and went downstairs to pour myself a stiff one. I made myself comfortable and ended up having two. As I sat on the sofa, I thought about how when I passed Trae's house, just down the street, I was scared to stop. Me. Muthafuckin' King Rick wasn't scared of anything know what I would say. Trae was my man and we were still cool before I had to get ghost. It's not like I did him dirty and left on bad terms like

I did with countless other muthafuckas. The truth was, I wasn't sure how he and Tasha would treat me since I was responsible for Kyra's death . . . in a way. *Fuck it!* I needed to man up and get the shit over with. I had to stop by there. That's why I came out here. I could hope he would hear me out. If not, at least I could say that I tried and take my ass back home. I needed closure. But either way, it felt so good to be back in L.A., the City of Angels. California. I got up, leaving the same way I came in. Made it to my ride, turned back for the last time, and looked at where I used to live, shaking off the memories.

"Rick? Is that you?" It was Mrs. Singer, my old, nosy ass neighbor. Some things never change.

I didn't even bother answering. Let her figure it out. I started the car and headed down my old block. Slowing down in front of Trae's, I noticed that there was someone sitting on his porch. She had her head in her lap, a little chick. It felt as if I'd seen this girl before. I threw my ride in park, turned it off and jumped out. Her head popped up and she was up and on her feet as I walked towards her.

"Excuse me. Do you live here?" she asked me. "I'm looking for Tasha Macklin."

Her voice went right through me. My heartbeat started racing. My mouth turned dry. I rushed up the walkway. But it couldn't be. I stood there face-to-face with . . . her. I wanted to turn my back toward her before a tear fell, but I couldn't. I couldn't take my eyes off of her.

"Do you live here?" she asked again, placing her hand on her hip.

I wanted to open my mouth to answer, but . . . how could this be? Finally, I asked her, "Kyra, is that you?"

She cracked a smile. "Do you know me?"

The sound of her voice made my heart race. Now I was scared for real. But she looked so different. "You don't remember me?" I asked her.

"Do you know me?" she asked again.

We stood there staring at each other for what felt like an eternity. This was not happening. I mean, what were the fuckin' odds? I didn't want to believe it was her. The dreads were telling me it wasn't her. But the scar. I could see the scar. She was shot. I had seen countless gunshot wounds. That's when I knew. Those eyes. I would never forget them. It was really her. My eyes again welled up with tears. "I didn't kill her," I whispered.

She reached out and wiped my tears with her thumbs. I kissed her hand. She was trembling. "Are you okay?" She tilted her head to the side. She stared at me with a little more intensity. Finally she said, "Rick?" She kept repeating my name. "Rick?" Tears were rolling down her cheeks. She hugged herself as she backed up. "Rick. Your name is Rick. I remember you." All of the color drained from her face.

And then she fainted.

I caught her just in time. My heart beat a mile a minute as I picked Kyra up from the porch and took her to my car. It felt as if I was performing a kidnapping. My palms were sweaty, and my adrenaline was high. Moving as if I was robbing a dope boy's stash house, I held onto her for dear life, opened the car door, and lay her across the backseat. My cell rang, and the ringtone let me know that it was my fiancée, Nina.

Immediately, guilt set in. "Shit," I spat. Now I was feeling like I was caught cheating, which urged me to take the call. "Nina, baby. I'm in the middle of something. Can I call you back? Is everybody okay?"

Silence lingered on the other end. Then she finally asked, "Is everything okay with you?" She was sounding as if she sensed that I was up to something.

"Everything's fine. Let me call you later." I hung up before she could say anything. I didn't want this moment to be ruined. I wanted her all to myself. I rushed back to the front porch and got Kyra's things. She had two suitcases, a purse, and a shoulder bag. I popped the trunk, tossed everything inside, slammed it shut, and jumped into the front seat. Cranking the engine, I took a deep breath and then turned to take another look at Kyra. My mind and my eyes were at odds with each other. There she lay, just as beautiful as she was the last time that I saw her. Then the loud voice inside me yelled "*She's alive!*" I couldn't believe this was happening. The woman I fell in love with, the woman I thought was dead and buried by her dope-fiend-ass husband, but here she was alive and in the flesh. My mouth filled with saliva, and my hands began to sweat. I turned and gripped the steering wheel as I pulled off, heading for the hotel where I was staying.

KYRA

I was dreaming that I was riding in a car. However, when I opened my eyes, I actually was. *How did I get here?* The last thing I remembered was looking for Tasha Macklin and then standing on the porch in front of Rick. I had recognized him. Tears were streaming down his cheeks and then everything went black. But now my head was pounding. It was hurting so bad that I kept swallowing to keep from throwing up. "My head," I moaned out loud, closing and squeezing my eyelids together as if that would stop the pain.

As soon as I did, the car stopped and jerked forward, damn near throwing me off the backseat. I sat up in a panic. The next thing I knew, the back door opened, and this beautiful specimen of a man leaned in and asked if I was all right, and should he take me to the hospital. I looked at him and felt my face frown up.

"Relax, it's me, Rick," he said.

I studied his face. "I know who you are. But is it really you? If it is then I'm Kyra. We dated."

"Yeah, it's me, and yes, you are Kyra and we didn't just date we were in love." He hugged me gently, as if I was too fragile for a real embrace. "I'ma get you to a hospital real—"

"No! Please, no more hospitals!" I grabbed his arm tight, causing him to pause. "Do you have any idea how long I've been in the hospital? I was in a coma for months and then in rehab for more months, and I couldn't and still can't remember who I was or how I got there. So please no more hospitals."

"Okay, okay. Relax. Do you realize that you fainted back there?"

"I just need something for my head. It's pounding from the fatigue and all of this excitement." Just as quickly as he was in the backseat asking if I was all right, he was back up in the front seat and pulling off. I had to lie back down.

We drove for a few minutes before the car stopped again. I pressed a hand on each side of my head as if that would make the pain go away. Rick jumped out, and after several minutes, he came back with some milk, cookies, and a bottle of Tylenol for migraines. He helped me sit up.

"You can't take these on an empty stomach." He opened the cookies and gave me two of them. I gobbled them down. He opened the carton of milk and held it to my mouth as if I was a baby. He then opened the pill bottle and shook two out into my hand. I swallowed them and drank some more milk, and then Rick motioned for me to lie back down. I did, because I badly wanted the headache to go away. It hurt to even think. I wondered if the headache was from me fainting or from the excitement of being possibly reunited with my family. "I'm taking you to a place where you can relax." He left me alone and got back into the front seat.

The car started moving again, and my thoughts were moving even faster. I was remembering people, places, and things. Now my chest was tightening up, making it hard for me to breathe. Visions and parts of my memory came flooding back. The doctors told me that if I saw something or somebody familiar, it would trigger certain events. *My baby!* I popped up. My baby daughter, Aisha Aaliyah. My heart raced. *Where is she?* I began rubbing my temples. *Rick.* I remembered creeping around 'with him while I was still loving . . . *Marvin.* And Marvin? *Where is Marvin?* I was now gasping for air. More flashes of events and faces began to crowd my head. There was a gun pressed up against my temple. *Mook.* I could still feel the cold steel against my face and the smell of alcohol on his breath. I remember screaming at Marvin to give that nigga the money and to stop haggling with him. Then Marvin shot Junie and yelled for me to put the car in reverse. I did, slamming on the gas and crashing into the car behind me. That was when Fish jumped out, shot Mook, and then shot me. The events came to me crystal-clear. It was night time and my daughter was in the back seat. I was petrified.

"If you want your wife, I suggest you give me my muthafuckin' dough right now," Mook said.

"Mook, get that fuckin' burner away from my wife," Marvin warned him.

"I'm telling you, Blue, he's going to split her wig. Just give me my dough. You owe me, remember?" Junie spat.

"I don't owe you shit, nigga! That was years ago. And here you are pressin' me about some fuckin' chump change? Why you pressin' me about that shit?" Marvin asked his cousin Junie.

"Stop haggling, Marvin. Just give the nigga the money," I blurted out, and slid him his burner.

"Listen to your wife," Junie said.

"Babygirl, these pussies ain't going to shoot nobody, not like I will." Pow! Marvin shot Junie in the stomach.

"See. That's how you do that. I didn't even have to get out," Marvin bragged. "Put the car in reverse, babygirl, and let's get the fuck out of here."

As soon as he said that, Fish jumped out of the ride behind us and started waving at us.

"Hold up, babygirl." Marvin told me. He then hopped out.

Fish snatched the gun out of Mook's hand and put a bullet in his head. I remember the BOOM! making my ears ring. "Pussy muthafucka." He clenched his teeth as he watched him slump to the ground.

Marvin started laughing. "Fish, nigga, where did you get these pussy muthafuckas from?"

He shrugged. "That's what happens when you send a boy to do a man's job." Fish pointed his gun at me and let one off. All I heard was . . . BOOM!

I could hear, but I couldn't move. Aisha! My baby! The last thing I remembered was hearing my daughter saying, "Daddy, we can't leave Mommy."

The anguish from all the memories overwhelmed me. I brought my hands to my face and cried. I was excited that I was remembering. But my daughter . . . Marvin left me? My stomach knotted up, and I couldn't hold back the tears. "He left me!" I screamed out.

"Kyra!" I heard Rick yell from the front seat. "Are you okay?"

"He . . ." I felt dizzy, and then everything went black again.

KYRON

I woke up to my brother and Trae staring in my face. These two pussy muthafuckas were standing at the end of my hospital bed with rocks in their jaws. I was disappointed in both of these niggas. I didn't know who these muthafuckas were anymore. Mad niggas were telling me that they were all wifed up and shit, crying about gettin' out of the game. Get out? I reminded those fools that we used to fuck the shit outta New York, raw. It was *me* who gave their lil' asses the muthafuckin' keys to this city. It was *me* who hooked them up with a connect that set them up for life. It was *me* who did a bid for these two pussies and got outta prison thinking we were gonna be out here makin' this paper, and what did I get? Knifed up over some pussy? And did my own brother have my fuckin' back? Hell, no! Since when was this a part of the game? So what if I fucked Trae's bitch, he was supposed to take that shit and keep it moving. Niggas, bitches, wives and girlfriends been getting fucked since the game started. Now niggas want to stand by their vows and shit. My only plan was to take back what was mine . . . the streets of New York. Do these muthafuckas think that my plan is supposed to change because they went soft and shit? Or because the Dons are complaining? Fuck my brother! Fuck Trae! And fuck the Dons. Shit, they ain't the only ones with work around here. I do shit my muthafuckin' way. I can ride solo. I told both of them to get the fuck away from me. I told them that I was no longer ridin' with them.

TRAE

I was glad when Kay got on the elevator and left me to do me. He knows that this shit between me and Kyron is not going to end until one of us was dead. We both knew that Kyron had 90's dreams about taking the streets over once again. That is what is wrong with the majority of these niggas, they come home and think that shit still supposed to be like it was. No matter how many ways we tried to explain to this nigga that snitching is accepted with these new generation wanna-be hustlers, he wasn't hearing it. I saw the greed and excitement in his eyes. Now it was time to put his lights our permanently. I took the five inch blade out of my pocket and went to work, wishing that I could have chopped his head off with an axe. I pulled the knife out of his throat and stood by the bed watching this grimy muthafucka take his last breath. All the while thinking to myself that out of all the lives I took and all the shit I did, not until this very moment had any of it felt justified.

Satisfied with the work I just put in, I went into his bathroom to wash the blood off my hands and my blade. I pulled the ski mask off and stuffed it inside my pocket. I then took off the hoodie, turned it inside out, and put it back on. I smiled at myself in the mirror.

After slipping out of this nigga's hospital room and bypassing the elevators, I entered the stairwell. I rushed down six flights to the second floor and then decided to get on the elevator. Just as I anticipated, when the doors opened, it was full. I stepped on, blending in with the crowd, and as soon as the doors reopened, I made my way out of the main lobby, passing security.

Outside, I started walking down 168th Street, thinking how that last move was done purely on emotion. Never a good thing, but it sure had me on a high. I hopped on the first bus I saw, the M4, and rode for a few blocks, got off, and flagged down a taxi. I gave the driver an address down the street from my apartment building.

Mission accomplished.

After enjoying a long hot shower, I lit a blunt and sat on the couch. I wanted to soak in and enjoy the peace and quiet around me, especially since I knew it was only the lull before the storm. The storm that I brewed up.

I also wanted to bask in my glory for a just a few moments. Old Kyron made Treacherous Trae come back out. That was my own nickname for myself back in the day. Being in the game wasn't easy. I had to take a lot from niggas and I had to give just as much by sending a lot of niggas to where I just sent Kyron. Straight to hell where I was sure that I would see all of them muthafuckas. But no nigga ever got what he didn't deserve. I almost went back down memory lane before Kyron went to jail and we was all out here lil' niggas trying to get it. But fuck that. I looked straight up at the ceiling and tried to think about nothing. But this apartment wouldn't let me. It was too dear to me for many reasons. I looked around my living room. I was attached to this apartment because it held so much history of where I came from and who I am now. That's why I would never sell it. I got this apartment as soon as I started seeing real money. Owning real estate on New York's Park Avenue back in the day let us know that we had arrived. Kay and I used to call this spot "'The Honeycomb.'" I remember how good it felt to get into my bed after weeks of nonstop hustling. We would rest for a day or two, and then we were right back at it. Those were the days.

I laid my head back and stared up at the ceiling. My thoughts drifted back to when I first brought Tasha here. She was the icing on the cake. Kay and I had a rule: No hos allowed. But as soon as I laid eyes on Tasha, I knew she was the one. I knew that she was going to be my wife. I will never forget the euphoria I felt to have snatched her up right when we were on our way out of the game. I was ready to settle down with that special someone who'd make me feel as if all that grindin' and throwing bricks at the penitentiary was well worth it. My baby stepped up to the plate and made me feel just right.

I'll always remember when I got shot, at Angel's wedding, getting out of the hospital and having Tasha nurse me back to health, right here in this very apartment. What used to be my bachelor pad now had tampons under the sink. My weight room was now the kids' bedroom, with bunk beds and Transformer curtains hanging over the windows. *Damn.* Nothing stays the same.

I had dozed off, not knowing how long I was asleep, when somebody woke me by knocking on the door. When the knocking got louder, I sat up, and in walked Kay. He had a key, so why was this nigga knocking as if he was the police?

"Yo, nigga, you slippin' tough," Kay teased.

"I knew ya ass was coming through." I held up the .380 I had tucked under my thigh. "She's never far from me. I keep my bitch close," I teased back.

I knew he would be stopping by, which was one of the reasons I didn't retire in the bedroom. I got up and went to the bathroom to piss, wash my face, and brush my teeth. Wide awake, I was now ready to face the music.

I went back into the living room and glanced at the clock. Three thirty-three in the morning. I sat down and watched Kay walk into the kitchen and come back into the living room with two Heinekens. He passed me one of them as he looked around, smiled, and sat down. I knew he was reminiscing about old times, too. You had to have been rollin' with us to understand what we were feeling. It was a rush to hustle nonstop and have to constantly look over your shoulders. I relit the other half of my blunt, took a few tokes, stood up and passed it to my main nigga.

"So you heard," I said to him as I sat back down. I looked over at him, and he looked tired as hell, as if he had been out in the streets for days. His eyes were bloodshot, and he wore the same clothes from the day before. "Nigga, you dumb. Of course, I heard. Do you know where the fuck I just came from? I'm just leaving the muthafuckin' precinct, a place where I said I was never stepping foot in again. I was one of the last niggas to leave the hospital room, so you know the police had to question me." Kay paused. "Your ass slipped up big time. You did that shit in a public place. You know they got cameras everywhere in a hospital."

"Who did you mention it to?" I was more elated with my deed than caring about some damn hospital cameras.

"Man, they got you on camera, I told you. You on the news. And you know me better than anybody. Who the fuck you *think* I mentioned it to? At the station, I only answered what my attorney, Harry, told me to answer. But you know I had to tell Angel bits and—"

"Damn, my nigga! Why did you have to say shit to her? You know she gonna run and tell Tasha. Tasha needed to hear this shit from me first." Hearing that took some of the fun out of what I did.

"Nigga, I told her not to tell anybody, especially Tasha. And what the fuck do you mean, 'why did I have to say shit to her?' Who do you think answered the door when the police came by? Who do you think called Harry? In your mind, you may think you did, but you ain't pulled off the perfect crime. Not this time. Actually, you may have fucked yourself, and my hands are tied."

I thought about what he said, and he was right. So I said, "For what it's worth, I apologize for putting you in this situation. I owe you for this one."

"You owe me more than an apology!" Kay barked. "You really got me in a fucked-up situation. Anybody else, you know we wouldn't be sitting here talking," my partner-in-crime said as we locked gazes.

They don't make niggas like Kay anymore. When he said that we were brothers, he meant that shit. Here I done killed his blood brother for fuckin' my wife, but because of our history, the circumstances, and him respecting the game, we didn't have to go to war. Of course, he didn't like what I did. Me and him being the same age and with Kyron going in and out of jail, Mama Santos raised us up as brothers. She is like a mother to me. And to this

26

day, I know Kyron hated me for that. But Kay understood that this was some man-to-man shit.

"So what's everybody saying? What's Mama Santos saying? You and she were the only ones stopping me from totally wildin.'"

Kay sighed. "Mama is disappointed. And do you really think that stabbing *my brother* in the throat wasn't wildin'? Angel said there was a mention over the local news. But shit, you ain't going to be able to keep it a secret. Angel and my moms is up at the hospital now. He's in critical condition. Hell, Harry said that's the only reason they let me go. But if he dies, Trae, you gonna have a hard time getting out of this one, in more ways than one. And you did all of that and ain't even kill the nigga. Don't get me wrong, that is my brother, and I love him. And I want to really do something to you for making my Moms hurt. But you really slipped up big time. Because if he doesn't die, when he gets out of the hospital you will be consumed with trying to get him. And we both know Kyron, he's coming for you. You need to get your lawyer Benny's ass on this ASAP."

Time felt as if it stopped. What the fuck did he mean, in critical condition? I was there when that pussy took his last breath. *How the fuck can a nigga survive a stab to the throat? Hell, I know I cut the jugular vein.* Real talk.

"Trae! Trae! What the fuck is wrong with you? Do you hear me talking to you?" Kay yelled. "Yo, you looked like you spaced out over there."

I leaned back into the sofa and shut my eyes. I was not gonna let this nigga tear my family to shreds.

Kay chuckled. "Oh, I know what your problem is. You thought you deaded him, didn't you? The Higher Power obviously ain't done with neither one of you niggas yet." My eyes popped open just as Kay stood up. "Not yet. But we'll see what happens. The next six hours the doctors say are the most critical. However, I know that he'll be alright. I don't know if you remember. But years ago, I told you about that dream that I kept having that was spookin' me out. Well, I had it again. But this time, it was crystal-clear. Before, I didn't know the ending. I know now. I shot my own brother in the head."

2

JAZ

"I feel so bad, Jaz. We need to be out there seeing what's up with Tasha. You know she would be here for us. But it's so much going on right now with this business, I couldn't leave if I wanted to," Angel revealed.

We were on the phone for the last twenty minutes, trying to justify why we weren't there for Tasha. However, I was on my way to see my girl. She needed us. Angel wasn't sure when she would be able to get away to get out there. She was doing something she said she would never do, and that was to let life come between our friendships. It didn't matter that she was in New York; hell, I lived in Georgia, but it wasn't stopping me. Tasha had just had a miscarriage and a fling that almost cost her her marriage and her family. We needed to be there for her.

"Let me go, Angel. I'm pulling up in front of my granny's." I disconnected the call and got out of the car.

Faheem had dropped us off at the Hartsfield Atlanta Airport at the crack of dawn. I had a six-and-a-half-hour layover in Jersey, so I went to visit my family, who were literally in the same place I left them years ago. However, I couldn't have cared less about them grown-ass niggas. But the clincher was when I stepped inside my granny's house. Her house was so caked with dust that I was choking and surprised that she was still breathing. Everything was neat and in place, but it was obvious that a dust cloth, broom, and mop had not been used in a long time. It was also obvious that no one was checking on her.

I rolled up my sleeves, found some bleach, a bucket, a broom, a mop and got to cleaning. Kaeerah entertained her grandmother with stories of her classroom, her teacher, her piano lessons, and her new brother. It took damn near three hours to get the house dust-free. I wiped the tears that welled up in my eyes as I wondered how they could allow her to live like this. Hell, this was the same woman who helped raise all of us. I put away all of the cleaning stuff and decided that I wanted to cook her a hot meal, but first I needed to clean her up. That pink, raggedy housecoat she had on was dingier than the slippers on her feet.

"Granny, I looked in your closet, and you have brand-new housecoats. Why are you wearing the raggedy one?"

"Don't come around here sassing me, girl," she snapped.

"Granny, I'm not sassing you. I just want to get you into something fresh and clean. And look, Granny." I held up a new pair of slippers. "You have slippers in here that you don't even wear. Now, let me help you get cleaned up." I had cleaned up the bathroom real good, and Kaeerah ran her tub water. I took off her robe, balled it up, and tossed it into the corner. First chance I got, it was going into the trash can.

"Mommy, look!" Kaeerah was pointing down at Granny's calf.

There was an open wound the size of a golf ball. I gagged. "Granny." I gagged again. "What happened to your leg?"

"Now, there you go meddling. Get on out of here so I can take my bath."

"Granny, no! I'm taking you to the hospital right now." I had never seen an open wound that size before, and it was grossing me out. Now I really felt like shit for not coming to see my granny much sooner.

"Hospital for what?" she countered.

"Granny, your leg is infected, can't you see it? This is not normal. It's not good. I'm taking you to the hospital."

So here I was almost twenty-four hours later, still in New Jersey, luggage probably still going in circles somewhere, never making it to California to check on Tasha. After eating all I could from the vending machine, I picked up my cell to call Angel. I needed to pass some time.

"How much longer do you think you'll be at the hospital?" Angel asked me.

"I don't know, but I'm sure they are going to admit her. I can't leave her until I know that she's squared away. She needs a nurse at home with her at least during the daytime. What about you? How soon can you get free?"

"Shit, I wish I knew. Lil' E still likes fucking with them hood niggas. And because of that, the feds came and kicked down her door, had a search warrant and everything."

"That girl is a white and a platinum-selling rapper. What dumb shit did she do now?"

31

"She ain't do shit. It's them hood niggas she likes to fuck with. Thank God her house was squeaky clean, because they didn't find anything. She knows Kaylin don't play that mess. So because of her, I'm stuck here babysitting her ass and trying to *keep* her squeaky clean. She's scheduled to go on tour overseas week after next, and he doesn't want to jeopardize that and have to cancel because of some bullshit."

"Hold on! Someone is trying to get through. I'll call you back." I hung up on Angel and clicked over.

"Jaz?" It was a male voice that I didn't recognize.

"Who is this?"

"Snell."

"Snell? You sound different."

"Jaz, you there?"

I didn't like the sound of his voice. "I'm here. What's going on?" My stomach began to knot.

"Fah told me to call you. He said to come home, now."

"Is everything okay?" My voice cracked, anticipating some bad news.

"Just get to the house. He needs you. He'll answer all of your questions when you get there."

"Snell, is he okay?" I pressed. Hell, I was in Jersey, not just across the street.

Frustrated with all of my questions, he snapped, "You need to get your ass off the phone and get your ass home!"

"Snell, what . . . Snell? Snell?" He hung up on me.

"Mommy, who was that?" Kaeerah was following closely behind me. Even my daughter could sense that something was wrong.

"Your Uncle Snell." I stood and began pacing back and forth. I called Faheem but didn't get an answer. I had to get somebody up here to the hospital so that I could take my ass back to Georgia to see what was going on with my husband.

FAHEEM

My heart sank to my feet, and my body became numb as I struggled to accept the fact that my son was lying in there on the floor, murdered in cold blood. The paramedic was treating my wound. It was two bullets that hit my shoulder. He said it appeared that a piece of bone was shaved off and that I would survive. I didn't care one way or the other.

"We need you to answer some questions first." The detectives were standing over me, as if I was a prisoner trying to escape.

"Not before my attorney gets here. For now, I'm going in there with my son."

"Sir, there are, from what we can see, at least three dead bodies lying in there. Your son is not going anywhere. You are shot, your son is dead, and you're still telling us that you don't know anything?" the detective asked.

I jumped up and headed for the club with the detective on my heels.

"Mr. Mujahid," the lead detective called after me. "Cuff him!" I heard him yell out. Three officers surrounded me and pushed me into a corner.

"Look. I'm just trying to be with my son. You haven't arrested me, my prints are on none of the weapons, so get the fuck outta my way. This is bullshit. I need to call my attorney."

"Mr. Mujahid, this is a crime scene. We are gonna have to ask you to sit right here and turn your cell phone off," the detective who identified himself as Boyd said to me. "We just need to ask you a few questions. Please, sir I know you are upset. But let us ask you a couple of questions and then we can let you go."

"That's my son, man."

"I understand. But this is a crime scene."

"How y'all gonna just disrespect my son and leave him on that cold floor?"

"Sir," the other detective with the limp interjected. "We need you to have a seat. You still have not answered our questions." Hostility was evident in his voice.

"I'm not answering shit until I speak to my attorney."

The muthafucka with the limp had the nerve to lunge at me, but Boyd jumped in between us. He mumbled something to Detective Limp and then asked me to have a seat.

"I need to call my attorney and my wife." I reached for my cell, and they both charged at me, and Limp snatched the cell from me. They finally got me into some cuffs.

"I told you to sit down and stay down." Boyd hissed. "I will place your phone right here. And like I said, we need to ask you some questions."

"My son is over there on the concrete, dead. I'm shot, and you take my phone, won't let me call my attorney, and you put me in cuffs?" I couldn't believe it.

"Hey, Boyd! Guess who we got laying over here?" Another one of the officers rushed over to where we were having our altercation.

Boyd turned around, and I was all ears. "Who?"

"Morgan. Dwayne 'The Gatekeeper' Morgan."

"No shit!" Boyd and the rest of the officers turned and looked at me. "Damn, Mujahid. You are running with the big dogs."

"I don't run with nobody. I told you, officer. I don't know these cats. I need to call my attorney." Just as I said that, who rushed into the warehouse but Oni's cop brother, Ronnie.

"Boyd, what's happening here? I heard the call and was in the area. Did I hear correct? A kid? What the hell happened here?"

"You heard right," Boyd told him. "It was a massacre, and this perp has the nerve to be tight-lipped."

Ronnie didn't want to look over at me. He knew all about today's meeting. I couldn't wait to see his reaction when he sees his bitch ass brother dead on the floor with a hole in his head and his nephew. How would he squirm his way out of this? His little cousin and his uncle both murdered at what looked like a drug deal gone bad. He was on my list of niggas to dead, but the more I thought about it, I figured that I wouldn't be the one to take him out of his misery. Let the nigga suffer. I was anxious to see how he would play his hand in front of his colleagues.

"Who is the perp?" he asked Boyd.

"His name is Mujahid. That's all we got from him so far. He didn't even have a driver's license on him."

Ronnie peered around Boyd. He took a few steps toward me. "Wait a minute. I know him."

"You do? See—"

Ronnie had left Boyd standing there in midsentence and was almost to where I was. I stood up.

"Ronnie, you better get these fuckin' handcuffs off me and let me call my lawyer and my wife." We stood damn near nose-to-nose.

"Chill out, and follow my lead," he gritted as he fumbled for his key to take the cuffs off my wrists.

"Your muthafuckin' family is gonna pay for this," I gritted right back.

"Shut the fuck up, and use the phone while you got the chance. I'ma stall him." He spoke through clenched teeth.

"Do you realize—"

"Boyd! Let me talk to you." He cut me off and went back over to Boyd.

He left me standing there, and I snatched up my phone and called Jaz, who answered on the first ring. "Baby, talk to me. What's going on? Snell just called me," she rattled off.

"Call Steve. Tell him they got me at Club Mix off of Candler Road. There are bodies, including my son, Lil' Faheem."

"Lil' Faheem? Is he okay? What do you mean, bodies? Baby, talk to me. What happened?"

"He's gone, Jaz. I hardly knew him. I'ma kill that bitch!" I tried to remain calm but I couldn't. "That bitch! I swear on every—" I couldn't get the rest of the words out before Jaz cut me off.

"Faheem, baby, listen to me. Don't do anything until I get there. Do you hear me?"

"Jaz, this shit is all her fault. My son is gone." I cried into the phone.

"Faheem, baby, I'm on my way. Please don't do anything until I get there. Please. I'll call Steve right now."

I ended the call, noticing the commotion. Boyd was signaling to a couple of the other officers who were on the scene.

Ronnie rushed over to the farthest body, which was Steele's people. He lifted the sheet, took a peek, and covered it back up. He then went over to Lil' Faheem. He bent down, lifted the sheet back, and I swear his rich brown complexion looked like it turned blue-black. He stood up and stumbled backward.

Ronnie went over to Wali's body and lifted the sheet. "No! No!

No! No!" he kept saying. Then he took out his phone and made a call. He looked at his uncle again, looked over at me, and came charging. Two of the officers tackled him down.

"I'ma kill you, muthafucka! I'ma kill you!" he yelled at me.

I managed to laugh. It wasn't your typical laugh. It was sinister mixed with sarcasm. "Surprise muthafucka! You see what his ho ass did to my son? You're all dead! You're all dead!" I yelled.

"I'ma kill you!" He kept yelling as they dragged him outside.

The white officer named Weber and the officer who came in with Ronnie, whose name was Johnson, came over to where I was. Johnson asked, "You want to tell us what that was all about?"

"Not without my attorney present. Once he gets here, you can ask all the questions you want."

"Oh, you're gonna answer some questions right now," Johnson said as he cocked his head to the right and then to the left, stretching his neck.

The way I was feeling, I wanted this muthafucka to jump. As Johnson and Weber turned to walk away, Ronnie, Boyd, and the other officers came back inside. They all migrated over to a corner, giving me the screwface and talked amongst themselves.

They all appeared to be trying to console Ronnie. I turned my attention to the three people wearing coroner's jackets. They were snapping pictures, using a tape measure, and taking down notes. One female was talking into a recorder. I noticed that a few walkie-talkies were crackling, the front door opened, and another cop motioned for Boyd. They all rushed to the door. I heard a female's voice, some arguing, and then Oni came rushing in.

I don't know what came over me. I was up and over to her in seconds, yoked her up with both hands, and shoved her into a corner. "Bitch, I hope you don't think for a minute that I'ma let you live."

"Get off me! That is my son, too." She was crying and trying to remove my hands from around her collar. "No, not my son!" she screamed.

"And it's your fault that he's gone. All because of you and your bullshit along with your punk-ass brothers." I was choking the shit out of her. I wanted to detach her head from her shoulders.

"Get off her! Get off her!" Ronnie yelled out.

Then I felt a sharp pain against my back and across my head. I turned around, and his punk ass hit me across the face.

"Get your hands off of her," the big officer Johnson threatened.

That's when I went ham on his ass, not caring that he was the police or about the fact that I was outnumbered. I remember grabbing him, lifting him up into the air, and slamming him onto the concrete. This nigga was going to get the beating of his life. "Training time bitch! I am sure the academy don't teach you this!" I heard myself saying. My intentions were to break his bones up into little pieces. I heard him cry out, and I knew I was beating the shit out of him. It's always them big, cock diesel muthafuckas that can't fight. Next thing I know, it seemed as if everybody was beating on my ass. Then shit faded to black.

When I woke up, my left leg was in a cast; it hurt like hell, and so did the rest of my body. Steve, my attorney, was surrounded by badges and what appeared to be some reporters. He never missed a chance to get in front of a camera. I was handcuffed to the bed. When I let out a groan, all eyes shifted on me.

"Everybody out!" Steve yelled. "I need to talk to my client."

A nurse rushed in and made sure everybody was out and then closed the door. The cop on duty remained with us.

"Give us a few minutes, please," Steve said to him. "He's not going anywhere."

"Sorry, I have to stay in the room as long—"

"Five minutes, man. Attorney-client privilege. Five minutes. You can even leave the door open. Damn."

"I'm on duty, man, sorry." He hunched his shoulders but did turn his back to us.

As the nurse probed and checked my vitals and whatever else, I asked, "What the fuck happened to my leg? Where's my wife, Steve? Why am I handcuffed to this bed?"

"I spoke to her. She is on her way here, and as far as your leg goes, they felt that you had it coming. There were bullets from weapons that were not on the scene. You are their main suspect for now. But listen to this." He turned up the TV, and on the screen was the club, police tape, footage of body bags, and Oni crying.

"Amelda Stone, tell us what happened there."

"Well, John, authorities are being pretty tight-lipped concerning this bizarre scene here at what used to be Club Mix in Decatur, Georgia. As you remember, John, Club Mix was shut down last year when a tip led the FBI and the DEA right here and a street value of almost six million dollars of ecstasy, heroin, and crack cocaine was confiscated. Back then, this club was owned and operated by the notorious East Atlanta Gresham Boys. And today a known and wanted member of the organization, Dwayne 'The Gatekeeper' Morgan, was found dead. He had one gunshot wound to the back of the head and one in the leg. Ironically, that is how the Gatekeeper was known to leave his own victims. One shot in the back of the head.

"The two other bodies are unidentified, but there is speculation that they are also members of the East Atlanta Gresham Boys. But John, the sad news is that there was the body of a child found dead at the scene. What a child was doing there, we don't know yet. And the child's father—"

"Turn it off, Steve. Turn it off." When they mentioned my son, it took me right back to that cold, dark warehouse. All I could do was turn my head to the window as the tears rolled down my cheeks.

JAZ

By the skin of my teeth, I managed to get a red-eye flight from Philly to Atlanta. I had to pay my cousin Pat to stay at the hospital for the rest of the week with my granny. We learned that she had Type 1 diabetes and that they were going to get her sugar leveled and run some tests on her leg. I was praying that they wouldn't have to amputate it.

Kaeerah and I arrived at the Emory University Hospital in Atlanta around three thirty in the morning. Just like me, she was wide awake. Stepping off the elevator, I knew what room Faheem was in because there were several policemen stationed out front. The sound of our shoes hitting the shiny hospital floors echoed as we walked faster. I felt my daughter squeeze my hand as I led the way down the hall that smelled of disinfectant, medicine, and death.

"Daddy!" Kaeerah let go of my hand and rushed to her dad's bedside.

I could tell that Faheem was drugged up. "There she is! What's up, Eerah?" He mumbled his pet name for her.

My heart sank when I saw that he was handcuffed to the bed and a police officer was on duty looking out the window. "Are you able to sit up?" I rushed over and propped his pillow up behind his head and raised the top part of the bed slightly.

"Daddy, what happened to your leg? Is it broken? My friend Camille had a cast on her leg when she broke hers. Why are you locked up to the bed?"

"Yeah, it's broke, baby."

"How did you break it?"

"Got into a scuffle."

"That's why you are locked to the bed?"

"Kaeerah, you can ask Daddy more questions later. Let Mommy talk to him. Go have a seat over there," I said.

"Aww, man," she whined as she headed to the chair in the corner.

"Excuse me?" I snapped my neck and turned my head towards her.

"Nothing, Mom."

I turned back to Faheem and kissed him on the lips. "What happened, baby? Why are you still handcuffed?"

He gave me the short version of what happened and mentioned all of the key players. Then he said, "Everything that could have gone wrong did go wrong. But my son, Jaz . . . they didn't have to kill my son."

I hugged him, because I did not know what to say. Words were not going to bring back Lil' Faheem. Something in me clicked. I was sick of this bitch Oni and her family. What if that would have been my baby? Now this ho had hurt him to the core. And that was enough to make me want to kill the bitch.

I looked over at the officer who had his back to us, and I whispered in Faheem's ear, "Let me take care of this. You have all of this heat on you. Let me handle this." I knew the one thing that would make him feel better.

"What did you just say?"

"Let me do this."

"Do what?"

I didn't speak. Even though he was groggy, I knew that he thought it was funny that I would even say some shit like this. But I was for real. "No. Oh, hell, no. Jaz, don't even think about it. You might as well get that shit out of your mind right now. You don't even know these niggas."

"What do you mean, don't even think about it? You laying up in a hospital bed with one good leg, the other one in a cast. You can't walk, and you are chained to the bed. The police are all over you; they will be watching the house and watching you. Face it, Faheem, you are hot right now. You already told me all I needed to know. Let me do this."

"Jaz, I'm not playing with you. You're not a fuckin' gangsta. Just because you did a few weeks in jail don't mean shit. Have you lost your fuckin' mind?"

"That's your problem, Faheem. You always underestimate me. But after this, you're gonna respect me. I'ma leave you alone to think about it." We continued to argue back and forth in whispers. Shit, there was nothing he could do to me right now but talk and shoot verbal threats. He damn sure couldn't chase me. "Let's go, Kaeerah. We'll come back in the morning to see Daddy."

"Jaz, don't make me—"

"Make you do what, Faheem? You're laid up with a cast on your leg. What you gonna do? Run over her and stop me?"

The nigga Steele needed to be dealt with. Oni was another story. I was not about to let what happened to Trae and Tasha happen to Faheem and me. No bitch was going to destroy my family. I was nipping the shit in the bud. Something I should have done a while ago. If I'd gotten rid of her when I first thought about it, Faheem would still have his son. The more I thought about taking her out, the more excited I became. I grabbed our daughter's hand, and headed for the door. He slammed his fist down on the bed as we walked out of the room.

3

KYRON

Whoever said pussy could get you killed didn't lie. How do I know? Shit, I am a living testament of that even though I am not dead. Not once but twice this nigga has come for me over some pussy. Don't get me wrong, the pussy is like that, but my hustler creed is MONEY OVER BITCHES.

I'm still laid up in this hospital and don't even know how long I've been here. I only know it's been long enough to think about how I'ma kill Trae's bitch ass. Because of his nose all up in Shorty's ass, he sees himself getting me out of the way by stabbing me in the throat. Who the fuck is stabbing niggas? My whole bid I had to worry about niggas trying to stab me. Who would have ever thought I would be on the streets and get knifed?

I'm lying here with my eyes closed, acting as if I'm asleep, listening to Mari pace back and forth in stilettos about to run a hole in the floor. She cries for a few minutes, and then she calls somebody, hangs up, and cries some more. I was introduced to Mari by my attorney right before I got sentenced and sent Upstate. She is a corporate attorney I hired to handle my business while I was locked up. Not only did I want to keep all of my shit, but I needed my shit to grow while I was down. She helped me to do just that and more. When I stepped out of the prison, I had more dough than I did when I went in. I came home with four prime pieces of real estate and a serious dope connect, all because of her. All she wanted in return was my heart and for me to work that connect, which belonged to her family. But she wanted me to move when she said move and act how she thought I should act. I wasn't built like that. She obviously didn't get the memo.

"I swear to you, Kyron, if I didn't love you so much and hadn't invested so much of myself and my time, I would kill you myself and leave you right here for dead." She turned to Kendrick and said, "I can't believe you are just going to let Trae get away with this! I don't give a damn about your no-snitch rule. He needs to be dealt with. And if you aren't willing to deal with him, then move out of the way and allow the law to deal with him."

"Let the law deal with him? What kind of bullshit is that? Do you hear yourself? Yo, Mari, you need to chill the fuck out. This is Kyron's beef. He will deal with him when he's ready. Not you, not me, that man there will handle it. We, you and I, don't have anything to do with this. So my advice to you is to fall back. Take your ass back to the boardroom where you belong."

"You're kidding me, right? Kendrick, tell me you are joking. Ha! Ha!" she let out a sarcastic chuckle.

"No, I'm not joking, Mari. This shit is between Kyron and Trae."

"The hell it is. Y'all had better handle this shit, or I will." She snatched up her bag from the chair next to me, stormed into the bathroom, and slammed the door. I opened my eyes just as the door shut.

"What the fuck, yo? You need to check her," Kendrick snapped as he pointed at the door. Kendrick had a twin name Kendra. Our fathers were brothers. Growing up, the twins and I rolled together since we were the same age.

I waved him off. I wasn't up for entertaining either one of them. I needed to get up and out of this hospital. I had moves to make and a shorty to see.

TRAE

The last couple of months was hell trying to get back on track after all the bullshit me and Tasha had gone through. But I had to admit that it's funny how you set your sights on one path and shit just gets fucked up along the way. One thing was for certain, I was determined to get my marriage back on track.

I wanted to feel that adrenaline rush and that school boy crush I got from Tasha when I first laid eyes on her. I wanted us to trust each other again and share that unbreakable bond we had way before the whirlwind called Charli and Kyron fucked up our world.

So tonight was going to be our new beginning.

I had just set everything up and was awaiting Tasha's arrival. Tonight, it was all about the love of my life.

TASHA

I had spent all day at the spa getting the *everything* treatment. Trae begged me to go out on a date with him. I agreed feeling that he had something up his sleeve. I drove to meet him at a resort out in Carlsbad. During the ride out there I couldn't help but go over in my mind all of the danger I put myself and Trae in by messing with Kyron. I would never do no revenge shit like that again. I had finally gotten to a place where I was no longer angry with Trae. Was it back to how it used to be? No, but I was hopeful that we could make it happen. The Trae I fell in love with had caused me major heartache but the Trae I needed was slowly resurfacing and I loved every minute of it.

I pulled up to the Villa that he had booked for us and butterflies fluttered around inside my stomach. I put the car in park and took a few deep breaths. After going over myself in the mirror and glossing my lips with what Trae called the sexy, suck my dick lip gloss, I reached over, grabbed my Gucci bag and got out of the car. As I approached the door I felt like a teen again. I was nervous and excited at the same time. Before I could knock the door opened and I was pleasantly surprised.

TRAE

When I saw the look on Tasha's face it was priceless. She was smiling and glowing. The sound of her girlish giggle accompanied with the way she sung out my name made me smile from the inside out. I knew that I was making her happy and that's all that mattered to me.

I had the whole room filled with vanilla scented candles. The bed that was strategically placed in the middle of the cabin was covered in red satin sheets, with white rose petals sprinkled all over them. I was planning to lay her sexy chocolate body over the petals and take some pictures for my stash. The soft music played in the back as I watched Tasha's eyes dance around the room.

"You gonna just stand there?" I asked as I watched her frozen in place.

"Awwwwww babeeeee," She cooed as she closed the door and placed her bag on the sofa.

"Come here."

As Tasha walked over to me I watched the way her hips swayed in those tight jeans and fuck me stilettos. My dick rocked right up. Shit was getting ready to jump off and a nigga was ready to put in major work. I hugged her tight and allowed my hands to glide down her back and settle on her ass before placing my lips on hers and kissed her gently. The increase in her breathing and the precision of her touch gliding over my arms and back caused my body to heat up. I pulled her tighter pressing that steel up against her clit. Shit had went from zero to ten in seconds. I had to slow it down because I had some things I needed to say to her. I had to make our shit back tight again.

"Hold up ma, I need to do something first." I broke our embrace.

TASHA

When Trae pulled back I didn't know what to think. He reached over and grabbed a velvet bag that was sitting next to a bottle of wine and two glasses. I watched as he reached inside and pulled out a small box. My eyes lit up when he lifted the top and there lay the biggest, prettiest diamond I had ever laid my eyes on.

"Tasha, I know we've been through a lot of shit. But tonight I need for us to put all of the mistakes, drama, hurt and pain behind us and start over. Right here, right now, today, I recommit myself to you, to our family and to our bond." He said as he took the ring from the box and began to slide it on my finger. "Baby, you know damn well that there is no me without you. I don't just want you in my life, I need you in my life. And you will always be a part of me. I don't want nothing or nobody to come between us ever again. I don't want you to ever again regret that you fucked with me. I want to thank you for giving me three strong sons that I get so much pleasure from." He paused, looked me in my eyes and continued. "Again, I am asking you to allow me to honor, cherish and love you for the rest of my life."

Tears had started streaming down my checks back when he said start over. I looked down at my hand and then back up at him. I said, "Trae, I never stopped loving you, and I never will. From this moment forward I promise to honor you, respect you and love you for the rest of my life." I leaned up and kissed his lips.

He led me to the couch, poured us both a glass of wine and we toasted to life, love and our new commitment. The one that we both vowed to let nothing or no one come between.

Once the last sip left my lips, my husband was all over me. Quickly he relieved me of every piece of clothing I had on. As he laid me so tenderly across the satin feeling rose petals, his lips danced all over my skin sending chills all over my body. His touch was firm and gentle at the same time. It was like he was touching me for the first time.

"Open your legs." He commanded. And I submitted.

I inhaled deep as he positioned his body over mine. The intense passion rose off of us threatening to set the room on fire. Slowly, he began to slip into my wetness. When his soft tongue began to pleasure my nipples I grabbed him tight, inviting him to go deep and he complied with long deep strokes that ignited my soul. His dick was calling my name and I answered by throwing the pussy back at him just the way he liked it. The soft moans left his lips accompanied by, "Tasha, I love you."

"I love you too." I replied as my body moved in sync with his.

"You are my world. Nothing can ever come between us again," he whispered in my ear.

"Never again." I agreed.

With that, we made love, we fucked, I cried and we made love some more, until we both were satisfied. Afterwards, I lay next to my husband, wide awake, watching him sleep peacefully. I ran my fingers up and down his arm. We had just sealed the deal on our new union; however, all I could do was pray that the universe would show the same forgiveness. Only time would tell.

TASHA

We were in the backyard. I loved the California weather; even though it was eighty-three degrees, to me it felt like seventy-five. The kids were splashing around in the pool, while Trae and I were relaxing in the lounge chair watching them. I was sitting between his legs while he was massaging my neck and shoulders. We had just come home the night before from our little romantic getaway. Just as I began to relax into my massage, my cell started ringing. I looked and I saw that it was a 718 number, meaning New York, and of course, I tensed right up.

"What's the matter with you?" Trae picked up on my tension immediately. "Who is that?"

"I don't know. I don't recognize the number," I admitted.

"Answer it," he told me. But I was too late. Whoever it was had already hung up. As soon as I let out a sigh, it rang again. *Shit*. "Answer your phone, Tasha." His tone was laced with suspicion, and I didn't like it.

I pressed the speaker button. "Hello."

"Is this Tasha?"

I looked at my phone as if it had a virus. An unfamiliar voice asking for me using my first name? "Who is this?"

"This is Mari. I'm actually trying to reach your husband. I don't have his number. I only have yours because it was saved in Kyron's phone."

Oh, okay. Kyron's woman. Yeah, I fucked her man, got pregnant by him, and lost the baby. But I think it's a little too late for her to be trying to call my husband. Especially since shit's already on the table. Between her and Kyron . . . the pregnancy . . . Trae fucking that bitch Charli Li, it didn't look like the madness was ever going to stop haunting us.

"Why are you looking for Trae?" I moved his hands from my shoulders and sat all the way up.

"Were you aware that he stabbed Kyron in the throat and that he's in critical condition? There's a strong possibility that Kyron could take a turn for the worse."

"Who the fuck cares?"

"Hear me out. I was calling to say that they plan to serve street justice on your husband. Me? I'd rather allow the appropriate authorities handle him. I'm simply reaching out before I turn him over to the law. Is he available? It's important that I speak with him."

"Is that all you have to say?"

"To you, yes. Is he available?"

"First of all, bitch, speaking to me is speaking to him. And do yourself a favor, and don't ever call my phone again. You need to be glad that he didn't stab *your* ass in the throat . . . just because. So my advice to you"—I paused to make sure she got my point—"is stay in your fuckin' lane."

I hung up on her and went to stand up. Trae grabbed me and hugged me tight. "I wonder what that was all about?" he had the nerve to ask me. I couldn't believe my ears.

I turned around and looked at him as if he had sprouted two heads. "You heard the entire conversation, just like I did."

"What's the matter with you?"

"You stab a nigga in the throat, his bitch knows that you did it, and you're sitting here wondering what it's all about? Did you really just say that? Or did I hear you wrong? And on top of that, I'm still trying to figure out why I gotta hear shit from everybody else except from my husband. I asked you about this several times, and you never had anything to say."

"And I still don't have shit to say. It is what it is, Tasha."

"Trae, she is the second person to tell me that you stabbed Kyron. She's talking about turning you in. What if she does? What if they come and arrest you? Don't you think I need to be up on what's going on?"

"No, you don't need to be up on this bullshit. I got this."

"Fine." I stood up. "But I tell you this, if your ass gets locked up, I promise you, I won't be the one coming to see you."

"Oh, yes, you will."

"I bet you I won't."

"Excuse me." Aunt Marva interrupted our argument. "There is someone at the door. I think you both need to get up here."

"Who is it?" I asked her. My defenses were already up, so I

knew that some more bullshit was about to go down. Once again, the madness appeared to haunt us.

"Who is it, Auntie?" Trae asked her.

"I'll stay out here with the kids. You two go let him in."

Him? I panicked but just as quickly relaxed, because it couldn't be Kyron; he was in the hospital. Now I was curious, and I guess Trae was, too, because he jumped up and grabbed my hand. When I tried to snatch away, he pulled me close and hugged me around the waist.

"Get off of me, Trae. I am not feeling you right now."

"Well, I'm feeling you," he said as he kissed me on the neck.

"Get off me."

"Why do you have to trip, Tasha?"

"Because we made a promise. No more secrets. No more lies. And it seems like I'm the only one keeping the promise."

"What do you want to hear me say? Fuck it! I'll say it. Yeah, I stabbed the nigga in the throat, because he talks too much shit, and he needed to die for fucking my wife! Now, does that make you feel any better? Hell, no, it doesn't, because you already knew that. You know me, Tasha. And you knew I was going to get him, and if I missed this time, I promise you I won't miss the next. Now what, Tasha? What else do you want to know?"

"How about if you get caught? What if you go to prison? What do you expect me to do? Ride the bit with you? I can't see myself going to see you in nobody's prison. I'm not doing that shit again." We were slowly walking through the house.

"You know better than I do, I can't let that pussy live, Tasha. I mean that shit."

"Baby, what's more important? Your freedom and your family or your pride and your ego?"

"The nigga disrespecting me by fuckin' my wife. So yeah, my principles are real important. Some shit you can't let ride."

"See, that is just plain stupid. Downright ridiculous."

"Call it what you want."

"I'm calling it as I see it. Trae, you really need to grow up. I think you are too old to be still trying to live by some little boy's creed. We both did things that we shouldn't have. But I think it is going too far."

"Nah, it went too far when the muthafucka got you pregnant." His nostrils flared. I could tell he was about to go off so I let it go. But I wanted to say, "It went too far when you fucked that bitch and got her pregnant." But I didn't go there. It was as if we didn't just spend four nights together recommitting ourselves to each other.

We arrived at the front door, and Trae mumbled, "Oh, shit! What the fuck?"

The three of us stood there looking at one another.

I broke the silence. "See, I told you. I told you I wasn't crazy. I told you I saw him at the restaurant."

We stood staring at the one and only King Rick. Finally, he said, "Y'all gonna let me stand out here while the mosquitoes eat me up, or are you gonna let me in?"

"Only if you're ready to put in some work, nigga. Just because you went on hiatus don't mean shit changed around here." Trae was smiling from ear to ear as he unlocked and opened the screen door. As soon as Rick stepped inside, they hugged as if they were long-lost brothers.

"Don't threaten me with a good time. You know how I gets down. Just tell me when and where." Rick told him.

"Ain't this some shit! I don't believe it."

"Man, you got a lot of shit with you! I remember crying over your dead body. I mean, what the fuck?" Trae wanted to know.

"Shit, the government kills people off, will give you a mock funeral and a whole new identity. They do that shit all the time," Rick said, and turned to me. "And you?" He hugged me and said, "You are still the finest chick I know."

"Aren't you supposed to be in a safe house or something? Not back to the same streets where you did your dirt?" I asked him. I had some reservations about Rick's sudden reappearance.

"You watch too much television! For us low-life, real niggas, ain't no such thing as a safe house. We on our own. Plus, I'm retired. I can go wherever I damn well please."

"So what brings you here on my doorstep? I know it's something. And don't tell me you miss a nigga or that you are trying to get your ex-wife back," Trae told him.

"This is my second time here. The first time I stopped by, y'all wasn't home."

"So what *are* you doing here? Are you trying to get back with your wife?" I wanted to know.

"Hell, no, she likes pussy more than I do. Plus, I have someone new and a baby on the way. But as fate would have it, just when I thought I was in a place that I was comfortable with, I got thrown a curve ball. Guess who I ran into right here on your doorstep? And I suggest you sit down, because if you don't, this is going to knock you down."

"Please, all the shit we've been through, I'm sure we can handle it," I said as I looked at Trae and rolled my eyes.

"Trust me. This is more powerful than me running into

you in New York." He looked me up and down as if he knew something no one else did.

"Oh, so now you're gonna snitch me out? What if I didn't want Trae to know? I see who your loyalty is with. So go ahead and share your ground-breaking news. I'm all ears!" Trae and I sat down on the sofa.

He looked over at Trae for approval. Trae nodded and then Rick continued. "I found Kyra, man. She was right there on your front doorstep."

There was silence in the room as we wrapped our ears around what we were just told.

"What do you mean, you *found* Kyra on our doorstep?" Trae asked.

"Yeah, what does that mean? And if that's the case, then where is she now?" This sounded like some bullshit to me. I know I said I could handle anything but this was not funny. Nor did I need for it not to be real. He was talking about my friend, my sister, my girl. He had to be fuckin' with us. Maybe it's like his funeral . . . all a lie. But at the same time, I hoped it wasn't.

"She's at the hospital. She's blacking out, having severe headaches."

I jumped up and went over to Rick. "Rick, don't fuckin' joke with me like this. You talking about *my* Kyra? First you, now Kyra? Rick, what kind of head games are you playing? Trae, I suggest you get your boy."

"I told you, you weren't going to be able to handle it. How do you think I feel? Can you imagine what went through my mind when I saw her sitting on your porch? I keep thinking that I am going to wake up and that it is all a dream. I thought I saw a ghost."

Damn. He did have a point. Just like the rest of us; we thought she was dead and that Marvin killed her. My mind was flooded with questions like, how? Who? What? When? But Marvin never did really say what happened. And we never knew anything about a funeral.

"Y'all wasn't home, and I saw her sitting on the front porch. When she saw me, she fainted. I put her in my car, and when she kept saying her head was hurting, I took her to the hospital, and they kept her. I went through her things and found her nurse. I called her and she had been with her since she was first admitted to the hospital. She brought me up to speed on everything that happened with her. She lost her memory y'all. All of this time she was right near me, in Phoenix, Arizona. So for the last two days I've been staying at the hospital with her, but I had to come by and let y'all know what was happening. They may let her out tomorrow. I was going to put her up in a hotel, but I figured I better check with y'all first." Rick was talking a mile a minute.

"Oh, my God." I grabbed my chest, sat back down, and laid my head back on the couch. I tried to control my breathing as a million and one questions flooded my mind and rolled off of my tongue. "How is she? What is she saying? I gotta see her! Trae, please take me up there." I stood up, not even waiting for Rick to answer my questions. Then I realized I didn't even know what hospital she was in. "What hospital?"

"Baby, calm down. I'll get you up there. But let me talk to Rick first." He kissed me on the forehead, and then he turned to Rick. He had this no-nonsense look on his face. "Man, let's go down in the basement."

"Just like old times." Rick chuckled.

"For real, Trae? Y'all gonna do this shit right now?" I was

standing there with my hands on my hips, ready to throw a tantrum.

"Just chill for a minute, Ma. Get yourself ready, and we'll be right back. I gotta talk to Rick."

And just like that, those rude niggas left me standing there. I knew Trae needed to talk to Rick, but damn. Just like Rick was his boy, Kyra was my girl. I could tell that Trae was glad to see him. Trae had saved his life one night when he was out terrorizing the streets being the dirty cop that he was. He had ended up becoming like family, and he treated Trae like a little brother. After that, Trae couldn't get rid of him. Despite him being a cop and Trae being a street nigga, they became thick as thieves. Trae says that he was loyal and that was all that mattered.

But later for him; right now, I had bigger fish to fry. I couldn't think about them right now. What was I going to tell Aisha? *Oh, my God.* How would I break the news to her? How is she going to react once I tell her that her mother is coming over? I had to call my girls, even though I was mad at them for not coming to see me. I bet their asses would come now. I went into the kitchen, grabbed the phone, and dialed Angel first.

"Oh, so you're not mad at me anymore?" she sarcastically asked me.

"Is that the way you answer the phone?"

"I'm just sayin'."

"Well, no, I'm no longer mad. It's all good, because I have some news that will make your ass fly out here today. But you best believe I will address me being mad at another time. I'm not letting you off that easy."

"Tasha, it's not like I'm not there with you on purpose. I had to—"

I cut Angel short. "Angel, it's all good. Just get Jaz on the phone."

"Damn you, Tasha," Angel mumbled, as she put me on hold.

I paced back and forth across the kitchen floor until I heard Jaz's voice. But to my surprise, she was crying. "Jaz, what's the matter?" I asked her.

"Shit's so crazy for us right now. I feel so bad for him!" she cried.

"So bad for who?" Angel and I asked at the same time.

"Faheem. His son. They shot and killed him." She started bawling.

I gasped not wanting to believe what I heard. It was fucked up because Faheem had just met his son a few short months ago.

"What happened? Who shot him? Where were they?" Angel asked before I could.

"Some drama his son's mother got him caught up in. On top of that, he's in the hospital with a broken leg, and the police beat him down and then arrested him. I'm at the hospital now."

"Oh, my God. Can this conversation get any worse?" I asked. "We didn't even get the chance to meet his son."

"I know. He was adorable. We didn't even get a chance to get used to him." Jaz blew her nose. "What's up? I gotta go and get myself together. As you can tell, I am a nervous wreck."

"Nervous wreck? I am devastated." And I was. "Why did this have to happen to him?" Faheem has such a big heart. I only saw good karma surrounding him. So why did this happen?

"I don't know," Jaz responded.

"Well, maybe what I have to say will cheer you up just a little bit. You ready for this? Kyra. She's here, at the hospital." When they didn't say anything, I said, "She's alive, y'all! She's here in California."

"Tasha, don't play like that." Angel said.

"Angel, don't get on my nerves. Do you honestly think I would play about something like this? Rick is getting ready to take us up there."

"Rick?" Angel screeched.

"You mean to tell me all of this time, she's been with him?" I could hear the shock and disbelief of Jaz's voice.

"No. He found her on my doorstep. It's a long story. Anyway, y'all need to get up here as soon as y'all can. For real, I don't think I can face this by myself. I understand y'all not coming here for me, but the both of you need to be here for Kyra, especially you, Angel. She is your cousin. Even if it is for only one day."

TRAE

Damn. The federal government be on some bullshit. Giving niggas fake funerals and shit. Rick was full of surprises. I attended his memorial and even shed a few tears. Now this nigga shows up on my doorstep. He told me how he was working as a detective in Atlanta and fell for this chick named Nina, who could pass for Kyra's sister. He said she was a true hustler and that they robbed some people, and now he was living with her in Tucson. She already had three kids and was five months pregnant with the fourth one, which was his. But now that Kyra was back in the picture, he admitted that his head was all fucked up.

We tried to kick it and catch up right quick about things that were going on in each of our lives. He was glad that I took Marvin out but pissed off because he wanted to dead the nigga himself. He said he was a pussy for leaving Kyra for dead. I told him those were my thoughts, too. Just for that and for causing my wife so much grief, I took care of him. It was the principle of the matter. Rick told me how Marvin and his crew caught him slippin', and because of that, he almost lost his life. I warned him not to tell Kyra about Marvin. I would do that myself when it came up and when the timing was right. I knew I would have to eventually face Kyra and Marvin's daughter. Aisha came up to me at least every other day and asked out of the blue, "Where is my daddy?" Or "Has he called yet?" And I couldn't say that it didn't bother me.

4

ONI

"Please Lord, oh please Lord bring him back!" I heard myself scream as I rocked back and forth, squeezing myself tight and wishing that I could hold my son one last time. My eyes were swollen shut from all of the crying. I was in the chapel inside the hospital, hiding from everyone. It had only been a couple of hours since I identified my child's body, and now the hospital wanted me to identify my brother Wali, but I couldn't. I didn't have the strength. So I gave them Mike's number. I felt as if I was living in hell. My son and my brother? I was overwhelmed with grief. I couldn't understand why my son was taken from me while he was so young. My only child. I began to cry again.

I got on my knees and prayed for an hour straight, asking God to turn back the hands of time so that I could do things differently. I prayed that Faheem would be okay and that he could find it in his heart to forgive me instead of hating me and condemning me to hellfire. But no matter how long I prayed, I noticed that I didn't feel at peace. I'm sure it was because of my guilt, my greed, and my lust. Calling them deadly sins is an understatement.

I had no business taking that package from Steele. We had no business robbing him in our own hotel. That was stupid. And two deaths was confirmation that my brothers and I hadn't planned things out thoroughly. It only became personal to Steele because I would sleep with him on occasion. For me, it was convenience, but he obviously thought differently. And because of that, he felt that he could hurt me by kidnapping my son. Someone I loved more than life itself. When I ran into Faheem, I saw the hurt in his eyes that told me that I was the one who needed to die. When he choked me, I was wishing that he would have killed me. Now I wish I could stay in this chapel forever.

JAZ

Well, well, well. Look at this bitch! Lord forgive me for that thought in your house. My jaws tightened at the sight of Oni as Kaeerah and I entered the chapel. I thought it would be a good idea for myself and Kaeerah to say a prayer for her father and her brother. We had to thank God that Faheem was alive and that losing his son wouldn't be too big of a burden that he couldn't bear. I was also praying that they would release him and not charge him with some bullshit. After all, it was Oni and her brothers who caused all of this drama. But as I entered the chapel the hairs on my neck stood seeing Oni kneeling. I came in peace but now I felt like warring. This bitch is the reason my husband is in pain both physically and mentally. I told Kareerah to take a seat.

"Mommy, there goes Miss Oni!" she yelled out, causing Oni to turn around.

"I see her," I mumbled. Oni looked like hell, for lack of a better word. She looked as if she had aged ten years. The sadness on her face almost softened my heart. She had dark rings under her red eyes, and her hair was pulled back into a messy ponytail. Even her clothes were crumpled and dusty-looking. Her cream blouse was ruined from the makeup all down the front of the shirt and on the sleeve. She looked as if she hadn't been home to change or bathe in days. If it had been any other day, I would have gloated that I was my usual fly self.

"Hi, Miss Oni," Kaeerah called out cheerfully. Despite my hate for her, I raised my child better.

"Hello, Kaeerah," she said, and then burst out crying. The type of gut-wrenching cry that comes from your soul. I took that as my cue to leave, because chill bumps were popping up on my arms. I know she didn't think I was coming over to console her.

I went over and grabbed Kaeerah's hand. "C'mon, baby, we will come back later."

"No, wait!" Oni got up off of her knees and rushed over to us. "You don't have to leave." She grabbed my arm and just as quickly as she did, I snatched it away from her, moving Kaeerah behind me.

"Jaz, please," she said with a crazed look in her eyes. "I need your help." She pleaded with tears streaming down her cheeks.

"There is nothing I can do for you," I said through clenched teeth. I was struggling really hard, trying not to tap that ass right there in the chapel.

"Please. You have to tell Faheem that I am sorry. I can't live with him hating me."

The pain in her eyes caused my heart to skip a beat. The mother in me wanted to comfort her, but the wife in me and the hate I was holding onto said, *Check this bitch*. I closed the space between us. "I will do no such thing. Are you fucking crazy? Bitch, it is *all*," I pointed toward her chest, "All your fault that your child is dead. You're *sorry*? Bitch, you are more than *sorry*! Because of you, your son is dead!" My mood went from anger to rage. "*Sorry* is not going to bring that child back. *Sorry* is not going to take back the pain that Faheem will live with for the rest of his life. *Sorry* is not going to take back the beat-down that my husband endured, and *sorry* damn sure ain't going to make the police leave him alone. You are absolutely right, you are sorry. A sorry, pathetic bitch. Your son is dead. He is never coming back and my husband, his father will never get over that. I hope you rot in hell. You were always sheisty, and you deserve whatever hell is coming at you, and believe me, it's coming. Stay the fuck away from my family! Let's go, Kaeerah." I pulled her arm, and we left the chapel.

I was not expecting to run into her and get that off. It actually felt better than prayer.

Most important, I hoped that she suspected that I was coming after her. I already knew who I was going to get to help me carry my plan out.

ONI

I couldn't believe that Jaz went off on me like that . . . and in front of her daughter. I already was at my wits end, guilt damn

65

near eating me alive. Now I felt as if there was no hope at all. She threw every shred of blame there was up in my face. It's my fault that my son is dead. It's my fault that Faheem will have to live with this pain for the rest of his life. I was hoping that Jaz would have helped me. But instead, she magnified my pain and cut my soul to shreds.

FAHEEM

"I'm baaaad, shut yo mouth!" Steve announced as he barged into my hospital room. "Tell me I'm the man! Go ahead! Tell me, Faheem."

"Steve, I'm lying here like a wounded, captured animal, and you want me to play word games?"

"You want to know why I'm the man?" Steve continued to ignore my sour mood. "You pay me the big bucks because I. Am. The. Man. That's right! I am the man!"

"I pay you the big bucks so you can get these chains off of me and keep them off, that's why." I focused on the television, which was on mute.

"Mr. Mujahid, exactly what in the hell is it that you think I did?"

He now had my undivided attention. "What do you mean, Steve?"

He leaned over and began to whisper, "Your prints were not on any of the weapons at the scene of the crime. Hell, they were on nothing but your son. But I did have to agree to bring you in for questioning. Key words: *bring you in*. Once we do that, our end of the deal is done. If you don't know anything, you can't tell anything. You understand?"

I breathed a sigh of relief. I knew Jaz would be glad to hear this. "So when will the cuffs come off, and when will the goon leave from out of my room?"

"They should be getting the call any minute now. As a matter of fact, let me call them." He left the room.

I was ready to get up out of there, but Steve wanted me to stay there as long as possible. He said that because of the beat-down, I had a potential lawsuit. But I couldn't have cared less about a lawsuit. I was anxious for my leg to heal, because I'd made a promise that once it did, each and every nigga who had anything to do with me losing my son was dead.

I looked up, and the minute I saw Jaz step into the room, I knew something was wrong. "What's up?" Jaz stood on one side of the bed, and Kaeerah went around to the other.

"I just saw that bitch Oni in the chapel."

"Watch your mouth!" I snapped. Kaeerah was looking dead in her mouth. "You need to get somebody to watch her. She doesn't need to be up here every day all day like this. And you should know that I don't want to hear shit about Oni."

"You watch your mouth, Faheem," Jaz snapped back, and Kaeerah started giggling. "It's not about her. The news I have for you is about my girl. Kyra is in the hospital out there where Tasha is, and I've gotta go out there to see her. I'ma take Kaeerah with me and hire a nurse to be here with you. Is that okay?"

"A nurse? I'm in a hospital. What the hell do I need a nurse for? And how long do you plan on being in California?"

"I'm only going to stay for a couple of days. And I'm hiring a nurse for my peace of mind. I can't be out there wondering if you're okay here."

"Kyra. Kyra?" My brain started processing. "I thought she was dead. She's in the hospital? What Kyra are you talking about?"

"My Kyra. Our Kyra. And she isn't dead. She is very much alive. Once they release her from the hospital, she's moving in with Tasha."

"So where the hell was she all of this time? Is she all right?"

"I don't know the answer to either one of those questions. But I want to leave in the morning. I hate to leave you here by yourself, but I gotta go see what's going on. You sure you're okay with that?"

"I'll be fine. Steve just told me that since my prints were nowhere at the scene other than on my son, they gotta release me."

Jaz came over and hugged me. "Yes! I love you, baby. I was so scared that you were going to jail, Faheem, you just don't know. That's the best news, well, the second-best news I received today, because Kyra being alive, that news floored me. Baby, we will get through this. I don't want to leave you, but I gotta go see Kyra."

"I told you, I'll be fine."

"Why is he still in here? Baby, the charges being dropped is not real to me until he is gone." She was referring to the cop still sitting in the corner.

"So, they aren't going to take you to jail when you leave here?" Kaeerah asked.

"No, Eerah, Daddy's not going to jail."

"Good! So you can come to Cali with us tomorrow!" My baby gave me this big Kool-Aid smile, and at that moment, it felt as if everything was going to be all right.

"How is your daddy going to get on a plane with this cast on his leg?" I reached out and tickled her neck.

She giggled. "Easy, Daddy. They can let you on first in a wheelchair."

"Nah, baby, I can't even walk yet. I'll wait right here for y'all to come back. Then, as soon as you do, you can roll me out of here in a wheelchair and take me home. Is that a deal?" I held my pinky finger up.

She wrapped her little pinky around mine. "It's a done deal!"

"That's what I'm talkin' about."

TASHA

I didn't know why I was so nervous. After all, Kyra was my family, but still, I really didn't know what to expect and was wishing that Angel and Jaz were there to help me out with this. Trae and Rick and I were on our way out the front door to go see Kyra when Rick pulled out his cell. His eyes lit up.

"This is her now! Hey, baby, I'm on my way up there right now, and I'ma bring some visitors." He hit his speaker-phone button.

"Well, save your surprise, and come get me out of here. No more visits. The doctor just gave me my discharge papers."

Oh, my God, that's her voice. I know that voice anywhere. It was really her. "Kyra!" I snatched the phone out of Rick's hand. "Kyra! It's me, Tasha!" I choked up.

"Tasha? Tasha!" She started screaming. Then she was quiet, and all I could hear was her crying.

"Kyra, everything's going to be all right. We got you. I just need for you to come on home. My home is your home. All you've got is love waiting here for you."

"I love you guys, too," she said through sobs. "Tell Rick to come and get me. God is good, he is so good. Tasha, my daughter. Is . . . ? Where . . ."

"Kyra, your daughter is here. I told you, we got you." All I could hear was her crying harder, which made me start crying. Trae took the phone from me and passed it back to Rick. He hugged me as I stood there. I was in shock. Even though Rick told us he had Kyra, I still was skeptical. After all, he was a lying ass cop. Standing there I was in a daze I heard her voice again, this time in my heart. I began to cry uncontrollably. I love my friends, we have been through so much. They are my sisters. And things haven't been the same since we thought that Kyra was dead.

"Rick, you go and get Kyra. Tasha and I will get everything here ready for her and talk to Aisha."

"No doubt. I'll call when I'm on my way back."

Trae whispered in my ear, "Are you gonna be all right? Or am I gonna have to sedate you?"

"Oh, so you've got jokes." I wiped my tears. "Baby, you gotta understand, just the sound of her voice after all of this time got me. Hell, the whole situation got me feeling some kind of way. I never dealt with something like this before."

"I know, baby, but you need to pull yourself together. You gotta go talk to Aisha."

"Why do I have to talk to her? Why can't we both talk to her?"

"Because one of us has to get her room ready," Trae had the nerve to say.

"Don't even try it. Let Aunt Marva get the room ready. Let's both talk to Aisha. I want you with me on this, Trae. I don't want to say the wrong thing."

"Baby, you are making this harder than it has to be. She's just a child. All you gotta do is tell her that her mother is coming home. Let Kyra tell her everything else."

"Fine, then. You do all of the talking, because I don't think it's going to be that easy. Let me go and get her. You want to do it in the living room, dining room, or porch?"

"Tasha!"

"Okay, okay, fine. I'll be right back, so wait right here." Mr. Smart Ass, always has all of the answers, which I was mostly thankful for. I found Aisha out back playing basketball with the boys. She obviously had fallen, because dust was all over her hair, and her clothes were dirty on the left side.

"Auntie Tasha, watch this!" she yelled out as she threw the ball up and it missed the rim. "Wait. Wait, watch this."

"Aisha, come here. Your Uncle Trae wants to talk to you. Marva, can you get the guest room ready? We have a surprise guest on the way. Please?" After I said "please," the sideways look that she gave me disappeared. I took Aisha up front to see Trae, who was waiting patiently, sitting on the banister on the front porch.

"Uncle Trae, I can play basketball now." She beamed. "I got game."

"You got game?"

"Yup. I don't just got game. I got mad game."

"Umph, I gotta check you out for myself," he teased her. "But listen to this. We just heard from your mother." He waited for her reaction. Me? I was holding my breath.

Aisha simply stuffed her hands into her short pockets, her eyes rolled back into her head as if she was in deep thought. Then she said, "So my mommy is not dead?"

"No, baby, she's not," Trae answered.

"Awesome!" she shrieked, and started jumping up and down. "So where is she? Is she home? What about my dad? Is my dad with her?"

"She's on her way over here, and no, your dad is not with her. So go get cleaned up so you can be ready to see your mother. She can't wait to see you."

"I can't wait to see her, either. Thank you, Uncle Trae and Auntie Tasha." She gave me a hug and ran up onto the porch to give Trae one. Then she turned to me. "Auntie Tasha, can you fix my bang? Oh, wait! First, I gotta tell the twins that my mommy isn't dead." And she took off running down the steps and around the back.

I looked at Trae, and he shook his finger at me as if to say, *I told you so.*

KYRA

I was so glad to be released from the hospital. The room was beginning to creep me out. I was seeing images of a black Jesus everywhere.

"Kyra, are you all right?" Rick snapped me out of my daze.

"I think I'm okay, just a little nervous. At first, I didn't have contact with anyone. I didn't know who or where anyone was. Now, just like that, I'm getting ready to see my daughter and my friends. I don't remember what Tasha looks like, but I remember her voice. I'm overwhelmed." I sat rolling the tissue in my hand.

"You should be. It's only natural. But it's going to be all right. Tasha can't wait for you to show up. Trust me. You're going to be fine." Rick came over to me and stood by my side.

He took my hands and pulled me to my feet. I thought about what he said. *It's going to be all right*. All right? I hadn't even dealt with my issues regarding him. He told me everything. He, who had a fiancée and a baby on the way. *All right*? How could I be all right with him, when I want to keep him all to myself? What was to become of the relationship we once had was still to be determined. What was I supposed to do? Tell him to just up and leave his family? From the little bits and pieces he shared with me, he seemed to be pretty committed. And truth be told, I still had a husband. What was I going to do when I saw Marvin?

It seemed that with each mile we rode in the car, my heart became heavier and heavier. Things were moving too fast. But now that they were moving, I was unsure of everything. Would my daughter be angry with me for leaving her? Would I be able to piece my family back together? And what scared me the most: would I be able to piece my broken self back together? I was in deep thought the entire ride.

"Okay, we are here." Rick interrupted my thinking as he pulled into the driveway.

"Oh, no. We are here already?" I heard the panic in my own voice.

"Kyra, you're going to be fine." He turned off the engine.

I could feel my palms getting sweaty, but when he jumped out of the car, my ass felt as if it was glued to the seat. Just as more panic started to set in, the front door came open, and my daughter yelled out, "Mommy!" She jumped off the porch, and that's when my body took over. I pushed the car door open, my legs swung around, and I jumped out of the car. "Mommy!" she screamed.

"Aisha!" I ran to meet her, and we hugged, falling onto the lawn. I was kissing my baby all over her cheeks and face. "Look at you! You are beautiful." We hugged some more, and I was living in the moment.

My daughter said, "I'm sorry I left you, Mommy."

"You didn't leave me, baby. Don't think like that."

"Yes, I did. I left you, Mommy. I'm sorry." She began to cry.

"Baby . . ." I couldn't hold back the tears. *She really thinks that she left me.* How long had she been carrying that burden on her little shoulders? What if I was dead and gone? "Aisha, Mommy is fine. I love you, I missed you, and we won't be separated again. I won't leave you, and you won't leave me. Do we have a deal?"

"What about Daddy?"

I didn't know what to say, but I knew I wasn't going to be lying to my daughter. And for real, at that very moment, I didn't give a damn if I ever saw his bitch ass again. He'd better hope that I didn't see him. "I don't know about your father. We've gotta find out what's up with him. I haven't heard from him. But for now, you've gotta give Mommy some more love. Can I get some more love, girl? Mommy missed you so much!"

Some lady was standing over us with tears streaming down her cheeks. The next thing I knew, she was down on the grass, hugging and squeezing Aisha and me. "Kyra, don't you ever pull no mess like this again. Do you hear me?" She threatened, even though she was all choked up.

Her voice. "Tasha?"

She leaned back and looked at me. "Yes, it's me, Tasha. Your bff. Oh my god. You don't remember me? It's me, Tasha. I'm the one who stopped you from drowning. Remember we were at—"

"Seaside Heights!" I cut her off. "Tasha!" And then like a movie on fast forward, events with me and her raced through my mind. It was . . . awesome. Then some kids came running out of the house. The boys obviously thought we were playing and dived on top of us.

"There's my husband, Trae. And Aunt Marva." Tasha said. With a glance I remembered them as well. I felt like I was back. My prayers had been answered.

5

KYRON

"Ma, I'm good. Just get everybody out of my house, and I promise you I'll be doing much better. Y'all are acting as if I'm a cripple."

"Your damn mouth is!" smart-ass Kendra, my first cousin had the nerve to say as she chuckled. "Look at you, you can barely talk, sounding like Whispers from the movie *Hoodlum*. You know your mouth is where all your strength lies." She plopped down in a chair across from me just so she could talk shit.

I gave her a look that said, *You better get the fuck out of my face and fast.* She obviously read my expression, because she got up and went into the kitchen.

My mother touched my shoulder. "Kyron, go lie down and get some rest. I will get rid of everyone."

"Ma, what do you think I've been doing for the last few

months? Laying up resting. Trust me, I'm good. I just need to clear my head in my own house all by myself. I'll be fine, Ma." I grabbed her hand and kissed it.

She sat down next to me. "Watch your tone, boy. You didn't try to get rid of me when I was cleaning your behind." She shot daggers at me, and I had to grin at the thought.

"My bad, Ma. I know you just want the best for your son." She smiled as I leaned over, kissed her forehead, put my arms around her, and squeezed her tight.

"That's your problem. You think you are the baby, but you're not. You are my eldest, and I want you to start acting like it. Now, turn me loose so that I can get you settled."

I couldn't do anything but surrender. Between the nurse's visits, Mari, and family crowding my space, I was feeling suffocated. I was thankful when my moms eventually went to kicking everyone out of my apartment before finally putting on her jacket and snatching up her big-ass purse off the sofa. I stood up, and she stood right in front of me with her hands on her hips. I leaned over and kissed her cheek one last time. Mama was my heart.

"Do you remember how to change those bandages?"

"Ma!"

"Do you?"

"Yes, ma'am. I do."

"Good, and don't get fresh with me, Kyron. I thought your brother was going to be the death of me, but now I see that it's you. You shouldn't have gotten yourself into this mess in the first place."

"I'll call you each time I change the bandages. How's that?" I needed to get rid of my mother as soon as possible.

"You are the oldest, Kyron. You are supposed to lead by example. A good example."

"I know, Ma. We all make mistakes."

"Why don't you want somebody over here with you?" My mother continued to question me as I led her to the front door.

"Ma, I need some time to myself. Time to think and strategize."

"Strategize for what? Kyron, at the rate you're going, I'll be burying you instead of you burying me. Don't take me through that. I'm not supposed to bury my son." She touched my face as tears began welling up in her eyes.

"Ma, I'm going to be fine. I promise." I opened the door to let her out.

"That's what your mouth says, but I'm not totally convinced." She rolled her eyes and shook her head as she walked out of the apartment.

I closed and locked the door and hurried into the bathroom to splash cold water onto my face. All of a sudden, I was having hot flashes. I wasn't sure if it was from the pain medication or the rush I was having from finally being out of that hospital and alone in my own space. To be sure, I opened up the pain-medication bottle and dumped the pills down the drain. I looked at myself in the mirror. I rubbed the stubble on my chin, while wishing that I didn't have to look at the gauze wrapped around my neck. The plastic surgeon hooked a brotha up, but the deep scar left behind would be a constant reminder that I almost lost my life over some good pussy. Pussy that didn't belong to me.

Trae's bitch ass had the perfect opportunity, but he fucked it up. It must have been meant for me to be here. He thought I was gone. But I was about to be his worst fucking nightmare. Now it was my turn.

I went and sat down on my sofa and stared at the blank television screen. I needed the silence. But what I needed more was to hear what this bitch Tasha had to say. I didn't even know that she had written me back until I was packing to leave the hospital. I wanted to read the letter in peace and quiet, one of the reasons I wanted everybody out. I was anxious, mainly because when I sent her my letter, I wasn't sure if she would receive it. But she did.

I ripped the letter open.

Kyron, Kyron, Kyron.

First of all, nigga, you bitch made. Here it is, you over there recovering from a life-threatening injury, and the first bitch you holla at is me? You talking all that shit about Jags and money and connections—who the fuck you tryna convince that you the shit, me or yourself? Talking about you love me and you hate me. What kinda fag shit is that? You wish you hated me. You don't know who you fucking with, so you better check my résumé. I will bet anything that your dick is hard right now as you read and anticipate my next line.

My nigga, why can't you just accept it? You were just something to do for me . . . simply a revenge fuck. I gave you some payback pussy on my terms, and you got pussy-whipped and fell in love. That's why you laying over there crying and shit. And you have the audacity to call me a ho? Fuck outta here with that bullshit. You don't even know how you mustered up the energy to call me a ho. No, nigga, I ain't your ho; you're my bitch. Sheeeit . . . gonna call me a walking billboard? If I am that, you best believe it reads, "Kyron's a fuckin' sucka!"

I recall you saying three important things: 1. You went out. 2. You made my money. 3. You kept me fly, then gave me the dick if and when I decided I wanted it. But then I fucked you so good you thought I was going to take you to the top of the world and had you begging: Marry me, Tasha! Be mine, Tasha! I had your punk ass pulling out rings and shit. So that sounds like you the ho. Nigga, I pimped your ass real good, had you trained well, and even after you got that ass whipped, you still brought Momma her money. Yeah, I rode your dick . . . good enough to make you lick where another nigga slides his dick. How does Trae's cum taste? Is it as good to you as it is to me? And then you brag about a bitch serving her purpose. No nigga, you served your purpose. I wasn't even fucking you, and you were coming up off stacks and scheming on ways to steal me from Trae. And you are boasting about a Jag? You a low-budget-ass nigga if you think a Jag gets you a come-up. Them fake-ass, so-called loyal niggas you got on your team are laughing in your face because they got a bitch for a boss, or should I say a broke-ass coworker? Bitch ass sitting here whining about a car, page after page. Nigga, please! I bought Trae a fuckin' Maybach. And you obviously forgot that I told you I have a Spyder C8 Aileron sitting in the garage that I don't even drive! That Jag was like a punch buggy compared to my shit. That's why Trae busted the shit up. You think your money is long? Get the fuck outta here; your money is as long as your dick . . . and that ain't long enough.

Since we keeping score, let me ho-check your ass real quick. You called me a ho, but I'm the same bitch who had you turn your back on your family. It was me, Tasha, the same bitch who had you eating pussy, and it ain't about you making me cum, nigga. I'm married to Trae Macklin. My pussy is well trained. And yes, I'm the same bitch who turned you into a marked fucking man. So watch your back, bitch-ass nigga. You do the math. Calculate that shit. Tasha, a ten . . . Kyron, a zero.

You asked yourself, are you insane? Hell, no! You in love, and I can't fault a nigga for that. You just like every other nigga that gets the pleasure of Tasha. You sprung the fuck out. The proof is in that long-ass letter going on and on and on about what you lost and what you wish you still had. Gonna write me a punk-ass letter. I can't get over this shit. What? You ain't got shit else to do? By the way, where your bitch at? You had a so-called bad bitch who held you down the whole time you was doing your bid, but as soon as you fell into this boss pussy, you forgot all about that bitch. I had your ass moaning and groaning my name. Tasha. While thinking, Mari who?

Oh, and I didn't kill your seed. The little muthafucka committed suicide when it realized it wasn't the child of a real boss. So fuck you and die, muthafucka!

The Boss Bitch,
Tasha Macklin Forever
P.S. Don't contact me no more. Bitch!

With each paragraph I read, I pictured myself killing this bitch. She really had no clue who she was flappin' off at the gums to. By the time I finished the letter, I couldn't help but laugh. *I'ma make this bitch eat all of these words.* We'll see who the fag is when my dick is all up in her guts. Did this bitch really say I was a revenge fuck? She don't know I will destroy everything and everyone around her until I get her. Including them bastard ass kids. Yeah, I'm crazy bitch and I plan on showing you just how crazy.

I called Kendrick and told him that I was getting ready to call Trina and that I might need him.

"Nigga, it's too soon for you to be hittin' the streets," he told me.

"Just be on stand-by." I hung up on him.

I called Trina.

"Hello."

"Hey."

"Who is this?" she snapped.

"Kyron."

Silence.

"Why are you whisper—oh, snap! Kyron. I forgot all about that."

"It's all good. I want you to set it up so that I can see Shorty." I got straight to the point.

"Oh, no no no no no, Kyron! My sister is barely speaking to me as it is. Her man hates me, her best friends call me all kinds of conniving bitches, and your own brother won't even give me the time of day. So no, no, no. I am not getting involved. No, Kyron. And listen to you, are you even well? You can barely talk, and you almost lost your life because of fucking with her. I would think that you learned some sort of a lesson from all of this and wouldn't even think about fuckin' with her."

"You done?"

"Yeah, I'm done." Trina popped off.

"Good. 'Cause I ain't trying to hear all that psychobabble

bullshit. Set it up. And do it within the next couple of days. Forty-eight hours, to be exact." I ended the call, and she called right back. "Trina, this is not a game. You got forty-eight hours."

"Or what, nigga?" she challenged me.

"Oh, you'll know." I didn't have time to be playing games with this ho. I turned my phone off and dialed Kendrick from the house phone. I needed this bitch to take me seriously.

"Yo, whaddup?" he answered.

"You got that address for me, right?"

"Which one?"

"Kevin's."

"I put someone on it. Let me check and hit you back."

TRINA

I needed to talk to somebody but had no clue who. That last phone call had me convinced that Kyron was a certified lunatic. Here this nigga was fresh out of the hospital, recovering from a life-threatening situation, and now he was running right back to the same trap that got him caught up in the first place. Insane! And he thought that I was going to get involved? I don't think so. I learned my lesson. As a matter of fact, fuck Kyron! As far as I was concerned, he and everything that looked like him was dead to me. And the conversation we had never happened. And as I thought over it some more, I figured that now was just as good a time to let him know. I called him, and it went straight to voicemail.

"Aye, Kyron, check this out. I won't be doing shit you tell me. Please leave me and my sister the fuck alone. You should be treating her like she got the plague and staying the fuck away! Don't call my phone no more."

KYRON

I couldn't wait to see how the bitch would react to this. She had me fucked up. I listened to her little voicemail message, and all it did was urge me to move a little faster. I had to let her know that it was not a game. I wanted what I wanted. As soon as Kendrick gave me the address to her brother, Kevin's house, we headed on over there. After I thought about it, I had a way to get this silly bitch's attention. I knew it would get Shorty's attention as well. This nigga stayed out in Coney Island. It was a nice, quiet spot, and his house was the last one on the block, sitting on the cul-de-sac. Kendrick and I camped out down the street for almost six hours before he pulled up. My muscle was already waiting on him; we were just waiting on their signal.

"What's taking them niggas so long?" Kendrick mumbled as he shifted from side to side in his seat.

"Stop fidgeting, nigga. You making me nervous."

"You think we should go in?" He reached for his hammer.

"Not yet. Wait for the word. I'm confident in these niggas."

Just then, Kendrick's cell vibrated. He looked at it and said, "Let's do this."

He started the car, and we parked right in the nigga's driveway and got out. It was dark and was beginning to rain. I pulled my hood over my head and followed Kendrick, careful to protect the bandages on my neck.

As soon as we came up the back stairs, the door popped open.

"Everything's ready. You sure you don't want us to stay?" my muscle, Herb, asked.

"We'll take it from here!" Kendrick told him.

We followed Herb to the kitchen, where our pawn was sitting at the table. "What do y'all want? Dope? Money?" He was sitting there looking confused, as Knowledge, muscle I had on my team from day one, had his foot propped on a chair standing over him with his pistol aimed at his head. I looked at Kevin closely and saw the resemblance. He looked more like Trina than he resembled Tasha. But there was no mistaking that he was family. Kendrick took off his jacket and pulled out his hammer.

"Y'all good?" Knowledge asked.

"We good. Y'all niggas wait outside," Kendrick told him.

"Who the fuck are y'all?" Kevin asked.

I pulled out this handmade crafted Sebenza knife that I had been wanting to use. Kendrick let out a whistle when he saw it. "Nice, ain't it?" I was talking more to myself. I pulled out my cell and dialed Trina's number, hit the speaker button, and set the phone on the table directly in front of her brother.

"Hello." She sounded groggy, obviously in a deep sleep.

"What the fuck do y'all want, man? I said take the dope. Damn! You got that," her brother yelled out. Kendrick quickly put him in a chokehold, and I stuck the knife into his shoulder, twisting it back and forth. "Ahhhhhhhh!" he screamed.

"Hello. Hello? Kyron, I don't have time for your bullshit," Trina snapped. She was starting to sound wide awake.

She didn't have time for the bullshit? Well, me, either. I got closer, grabbed the nigga's face, sliced the nigga's ear off, and threw it on the table.

"Owwwwwwwwww! Shit! Fuck! Ahhhhhhhhh!" His eyes

widened as he shook and twisted. You would have thought I'd sliced the nigga's dick off the way he was yelling in anguish, holding the side of his face as Kendrick unlocked his grip. Blood poured through his fingers. "Take the dope! Shit!! Ahhh! Take the dope!"

I picked up the phone and took it off speaker.

"Kevin?" Trina asked in apparent panic. "Kyron, is that my brother?"

"My fuckin' ear! What the fuck? I don't even know you." He was still screaming.

"Kevin! Kevin? Oh, my God. Kyron! His ear? What are you doing to my brother?"

"You took care of that yet?" I asked her.

"Kyron, is that my brother? Don't do this. Why are you—"

"Did you take care of that?" I asked again as I walked to the living room and peeked through the blinds.

"No, not yet. But I'ma do it. Please, Kyron. That's my brother. I'ma do it."

"Now, do you see how easy that was?" I asked her.

I thought about the look in Kevin's eyes, and it was void of fear. I had to give it to him.

"Please, Kyron, stop hurting my brother." Trina pleaded with me.

"You got that. Just handle my business. Me and you good, right?"

"Yes, we good." She started crying.

That was all I needed to hear. I ended the call, went back into the kitchen, pointed the knife in his face, and said, "This shit is between us." I rubbed the blood from the blade on his lips. "If not, everyone you love will die a slow and painful death. Sorry for the inconvenience."

I was now more anxious to see Shorty.

MARI

"I'm outside," I heard Kyron say, and then the phone went dead. I went into the bedroom and stood in front of my long mirror, giving myself the once-over. I was thinking about dyeing my long, thick black mane to a medium brown. I needed a change and was no longer feeling the black. And if one more person asked me if I was Eva Mendes, the chick who played Denzel's mistress in *Training Day*, I was going to snap.

My Chanel dress was hugging me in all the right places. I wanted Kyron to see what he had been neglecting and what he was about to lose. He, of course, didn't say where he was taking me; he simply said to be ready. Little did he know, tonight I was giving him his walking papers.

I grabbed my Chanel bag, turned out my bedroom light, and headed for the door, only to hear the locks turning. I stepped back, and in walked Kyron.

"I thought you wanted me to meet you out front."

"I changed my mind." I barely heard him. He closed the door behind him and locked it.

He had on all black, even down to the gators. He looked and smelled like money and appeared to be wearing the gauze around his neck proudly. I hated to admit it, but I was a damned fool in love. His love. I put so much into him. Into us. But it was so one-sided. Just the thought pissed me off and made me realize that I didn't need to end things tonight. *Hell, no*. Not before getting back at least half of what I put into this relationship.

"Why is your face all frowned up?" he had the nerve to ask me.

"Because seeing you only makes me angry."

He smiled. "This was always about business. You know that."

"Business? Is chasing that bitch business?" I paused and looked at him. "Why would you let some new pussy fuck up everything we've worked so hard for?"

He smiled again. "Who's been puttin' shit in your ear?"

"Puttin' shit in my ear? Kyron, I am not stupid, so don't insult my intelligence. I have eyes. Were you not just laid up in critical condition? Don't you have a patch covering your throat? Can you barley speak? Are you not chasing a married woman, acting like some common hoodlum from the block?"

He nonchalantly turned around and opened the door.

"Oh, so now you don't have anything to say."

"Are you coming with me or not?"

"Oh, I'm coming. This conversation is long overdue." I brushed past him. "Remember the big picture, Kyron."

"Why the fuck are you still here? If you don't want to ride this thing out with me, you can go. "

"You're kidding me, right?" I stopped and turned to look into his eyes.

"When have you known me to kid?" He was dead serious.

"Kyron, we have a game plan. We were supposed to stick to it, not come home and fall for some hood bitch and lose focus."

"Game plan. Did you hear what you just said? *Game plan.* Mari, this ain't no game out here."

"You are the one playing the games, Kyron. Chasing some married bitch. You are more concerned with this whore than you are with business."

"The game plan." He chuckled.

"If you want me to scrap everything, let me know. My brother is waiting on you. And when he asks me about you, I have to choose to lie or be totally truthful. My reputation is on the line here, Kyron, and I'm not going to let you fuck that up!"

We stood in an intense stare-down. Then he smiled. Something he always does when he thinks I'm bullshitting. "Stop stressing over irrelevant shit. You look too sexy to be stressing."

He opened the front door. I stormed to the car, stood there with my arms folded, and could only shake my head. I got into the car, entertaining the thought of going right back into the house.

When he jumped into the car, he said, "Your brother ain't going nowhere. When I'm ready to get with your brother, I will do just that. I don't work for nobody, and I don't owe nobody shit."

"So this is what's stopping you? The fact that you're a boss, you don't work for anybody?"

"Exactly. I don't need muthafuckas. Muthafuckas need me." He looked over at me and then put the car into gear and pulled off.

I couldn't believe the shit that was coming out of his mouth. I wanted to reach over and slap that smug look off his face. I turned away from him and looked out the window. I was the dumb one. I was the one guilty of sticking around and taking all of his bullshit.

We drove in silence all the way until we stopped at a light on Manhattan's Eighth Avenue. A white guy on a bike next to us hawked and spit, and the wind blew it onto the hood of Kyron's car. The next thing I knew, he was out of the car, running and grabbing the back of the guy's bike. He pushed him over and went to stomping him. I couldn't believe it. "Kyron! The bigger picture! The bigger picture!" I heard myself screaming. I jumped out of the car and grabbed his arm in an attempt to end the situation before it got worse.

"Get the fuck off me!" he barked, no longer whispering and he snatched away from me. He was in a fitful rage.

I was furious as I stepped back and looked at him. I had to ask myself, was it worth it? Why the fuck was I so obsessed with him? And if he didn't give a fuck about his future, why should I? Just like I guided him to this point, I could just as easily guide the next man, and it probably wouldn't take half the time.

"You know what? I'm out of here." I left him there stomping the daylights out of a total stranger on a bike. "Taxi! Taxi!" I jumped into the first one that stopped. I was convinced that Kyron had lost his mind.

6

TASHA

I was glad that I had Kyra all to myself first. We cried, hugged, and caught up to what had been going on during our time apart. Now it was Angel's and Jaz's turn. They had finally made it to sunny California. I stood in the doorway and watched the three of them cry, laugh, cry, and laugh some more, just like I did. The reunion was bittersweet.

Not only did Kyra look different, but she seemed different. For one, it was surprising to see her reading the Bible and down on her knees praying. One minute she would appear all holier-than-thou, and the next minute she would be the old, talking-smack, neck-twisting, from-the-hood Kyra. The Kyra I was used to.

"Ooh! Why are you sneaking up on me like that?" Trae had eased up behind me and was brushing his lips against my neck.

"Because I want to steal you away from your girls for a few minutes."

"A few minutes? Yeah, right. That's what you said the last time." He began easing me away from the door. "Trae, stop. We are getting ready to go get something to eat."

He stopped and peeked in at the girls. "They ain't trying to go nowhere no time soon. I just need a few minutes. They won't even know you're gone." He pulled me away from my girls and eased me into the hall bathroom and shut the door.

"You ain't right," I said, smiling at him.

"You ain't right! Stilettos on, ass cheeks hanging out the dress. What kind of restaurant are y'all going to?" He backed up against the door, and with both hands on my ass, he pulled me close to him.

"Stop exaggerating! My ass cheeks are not hanging out."

"Bullshit. You ain't going to no restaurant wearing a club dress."

I sucked my teeth. "Since when did you start having problems with me wearing short dresses?"

"Since I'm not going with you. That's when. You know my rules."

He was trippin', and I wasn't liking it. I damn sure wasn't about to take the dress off. Hell, we were only going out to eat. We stood there staring into each other's eyes as he continued to caress my ass. Just as it started to feel good, he abruptly turned me around and guided me toward the sink. I felt his hand ease up my back, and he pushed me forward. I grabbed onto the edges of the sink.

I looked back at him. "What do you mean, I know your rules?"

"Assume the position, and shut up."

"Shut who? Assume what?" I went to stand up, but he was holding me down with one hand and holding that steel with the other.

"You heard me." He used his knee to force my legs apart.

I watched him in the mirror as he admired my ass and stroked himself.

I felt the head of his dick enter me. "Don't be telling me to shut up." I moaned as I felt him push all the way inside me. I wanted to fuss, but it was feeling good, and I couldn't help but throw the pussy back at him and talk shit. "Niggas willing to die over this pussy."

"And I'm willing to kill 'em." He shoved the dress over my ass, ripping it. I knew he did it on purpose.

"Trae!" I looked back at him. His eyes were closed as he held tight onto my waist, putting in work. I had an attitude about my dress, so I had to say something. "You tore my dress." I even wanted to argue, but the dick now had my undivided attention. He stroked long and deep as subtle moans escaped his lips. I grabbed tighter onto the edges of the sink, and then he started coming. He pulled out and skeeted all over my ass and my dress. I stood straight up, turned around, and pushed him. "You dog!"

"Now, go change into something more conservative!" he said as he tried to catch his breath. "But you gotta admit, that was the shit."

"You'll see how conservative I am when you realize how long it'll be before you get up in this pussy again," I snapped as I brushed past him to get out of the bathroom. He blocked the door, staring at me as he fixed his clothes.

"What's the matter with you? I know you ain't trippin' about a dress that I bought!"

"Yes, I am trippin'. I'm trippin' about you tearing my dress, fucking me, spurting all over me, and I didn't even come! What the fuck is your problem?" I snatched the bathroom door open, and he slammed it shut. "Move, Trae, with ya selfish ass!"

"Man, fuck that dress. I said I didn't want you wearing it." He grabbed the part he already ripped and ripped it some more. "Now what? And all of a sudden, you want to come, when at first you didn't even want to fuck. Now you wanna come?" He grabbed me roughly, picked me up, and slammed me onto the sink.

I tried to get down, but he held me there. "What do you think you're doing, Trae?" He was fumbling with his pants. "What is your problem?"

"You want to come, right?"

"Nigga, please. Let me outta here. You ain't even hard. I gots to go."

"Nah. I'm selfish. You ain't come. You ain't going nowhere." He stood there between my legs, pulling out his dick.

"Forget it, Trae," I said, only to have my leg raised up into the air and a half-hard dick thrust up inside me.

"Why the fuck are we arguing over nothing?" he asked me as he stroked in and out.

I could feel him growing harder and longer. I spread my legs wider, grabbed onto his ass, and pulled him deeper inside me.

"Oh, so you like that, huh?" He kissed me roughly around my neck.

"You ruined my dress." I moaned as I shut my eyes tight and matched my strokes with his.

"Fuck the dress, and concentrate on fucking me." He increased his fucking pace. "How does this feel?" he whispered in my ear.

"G-good." I moaned as I tried to get and keep as much dick in me as I could. With me holding him tighter and him fucking me harder, I began to embrace and ride the wave of a much-needed orgasm. My husband waited for my legs to stop shaking before he eased out of me. I leaned forward and gently kissed his lips. He helped me off the sink, and before he could say something smart, I said, "You still didn't have to fuck up my dress." And I stormed out of the bathroom on wobbly legs.

I slipped past the family room where my girls were talking and laughing and the kids were running wild. On my way upstairs, as I made it into the living room, I heard knocking. I went to the door, cracked it, and there stood Trina. She looked as if she had been crying. I opened the door and asked, "What are you doing here? What's the matter?"

"I didn't want to come, but I need to talk to you."

"Why didn't you just call me? You know Trae don't want you over here. I told you I would let you know when things cooled off."

"Tasha, let me in. I need to talk to you. Kevin is hurt."

"What? My little brother?" I hadn't heard from him since Stephon's funeral. Now I wondered what he was mixed up in. He usually handled his business. I looked back to see if Trae was coming before I let her in. "Hurry up!" I opened the front door. "Where's your car?" I was now whispering.

"I parked down the street. Come outside. I don't want to have to cuss Trae out."

"I have to change. Come on, girl. I'll sneak you upstairs. Close the door, and tell me what happened. Hurry up." I made a dash for the stairs. She was right behind me. I knew that my ass was hanging out.

"What happened to you? Never mind. I don't want to know," she said.

We went into the bedroom, and I shut the door. I went into the bathroom and closed that door, leaving it cracked. I turned on the shower and began to undress. "So what happened? Is he okay? He got busted?" I yelled through the crack in the door.

"It's Kyron."

I stopped the bitch right in her tracks. Opened the bathroom door all the way, naked and all. "Kyron? Trina, get the fuck outta here with that bullshit. I can't believe you." I snatched up a towel, wrapped it around me, and started pushing her out of my bedroom. I couldn't believe she was bringing me this bullshit. I wanted her out of my house. "Get out, Trina!"

"Tasha, no, listen to me. He threatened me. He said if I didn't set up something with you, it would be my ass. And when I didn't, he went to Kevin and cut his ear off. He—"

"He did *what*?" I shrieked as I stopped pushing her.

"He cut his ear off. He did it with me right there on the phone. I don't think Kevin knows why. And I wasn't planning on telling him!" Tears welled up in her eyes.

"This shit is crazy. This has to stop." I began pacing back and forth.

"Make it stop, Tasha," she said with sarcasm dripping from her voice.

"How can I make it stop? I'm not fucking with Kyron like that no more. You must be crazy!"

"What if he comes after you? Or Kevin again? He's your brother, too, Tasha. Or even worse . . ."

"Or even worse what?" I stopped my pacing. "Trina, this is mostly your fault—"

"My fault? Was it my fault when you fucked him?" She pointed at me. "I'll take half of the blame. But not all of it. But now we have a crisis, and we gotta do something."

"Do what? You know my situation."

"Do something. Shit, I don't know."

I went back to pacing back and forth. Kyron wanted to see me? I was scared to even mention his name to Trae. But I knew for a fact that I wasn't meeting him under any circumstances, not in this lifetime. And our baby brother— this was outrageous. "You gotta stall him somehow until I can figure something out."

"How am I supposed to do that?"

"Bitch, I don't know. Think of something. Tell him you spoke to me and that I said I would get back to him. Shit, make up something. In the meantime, I gotta call Kev."

"Nooooo! Tasha, don't! We can't let him know we had anything to do with it. He doesn't know Kyron and don't know that we know him."

"Bitch, you sounding real stupid."

"I'm serious, Tasha."

I thought about what my sister said, and it just reconfirmed how cold-hearted of a bitch she was. Here it was, our own flesh and blood; all three of us came from the same loins. Our brother was cut the fuck up and over some of our deeds, and she was talking about don't call him.

"Trina, I got to figure this out. This is too much for me to swallow right now. Let me think about it, and I will call you later." I had to tell Trae about this.

"Don't call Kevin, Tasha. And call me. Don't leave me hanging. All right, Tasha?"

"All right, Trina!" I snapped, agitated that she had brought me this Kyron bullshit. Why didn't that muthafucka die? And now he was using my brother and Trina to fuck with me. I needed to get her and her negative energy away from me. "Come on, let me get you out of here." I tossed the towel and grabbed my robe and pulled it tight. I cracked the bedroom door to make sure the coast was clear. I peeked out and motioned for her to come on. As I began to creep down the second-floor stairs, Kyra turned the corner and dashed up the steps. I almost shit on myself. "Kyra, you scared the devil out of me. Where's Trae?"

"Why are you whispering? And Trina? Is that Trina? Get out of here! Praise God!" she squealed.

"Kyra!" Trina dashed back up the stairs as if she was running from a ghost. That shit was so comical, I wish I had of caught it on camera.

"What is her problem?" Kyra asked me.

"She thought you was gone just like the rest of us. No offense. Trina, get your ass down here!" I called out. She peeked over the bannister.

"What the . . . where—"

"Girl, it's me and I wish y'all would stop with the dead bullshit."

"Kyra, look at you. Dreads? Your skin is so smooth. Where have you been?" Trina came dashing down the stairs, damn near knocking me over to go hug Kyra. "Tasha didn't even tell me you were home. You had us worried half to death. Where were you?"

"Trina, you need to be going. Going now." I grabbed her arm and damn near yanked it out of its socket.

"No, don't go. We are getting ready to go out to eat. Me, your sister, Angel, and Jaz. Come with us." Kyra extended a dinner invitation to my sister. I wasn't trying to hear it, though.

Trina lit up; then, just as quickly, her face turned into a frown. I was sure that she was thinking about how Angel and Jaz both wanted to kick her ass. "Not this time. I already have a previous engagement. But let me take you to breakfast."

"That'll work," Kyra said. "Don't stand me up, girl, and have me getting up all early for you, Trina. We gotta catch up."

"I'm looking forward to it, Kyra." Trina hugged Kyra again and then flew down the stairs and out the front door.

I rushed up the stairs, took a quick shower, and got dressed. I had decided to wear a blue Alexander McQueen pant suit with a pair of cream Giuseppe heels. Angel was wearing an Anna Sui brown chiffon dress and gold Louboutin stilettos and Jaz had on a pair of Givenchy jeans with a red Dolce and Gabbana blouse and red strappy heels. We all looked at what Kyra had on, looked at each other and now words needed to be spoken.

Kyra glared at us, snapped her neck and asked, "Why y'all lookin' at me? Y'all know I ain't got no clothes."

"Don't even worry about it, I got you." I told her. "I'ma call my girl Detroit Keish at Boutique Bleu on S. La Brea and tell her I'm coming through. I'ma give her your sizes and she'll have shit laid out for you as if you are royalty. We get in, get out. Now let's bounce."

When I got downstairs, Trae was kicked back on the couch with his eyes closed. I kissed him lightly on the lips and grabbed my girls, and we were on our way out the door.

"Don't make me come and get you," he yelled after me.

"Stop being so mean, Trae," Angel snapped at him before I could. "She's with her girls."

"Don't let me find out y'all doing more than eating."

"And if you do?" Angel challenged.

"Me and Kay going back to our old ways."

"Whatever!" We all laughed. We were already celebrating so I pulled out the Maybach. Y'all must have forgot who the fuck I was.

My girl Keish blessed Kyra with a slick Armani khaki mini skirt with a black Armani jacket, a pair of black and brown Fendi ankle boots. We were now ready to roll.

"Wait until Rick sees your ass in that." Jaz teased her.

We had reservations at the Geisha House on the Boulevard in L.A. Kyra and Angel wanted sushi. The waiter had just cleared the table of our dinner and poured us our third round of sake. We laughed and reminisced for what felt like hours. Everyone had their glass filled to the rim at least twice, except for Kyra; she didn't want anything to drink. She was listening intently as Jaz told her about Faheem, Oni, and his son. Then she started crying and praying. Everybody was, like, what the fuck? She quickly recovered and began asking more questions. But it was too late; she had changed up the whole atmosphere.

Since Angel didn't have any major drama of her own, she happily told Kyra all about mine. My drama didn't cause her to cry, but from the change in complexion of her skin, I thought she went into shock. And Angel thought that shit was so funny, she couldn't stop laughing, and I wanted to bust her in the mouth.

However, I was dying to know what Miss Holier-Than-Thou Kyra was going to do about Rick. Because Rick had a woman and a baby on the way, so I decided to ask her. Hell, I knew I wasn't the only one at the table who wanted the scoop. So I decided to go all in.

"Enough about us, Kyra. What are you going to do about Rick?" Her eyes got as big as saucers. "C'mon, Kyra. You don't gotta front on us. Hell, we know you. We're your girls. So what's up? Just because you were gone for forever, I hope you remember that we don't keep secrets from each other."

She buried her face in the palms of her hands. We were all sitting on the edges of our seats. "I don't know. I don't know. God, I don't know."

"You sure you don't want any of this wine?" Jaz asked her.

Kyra waved her hand back and forth. "I need a blunt right about now, not some soft-ass rice wine." We all gave her the side eye.

"Sooooo . . . what's up? He has a fiancée who is pregnant. They live together as a happy family." I pressed.

"I know, Tasha. You don't have to remind me. We talked, and he's just as conflicted as I am. But, for real, I think he's leaning toward staying with her."

"I can't tell. Why isn't he gone, then? He's still here with you," I said. "That sounds like some bullshit to me."

"Do you want him?" Angel asked her.

"Y'all know I do," Kyra admitted. "Shit is just complicated."

"Have y'all fucked?" Jaz whispered, as if any of us wasn't fucking.

"No. No, we haven't. Our situation is so . . . delicate. I don't know."

"Have you told him what you want?" Angel asked.

"No, but I plan on it. Believe me, I plan on it."

RICK

Trae and I were sitting on the porch when the ladies pulled up. My palms got sweaty, and my throat got dry, because I had made up my mind to tell Kyra that I was leaving tonight. I was going back to Nina. Was it the right thing to do? I couldn't answer that. Was it the easiest thing to do? I couldn't answer that, either.

Trae got up and went to meet Tasha. When she got out of the car, he picked her up and swung her around. She squealed in delight and begged him to put her down. He had the relationship that niggas envied. Through the ups and downs, their shit was bulletproof. I still couldn't believe the drama he had with the Chinese chick and that other nigga Kyron. I had years on the force and thought I had seen it all. But he proved me wrong. He admitted that his relationship with Tasha was rocky, but he was determined to smooth it out by any means necessary. And I knew he meant that shit.

Kyra came up onto the porch and sat next to me. I waited until everyone went inside before I spoke. I cleared my throat. "Kyra, I'm going back tonight."

"Why?" she asked me. "Why do you have to go back? I need you. I need you here with me, Rick."

"Kyra, you're in good hands. I'm at ease now, knowing that you are safe and pretty much settled in."

"Rick, you know damn well what I mean. I want you here with me. I don't want you to go back."

"Kyra, you know my situation. What do you want me to do?"

"Stay here with me. It's only a situation if you make it a situation."

I laughed. "Shit, I wish it was that simple."

"So you're going to choose her over me? Why? Because she's pregnant? Shit, I can get pregnant, too. Then what?" And to my surprise she climbed over onto my lap and straddled me. *Shit.*

"Kyra, don't make this harder than it has to be."

"What am I supposed to do, Rick? You know I'm a fighter. You don't expect me to put up a fight for you? Why not? I had you first." She kissed me on the lips. It was the first kiss we had shared since she came back into my life. I couldn't even say we shared it, because I was scared to kiss her back, fearing that I wouldn't be able to stop myself. "Answer me, baby. What am I supposed to do? This is not fair to me, and you know it." She pressed her lips against mine and forced her tongue inside my mouth. I tasted wine and peppermint. She wiggled a little to get a better position on my dick. She kissed me again, this time rocking back and forth on what was now my growing hard-on. I knew I was in trouble.

"Kyra . . . baby."

"I like the way you call me baby."

"Kyra—"

"Rick, if I'm going to lose you, at least let me have this moment. I haven't been kissed in God knows when. I haven't been fucked in God knows when. I want you to fuck me, Rick." She was kissing and sucking on my neck. I was the one who was fucked.

Because my shit was getting too hard, I had to get her off my lap. I went to stand up, and she wrapped her arms around my neck and her legs around my waist.

"Kyra . . . baby. We need to talk. Don't do this."

"Do what?" She held me tighter as I eased over to the banister and set her on it. She still refused to turn me loose. I felt her hand slide down in my jeans and grab my joint. "Do what, Rick?"

"That, Kyra." She was squeezing and massaging. "C'mon, now. Let me go. I'm going back to her tonight, Kyra." I tried to move her hand.

"Not before I get me some of this dick, Rick. Remember the time we fucked in your mother's house, in your old bedroom? I remember that. It's crystal-clear in my mind. I can even feel you inside me." She purred in my ear, as she nibbled my ear lobe.

This time, when her lips touched mine, I kissed her back, and

I couldn't stop. The king anaconda was fully awakened, and he had a mind of his own. He was doing all of the thinking and was ready to dig into his prey. "Let's go inside." I was breathing hard. At this point, I couldn't contain him if I wanted to.

"Nope. You might change your mind. We are not going anywhere. You're gonna fuck me right here. Right now." She said it so seductively that I couldn't help but lift her up and snatch off her panties. I hoped that Trae didn't come to the door only to find me fucking Kyra on his porch, on his banister. I knew he had to have fucked Tasha out here, because the height was just right, the width was perfect, and the night sky put you in the mood the same way a nice, slow love song would.

"I want you to feel how wet you're making me, King Rick," she whispered into my ear. She grabbed my hand and guided it between her thighs, and I ran my fingers lightly up her pussy, teasing her clit, causing her to jump and release one of the sexiest moans I had ever heard.

"It's too late to get jumpy now." I kissed her throat, causing her to throw her head back and moan.

"I'm not jumpy. I'm just horny."

She slid my jeans over my ass. I grabbed my steel and put it to her opening. She stiffened up. "Relax," I ordered her. I buried the head of the anaconda in her tight but wet opening, sliding slightly in and out, causing her to groan as if I was all the way inside of her. "You sure this is what you want?"

"I'm so . . . sure." She moaned. Her body was shaking.

I then slid all the way in, enjoying the tight grip of her walls. I felt her nails dig into my back as I went deeper and began to fuck her the way she wanted me to. Her tightness had me ready to come.

"Rick. Rick. Rick," she kept repeating. "Oh . . . Rick. I wanted this as soon as I realized who you were," she said as she threw the pussy at me.

"Kyra, I missed you so much." The good pussy was forcing me to confess. "I want her to be you. I need her to be you." I was saying shit I shouldn't be saying.

"I'm here now. I'm . . . Rick, baby. Oh, that feels . . . so . . . ssso good. Fuck me. Keep fucking me like that." She squealed, and her body began to tremble. It vibrated like it had the few times I had taken her tender frame to ecstasy. She wasn't lying when she said that she was thirsty for a good fucking. Her pussy was on fire and she was riding my dick as if it was the only one on the planet. I grunted as I plunged into her harder.

"Shit," she mumbled as her eyes rolled into her head and she gasped for air. She clung to my body. I could tell that she was glad to have me in her arms again. Each stroke brought me closer to her. My flesh rubbing against hers, her soft hands clutching at my back, her eyes locking with mines—the way we connected with each other went far and beyond mere sex. When we were together, we were on another plane.

Just then, a van slowed down in front of the house. I pumped inside Kyra's pussy faster. Van or not, I couldn't stop. The pussy was feeling just that good. I was at the point of no return. She was coming as the van pulled into the driveway. I could see the heads of three kids. Nina, my fiancée, got out of the van as I spurt my seed deep into Kyra's womb.

7

NINA

I'm Nina Coles, and no, I'm not some chick who just popped up in the mix. I came on the set in *What's Really Hood*, Wahida's anthology with the short story called "Makin' Endz Meet," and then I'm the star in *The Golden Hustla*. Those two stories go together. Yeah, I had to plug Wahida's books. She's like that.

Enough of the formalities. I met Rick while I was living in Atlanta. He became my thug knight in shining armor. It didn't matter to him that I had three kids, a crazy ex and was mixed up in some made-for-reality-TV drama with my job. With his guidance, I flipped all that shit around and made it work for me—or, rather, us. We robbed my boss of his stash money, packed it up and moved to Miami. I wasn't feeling the superficialness of Miami, so we decided to try Arizona. Especially since my oldest son had asthma.

I knew that Rick used to live out in Cali and that his ex-wife was still there. I knew all about Kyra, the chick he was in love with who got killed. Hell, he admitted that I reminded him of her. He told me that several times. And I hate to admit it, at first, I was jealous of her. It was obvious that she had his heart, and I felt that I couldn't compete with her. He had the hardest time making me believe that it wasn't a competition. The girl was gone. Dead. Once I accepted and believed that there was no competition, our relationship went to the next level.

I was and am still madly in love with him. He completes me. He is my soul mate, who loves me for me, and once we found out I was pregnant, he was ecstatic. He didn't have any kids of his own, so he was beside himself.

Everything was going picture-perfect until he made this trip to his old stomping grounds. I didn't have a problem with him going back to where he made his career. Especially when he said he would only be gone for a few days. He said it was something he had to do. Some bullshit about a cop's intuition. Now, that part concerned me. I wasn't sure if that meant he was going to kill somebody, investigate a crime, or what. But he assured me it wasn't anything like that. He said he needed to clear his head and wanted to hit the road. Okay, cool. Driving from Arizona to Cali—I didn't have a problem with that. Shit, I couldn't stop him if I wanted to. But then, the more he would call home, the more distant he began to sound. I would ask him if everything was all right, and he could never give me an answer that I was satisfied with. And now that he'd been gone for almost two weeks, I said, "Oh, fuck that!" Something was up. And that's when I started piecing events and conversations together. Niggas don't realize that women are the best detectives. When we want to find some shit out, we can, and we will.

It took me a couple of days, but I finally faced the facts. I saw exactly where Rick was driving around in our Mercedes ML550, thanks to the "mbrace" system we had installed. I was able to find out all that I needed to know. I saw that the car was back and forth between his old street address and a hospital. My first thought was that this nigga had obviously gotten back with his wife.

So I packed up my three kids and headed to his old address. However, I was not ready for what I was confronted with. When I pulled up into the driveway and got out of the car and got closer to the porch, to say I was confused was an understatement. I was appalled! It was obvious that he was fucking this bitch right there on the front porch. When our eyes locked, he backed away from her and came and stood at the top of the stairs.

"You had a cop's intuition or a gut instinct, all right! But Rick, your ex-wife? The way you talked about how you hated her? You hypocrite!"

"Nina. What—" He was busted. And ex-wife or not, I was putting my foot in her ass.

I stormed up the stairs. "Don't *what* me! You got me at home worried as hell about you! I'm wondering if you are all right, and you're out fucking your ex-wife on porches." The Trenton, West Side, Jersey hood came out of me.

I looked at the bitch. She looked at me. *It can't be.* I was so mad that I was seeing my dead competition. As I looked closer, I froze. *It can't be!* My gut was telling me, *Oh, yes, it is.* I walked up to Rick and slapped him clean across his face. "You told me that she was dead! You lying piece of shit!" I slapped him again. This time, he grabbed me, but I pulled away and went stumbling backward onto my ass, knocking over a plant. "You pushed me!" I screamed.

"I didn't push you." Rick came toward me and tried to help me up. I started throwing blows as soon as I was on my feet.

"Get away from me! Rick, you lied to me. How could you lie about something like that? That is so cruel. And you? Did you know that he has a family? Three kids? And I'm five months pregnant! Didn't he tell you that?" I shouted at her. She just sat there speechless, staring at me.

TRAE

"Did you hear that?" I asked Tasha. We were just chillin', lying across the bed watching *The Real Husbands of Hollywood*.

"Hear what?"

"Arguing."

"It's not me and you, so no." Tasha had this smug look on her face.

I got up and looked out the bedroom window. There was another van parked in the driveway. *Who the fuck does that belong to?* I went to my spot and grabbed my strap and tucked it. "Stay put. I'll be right back." Tasha popped up and went to the window. By the time I made it to the front door, Angel and Jaz were already there, and Tasha's hardheaded ass was right behind me. My eyes scanned the porch as I grabbed the door. Then I saw this little pregnant chick walk over to Kyra and slap the shit out of her. Kyra fell over backward off the banister, and then all hell broke loose. The little pregnant chick dashed off the porch headed for Kyra, and then Angel and Jaz were on the little chick like white on rice. Tasha went to see about Kyra, and Rick was trying to get the girls off of this little chick, who I assumed was Nina, Rick's woman. I snatched Jaz up and tossed her into the house. Rick passed Angel to me, and I pushed her inside the house and stood in front of the door.

When I turned around, Kyra was charging up the stairs like a bulldog heading for Nina. Rick was doing his best to protect her.

"Get off of me, Rick! I'm leaving, and by the time I get home, you'd better have your ass there, too." Her little ass shoved him out of the way, but not before Kyra punched her in the face and Nina countered. Rick broke them up, dragging Nina to her van.

"Bring Kyra into the house," I told Tasha, still blocking the door.

"Who the fuck do she think she is? She don't know who she fuckin' with," Angel said while trying to get back onto the front porch. "You should have tapped that ass, Kyra. Pregnant or not."

"Bitch, you might as well go back home. He's mine! Even when he thought I was dead, ho he was still mines!" Kyra yelled. "He's mine! Always has been! Always will be!"

Damn.

"Bitch, in your dead-ass dreams!" Nina said with confidence as Rick continued to push her into the car.

What the fuck? I had to laugh at all of what just went down. Ol' King Rick got his hands full, and I was glad that it was him instead of me. You talk about drama! I did not see this one coming.

KYRA

I stood at the window, crushed, watching Rick talk to the Nina girl. It seemed so easy to me. All he had to do was leave her and come back to me. But I was anticipating him jumping into his truck and leaving me.

Who would he choose? Me or her? He had to make a decision. I wanted desperately to go out there, but Trae was at the front door guarding it. I couldn't take this anymore; if he left, I swear I don't know what I'm going to do.

I opened the window. "Rick, I need to talk to you. Now!"

"Bitch, what part of 'he ain't your man don't you understand? Do you see this rock on my finger?" she screamed at me, head and ring hand sticking out the car window. Then she tried to get out of her truck, but Rick wouldn't let her.

"Rick!" I yelled out again.

"Bitch, you can beg all you want! Tell her, Rick. Tell the bitch to comprehend the fact that you are coming home to me."

Rick was trying his best to calm her down, but it wasn't working. I knew the longer he spoke to her, the more likely he was not going back to her. Not tonight. So I remained right there, gaze locked on Rick and his gestures, but my patience was dwindling.

"Rick!" I yelled.

"Kyra, Trae said get out of the window." Tasha came bursting into my room.

"I can't. If I get out of the window, he's going to leave. I don't want him to leave. I won't be able to handle it, Tasha!"

"Kyra, stop it! Stop talking like that! You are much stronger than that." She came over to where I stood and grabbed my shoulders. "Girl, pull yourself together."

"I will. Just give me a few minutes, please." She stood there looking at me as if she didn't believe me. "A few minutes, Tasha."

"All right, I'll let Trae know. But don't play yourself for that nigga. And please don't throw anything out of the window, including yourself."

I stood there and watched for another, I don't know, it seemed like eternity. Finally, her truck began to ease out of the driveway. My competition screamed some obscenities as she backed up, crashing Angel's or Jaz's rental, jerked the van forward, and then pulled onto the street. Rick stood there watching her. I pulled myself away from the window and ran downstairs. When I got outside, he was in his truck, lighting up a blunt. When I came up to the car, he asked, "Are you all right?" He had this somber look on his face.

"Get out, Rick, we need to go inside and talk." I needed to know who had won. Me or her? I grabbed the car door and pulled it open.

"I need a minute," he said as he released a cloud of thick smoke. "You all right?" he asked me again.

"What do you think? Get out of the car. We need to go inside and talk."

Rick took another deep pull on his blunt and stared into my eyes. I stood there staring back, with one hand on my hip, the other on the car door handle.

Angel and Jaz were now outside, cursing and checking out the damage on Jaz's rental, while talking shit to Rick about Nina. Rick didn't bother to respond to either of them. I grabbed his hand and began pulling him out of his ride. I led him into the house and up the stairs. We went into my bedroom. I shut the door, locked it, and turned around to face him.

"Rick, you need to de—"

"Shhhh." He gently placed his finger against my lips. "Let's

112

argue and fight later, but not now, all right? You wanted your moment. I gave it to you. Now I want mine."

He reached forward and began unbuttoning my blouse. I was jumping up and down for joy inside as he began to undress me, one item at a time. *I won! I won!*

"I never stopped loving you, Kyra. And I never will," he said in a whisper as he laid me down on the bed. He began to kiss me and caress me all over. As I held him tight, nothing else mattered. At that moment, the only thing that existed for me was Rick.

He made love to me until I was satisfied. I was in heaven. Secure and full of peace. I rolled off of him, snuggled up under his arm, and hugged him around his waist.

"I don't want this to end, Rick," I admitted.

He kissed me on the forehead. "Me, neither." Those words caused a smile to form on my lips. *I won.* I closed my eyes and found myself basking in the glow of love after sex.

When I opened them again, the right side of my bed was empty and cold. I sat up, and my eyes darted around the bedroom looking for Rick's things. They weren't there. I jumped out of the bed and ran to the window. His truck was gone.

TASHA

There had been enough drama in my house the last few days to last for the next few years. Angel went back to New York, and Jaz went back to Atlanta. Rick was gone, and Kyra had been moping around the house for a week. Rick and Kyra? Of course I wanted my girl to have the man she wanted but what about Rick and his relationship with Nina?

That was a situation that I honestly didn't want any part of.

Trae and I, knock on wood, had been chillin'. No fights, no arguments, trying to stay on course of getting back to what we knew we were. It had been quiet and peaceful for the most part. The last time my stress level rose was when I spoke to Jaz. She sounded as if she was about to be on some ignorant shit. I was hoping that she was just running her mouth.

I had just fed the kids their lunch and was cleaning the kitchen when Trina called me. So much for being stress-free. I hadn't heard from her since she came over with that bullshit message from Kyron. Despite the fact that Trina didn't want me to, I had been calling my brother, but he never would answer his phone. I didn't want to answer her call, but with all of the shit going on, I decided to pick up.

"Hello."

"Hey, it's me. Can you talk?" she asked me.

"What's up?"

"Hold on." She clicked over. "Tasha, you there?"

"Yeah, what's up, Trina?" I asked her.

"You are." Hearing his whispery voice caused my stomach to flip and my knees to buckle. "What's up? I got your little letter. I need to see you."

I had to regain my composure. "You have to be the dumbest nigga in America. I don't want to see you or speak to you. I am done fucking with you. Period. It shouldn't be that hard to comprehend. And like I said in my letter, don't call me anymore, don't say shit to me. No letters, no messages, just leave me the fuck alone, Kyron. Damn."

"And you're sure about that?"

"Why wouldn't I be sure?"

"All right, then! I guess your brother don't mean shit to you. But I got something that will give me your undivided attention."

"Whatever, Kyron. I'm calling Kaylin and telling him what you did to my brother and that you are harassing and threatening me."

"I'll catch up with you sooner or later. Give my regards to Trae." He hung up.

"Whatever, nigga! And Trina, stop with the three-way phone calls and messages! Stop letting this nigga intimidate you! Call the cops on his ass! Call Kaylin right now, and tell him what he has you doing!" I spazzed out on her.

"Tasha, I—"

I hung up, not realizing how badly I was shaking. I needed to tell Trae about Kyron, but I was scared to death to do so. Maybe I would tell Kaylin and let him be the one to tell Trae. I went to dial Kaylin, but then I heard Trae calling me. He came into the family room.

"What, Trae?" I snapped.

He looked at me sideways. "What's the matter with you?"

"Nothing." I tried to play it off.

"Tasha? What's up?" He came toward me. "You're trembling."

"I just spoke to Trina, and she's trippin', that's all."

"Trippin' about what?" He came and stood in front of me, staring into my eyes as if he could read my mind. "She got you trembling like that?" He took my cell and looked at it confirming that it was her who just called me.

"Why I won't come over to see her, why she can't come over here to see me, same ol' shit. I'm just mad at her, that's all." I struggled to maintain eye contact.

"Don't accept her calls. I don't want you talking to her."

"See what I mean? You're pulling me one way, she's pulling me the other."

"So what are you saying? You gonna do like I said or not, Tasha?"

"You already stopped her from coming over. Now you don't want me to talk to her?"

"That's what I said." He raised his voice. "The girl is trouble, and when she gets you hemmed up into some bullshit, then what? So fuck it, I'm not asking you, I'm telling you. Cut off communications as of now! Do we understand each other?"

"I heard you, Trae."

"I didn't ask if you heard me. I said do we have an understanding?"

I took a deep breath. "Yes, we do."

"Good. Get the boys ready. I gotta run to Home Depot."

I rolled my eyes at him and left him standing there. I regretted every second I spent with Kyron, and now that nigga was bold enough to call me and ask to see me? I definitely chose the wrong nigga to use as a revenge fuck. I went and got the boys ready to go with their father. Home Depot was one of the spots that Aisha wasn't trying to go to, but the boys loved it.

"You want me to stay here and keep an eye on Mommy, Dad?" Kareem had the nerve to ask his father. I didn't know what the hell Trae was filling their heads with.

"Nah!" Trae looked at me with that damn smirk on his face. "Aisha can keep an eye on her."

"Whatever!" I pushed Trae from in front of me, and he grabbed me. "Stop, Trae. And what are you telling my sons?"

He laughed. "I haven't told them anything but to keep an eye on their momma. You know my lil' soldiers are very attentive and smart. They don't miss *anything* so you better stay on your p's and q's," he joked.

"Yeah, whatever."

Just then, there were knocks at the door, and the doorbell was ringing. We both turned and headed for the door.

"Who the fuck is it?" Trae barked.

Trae went to the screen door and I shot the officers a dirty look.

"Police. I'm Detective Ramos, and this is my partner, Moss. We are looking for Trae Macklin."

"I'm Trae Macklin. What can I do for you?" We both stood at the screen door.

"We have a warrant for your arrest."

8

JAZ

I was at the hospital waiting for them to discharge Faheem. I was over there looking out the window, purposely keeping my back to him and Oni, at the same time ear-hustling on their conversation. *I swear, if I turn around and look at that bitch, I will smash kill her. That is, if Faheem doesn't get to her first.*

"Bitch, every time I think you have outdone yourself, you do one even better," Faheem hissed. I almost wished that the police was still here. The room was that intense. At any moment, I was thinking that her ass was going to get knocked the fuck out. Her once smooth, silky skin looked ashen and gray. Her hair was pulled back into a ponytail and her eyes were damn near swollen shut. She had a blank stare on her face as Faheem struggled to control his anger.

"It has to be something seriously wrong with me to have ever fucked with you or fucked you! Bitch, do you hear yourself?" He gritted.

"I'm sorry," she pleaded. "He was my son too. I wanted his soul to rest. Do you think I should have left him here in this hospital until you got out?"

"If it took years for me to get out of this muthafucka, damn right you should have waited! You didn't let me get any closure. So later for me and my family wanting to say our last goodbyes. Fuck is wrong with you? Then I know you was being your little grimy-ass self because you could have called and asked me. But no, instead you sneak off and have a funeral without me. Well guess what? There is going to be another one. I swear by the time my discharge papers are signed you better have talked to somebody about digging him up!"

I heard her footsteps stomp out of the room. I turned around, and Faheem was so mad he had tears welling up in his eyes. I stepped out of the room to give him a few moments to himself. I went down to the cafeteria, bought a banana, and stopped at the nurses' station.

"What's taking Dr. Ravi so long to discharge my husband? We've been waiting all morning," I reminded the head nurse.

"I'm not sure. Give me a few minutes, and I'll look into it for you."

"Thank you."

I had to get my husband out of that gloomy-ass room. The walls were caving in on me, and I wasn't in there 24/7, so I knew they had to be crushing him. I walked straight over to Faheem and gave him a hug.

"I can't believe she did some bullshit like that," he mumbled.

"I do. She's grimy like that."

"Well, I know she better allow me to bury my son."

"Baby, let me take her out." I whispered in his ear to be sure

119

that he heard me. But he didn't respond. "Faheem, I'm serious. Let me dead that bitch."

"Jaz, this whole situation has got you trippin'. Why are you even talking like this? Look, stop it. Stop the shit right now. And I don't want you bringing it up again. Got the nerve to be asking me if you can kill somebody and in the same tone that you would ask me to take you shopping. What the fuck is the matter with you? Go tell them to get the doctor so I can get you the fuck outta here. You talkin' about me? I think this room is fuckin' with your head. Go! Get out of here!"

"Faheem, I already told them. And I'm serious. I can do it. She needs to be dealt with, and you can't do it."

"What?" He looked at me as if he was insulted. "You forgot who I am?"

"I didn't mean it like that."

"I can't fuckin' tell."

"Faheem, you know I would never forget who you are. It's just that I'm not having this bitch breathing or being able to bring anymore bullshit to my door. Don't you know I'll ride for you and die for you? I'll even kill for you?" I looked at him intensely. And what does he do? The nigga laughs.

"Jaz, just because I've been awarded husband and daddy of the year, don't get it twisted. I have been inducted into the Gangsta's Hall of Fame. All I gotta do is make a phone call, and Oni and her whole family tree can disappear. So what would it look like if you out there killing people?" Again he laughed. "Stay in your place. I got this. You talkin' crazy, and we are not having this conversation again."

"You know what? Fuck you and that broad. I'ma do me! Then you can laugh at that!" I walked out and left his ass in that hospital bed. I could hear him yelling out my name, but I didn't care. I didn't want to admit it, but I was becoming obsessed with killing that ho. I couldn't stop fantasizing about doing the deed, and it was both scary and exciting at the same time. I wanted to feel those same feelings he felt when he killed someone. I wanted to feel it at least once. I didn't care what Hall of Fame he was a part of.

TASHA

"Call Benny, Tasha." Trae said to me as they put him in handcuffs and read him his rights.

"What are you charging him with?"

"Attempted murder, ma'am." Detective Moss answered my question.

"Attempted murder?" I repeated out loud. I couldn't believe what I was hearing. "Where are y'all taking him?"

"Here you go, ma'am." Detective Ramos, who was sweating profusely, handed me a card. "There's all the information right there. We'll take good care of him. And if you don't mind me saying, this is a lovely piece of property you have here."

I wasn't up for all of the niceties. I snatched the card and called Benny as they were walking Trae to the squad car. His voicemail clicked on, and I dialed the office phone to get his secretary, Jillian.

"Law offices of Buns and Pratt, how may I direct your call?"

"This is Tasha Macklin. Is Benny available?"

"He's gone for the day."

"What about Jillian?"

"Please hold."

"Mommy, where are they taking my dad?" Shaheem asked.

"This is Jillian."

"To court, baby, he'll be right back. Hello, Jillian? This is Tasha Macklin. They just took my husband, Trae, away in handcuffs."

"For what?"

"The detective said for attempted murder. I need Benny to see what's going on. They gave me a card naming who to contact. Are you ready?"

"Mommy, they had Daddy in handcuffs?" Kareem asked while pulling at my arm.

"Let Mommy finish this call, baby." I gave the info on the card to Jillian and hung up.

I had to calm the kids down and get them focused on something else. They were acting worse than me. *Attempted murder?* My mind was reeling. Who in the hell did Trae attempt to kill? Did Kyron's bitch-ass snitch? Or, knowing Trae, is this some old shit that finally caught up with him? After I got the kids straight, I was going to make some phone calls.

"Who wants to go to the park?" My voice cracked as I called out.

"I do! I do! Me!" they all yelled.

"Okay, let Mommy call Uncle Kaylin first. Everybody go to the bathroom. Aisha is in charge. After you use the bathroom, get one toy and go wait for me on the front porch." They took off running.

Just as I was getting ready to dial Kaylin, my cell rang. I answered immediately.

"Do I have your attention now?"

If Kyron didn't have my attention before, yes, he had it now. If that nigga was responsible for Trae getting locked up, then he was more bitch than I thought he was. "I know that you need to stop playing these games. I'm getting ready to call your brother right now. I don't give a fuck if Trae goes to jail for life, I still wouldn't fuck with you." Furious, I ended the call and dialed Kaylin.

"Tasha Macklin, what's up? Angel has been in meetings all day. You can call her back in about an hour."

"I'm not calling to speak to Angel, I'm calling to speak to you."

"Oh, my bad. Is everything aiight?"

"No, they just came and took Trae outta here in handcuffs for attempted murder."

"What?"

"Yeah, and Kyron just hung up. He may be the one behind this bullshit. He's been calling me and threatening me. I called Benny's office already, so I'm hoping he can make this all go away. But it's your brother, Kaylin. Tell him to leave me alone. It has gotten out of hand."

"Wait a minute. You said Kyron is behind Trae getting locked up?"

"I think so but I am not sure but I won't put it past him. He's been trying to get with me. First he had Trina call, then he fucked up my brother, and now this. He calls after each incident. Me and my dumb ass, I've been hiding it from Trae because I'm scared that he'll think I'm back fucking with him. I need your help, Kaylin. Make your brother stop this bullshit."

I heard Kaylin sigh. I knew he didn't want to hear what I was telling him, but it was what it was.

"All right, I'll take care of it, but have Benny call me."

"I will." I hung up and went to take the kids to the park. I was a nervous wreck. I told Kaylin, and I knew he was going to tell Trae, that Kyron had been calling me and starting shit. On the way to the park, I decided to stop at the grocery store to pick up a few snacks. I could have easily packed something, but I needed to get out of that house fast.

"There goes my mommy!" Aisha yelled out. We were riding past the front entrance of the supermarket.

"Auntie Kyra, Auntie Kyra!" Caliph squealed as he squirmed in his seat, trying to get his seatbelt off. I think my five-year-old son has a crush on Kyra.

I looked to my right, and yes, it was Kyra, but she hadn't told me she was going to the store. *Wait a minute.* How did she get there? I didn't notice any vehicles gone other than Aunt Marva's. *What the hell is she doing?* It looked like she was selling something. She was stopping people and talking to them, but everyone was keeping it moving. She had a book in her hands. *Was she selling books?* I pulled into a handicapped spot and threw the car into park. "Kids, stay here. Aisha is in charge. I'll be right over there talking to Kyra. I'm not going into the store yet." I jumped out of the car and rushed over to where she was.

As I got closer, she opened the book and said, "Two Kings, chapter twenty, verse one says, 'In those days Hezekiah was sick and near death, and Isaiah the prophet, the son of Amos went to him and said to him, Thus says the Lord: Set your house in order, for you shall die, and not live, then he said—'"

"Kyra? What are you doing?"

She looked at me, and with a straight face, and said, "Tasha, I'm just calling these sinners back to the Lord. It's time for the people to get their house in order. You are here to listen to the word, aren't you?"

"But why are you out here in front of the supermarket? How did you get here?"

"The Lord makes all things possible! Verse two says, 'Remember now, O Lord, to pray, how I have walked before you in truth and with a loyal heart.'"

What the hell? She rambled the verse off like she was a bible scholar. "Kyra!" I grabbed her arm. "The kids are in the car. Come help me with them."

"I can't right now. I'm doing the Lord's work."

"Your daughter, Aisha, is in the car, Kyra."

"'I have done what was good in your sight and Hezekiah wept bitterly.'" She continued to quote the Bible. "Come to Jesus! Come back to the Lord!" she yelled, and began following a group of strangers.

I was at a loss for words. Could this day get any crazier?

9

TASHA

"Benny, how long does it take to bond someone out? I'm coming down there!" I screamed at Benny. I had the day from hell. Kyra out preaching hellfire to strangers. Trae getting locked up and still not home. I was losing it.

"Mrs. Macklin, coming down to do what?" Benny called himself calming me down. "You can't rush the courts, and it's not like it's a simple traffic ticket. We're talking murder and attempted murder."

"Benny, I am freaking out. I can't lie to you."

"Mrs. Macklin, please. Don't freak out. I'll have him home in a few hours. I promise you. Let me do my job, all right?"

"I need my husband home. We have a family here."

"I know, Mrs. Macklin. Trust me. I will bring your husband home."

I hung up, not feeling any better. Was I the cause of all of this bad shit happening to our family? Or were we both the cause? I was mad at him, but I didn't want to lose him. Here it was going on 11:00 P.M. and he still wasn't here where he belonged. Earlier, around 8:00, that's when I was beginning to get that uneasy feeling in the pit of my stomach. Shortly after, I got a call from Benny talking some nonsense about them running his prints and them being found at the scene of a murder. It took a few minutes for his words to sink in, but when they did, I panicked. All I envisioned was him on death row somewhere and me never being held in those strong arms again. I had to go and pour myself a drink. I downed it and poured me another one. I didn't even care what I was drinking.

Aunt Marva came into the living room. "Why are you sitting here in the dark?" She turned on the light. "Look at you. You look a mess! Go upstairs and get you some rest. You ain't doing yourself any good, sitting in the dark drowning your sorrows in this bottle. And it's my bottle!" She snatched the bottle up.

I couldn't stop thinking, *attempted murder*? If Trae couldn't wiggle out of this one, he could be taken away from me and this family for a long time. He promised me that would never happen. And at the time I believed him. "I know. I'm just anxious to find out what's going on." I was feeling light-headed.

"And you will. He'll tell you everything as soon as he walks through that front door."

"Where's Kyra?" Since we'd come back from the store and the park, she was staying out of the way.

"Everyone is in bed, where you should be."

"What about you, Aunt Marva? You aren't in bed."

"Don't worry about me, missy."

"Did I tell you about Kyra? I'm sure I didn't, because I don't even want to repeat it. I actually want to forget what I saw."

"What about her? What did you see?" she asked with her brow raised.

"I'm worried about her. Earlier, we went to Vons, and when we pulled up, she was standing in front of the store, holding a Bible and preaching hellfire to all who would listen."

"What?" Aunt Marva had a puzzled look on her face.

"I kid you not. She was yelling and following behind total strangers. I don't even know how she got there. All of the cars were still in the driveway. It was crazy. I should have videotaped it, because you would have to see it to believe it."

"So what did you do?"

"I got out of the car, made her ass get in, dragged her to the park with us, and then brought her ass home."

"What did she say?"

"In the car, nothing about that. She talked to the kids the whole time, and when we got to the park, she acted as if nothing happened. I didn't even know what to say to her."

"You didn't know, or you were scared to say something?"

"Both. I ain't gonna lie. It was awkward."

"We're gonna have to keep a close eye on her. Now, come on." Marva clapped her hands together. "Go upstairs and get some rest. He'll wake you up when he comes in. Go ahead, now. I'll clean up this mess."

"Okay, okay. I'm going." I got up and went upstairs. I stopped and checked on the children, who were knocked out. I went into my bedroom, and the last thing I remember was lying across my bed.

TRAE

Benny dropped me off around two thirty. I didn't have my key, so I had to go around the back where Marva kept a spare to the back door under the base of the patio table. After I got into the house, I cut the alarm off and looked around the living room, expecting to hear some sort of movement. But the house was dead silent. I hit the stairs to look in on the kids, who were sprawled out and snoring. When I stepped out of their bedroom, I bumped into Kyra.

"I thought I heard you come in. Are you all right? Did I hear correctly? You got locked up?" she asked me.

"I had some old shit that they pulled up. Nothing that a little money can't make go away. Go back to bed, and we'll talk in the morning."

"I need to ask you something."

Oh, shit, here it comes. I was not in the right state of mind to have the what-happened-to-Marvin speech. "What's up?"

"Rick, have you spoken to him, at all? What is he saying?"

I breathed a sigh of relief. I thought for sure Marvin's name was going to slip out of her mouth. It seemed as if she had blocked him out of her mind. Hell, he was her baby's father and her husband, and she wasn't even asking about him. Didn't she want to see him? Know where he was? That had me baffled.

"No, he hasn't called me. Why? You haven't heard from him?"

She shook her head no and then lowered her voice. "What do you think is going through his mind? And don't bullshit me, Trae. You are a man. You have been in this situation. What is he thinking?"

I thought about it for a minute. "Kyra, I don't think it's the same things that are going through yours. Here this man

129

was in love with you, and then thought he lost you forever. So he moves on. He gets a new love and has a family. But when his love shows back up and figures that she can start right back where things left off, I'm sure that has the man in turmoil. Shit, if that happened to me, I know my head would be fucked up. Think about Romeo and Juliet. What if Romeo didn't drink the poison and left town and moved on? Only to find out years later that Juliet was not dead, she had only drunk a drug to put her in a coma for two days? And she finds him, but he is now married with children, the whole nine. You feel me?"

Kyra laughed. "Romeo and Juliet, huh? Now that you put it like that, yes. But I've been calling him, and he doesn't even bother to answer."

"Give him some time. He'll come around," I assured her.

"I hope so. But at the same time, I'm a little worried. I'm worried that he won't choose me, and it's driving me crazy!"

"Kyra, you know he'll come around. Let him work it out."

"God, I hope you're right. And thanks for listening."

"No doubt." I left Kyra standing there. I needed to get my ass into a hot, steamy shower and scrub the day off of me. Then I needed to ease some tension. The whole time I was in custody, I wondered if my luck was finally running out. Everything seemed to be closing in on me all at once. I was ready for anything. But doing time? I didn't forsee that. I had to figure out how to get out of this one.

When I went into my bedroom, Tasha was lying across the bed in all of her clothes. Obviously, she'd tried to wait up for me but couldn't.

"Baby." I shook her. Her eyes popped open, looking all wild

and shit. "It's me. Are you all right?" I couldn't help but smile. She was even beautiful when I scared her out of her sleep.

"I'm sorry, baby, I tried to wait up for you," she said, sitting up.

"Come get in the shower with me." I grabbed her hand.

"How long have you been home? What happened? What did they say?" She got off the bed and gave me a hug. "I was freakin' out, Trae. Murder? Are you going to beat this? A murder charge?"

"Murder and attempted murder."

"Who did you murder?" she asked, rubbing her eyes.

"Nobody, baby. My prints were at a scene, but I didn't do shit, and they can't prove it. Benny said it won't even get to court."

"Who did you attempt to murder? Kyron? Or is this something old? Is it two different murder charges? The other murder, who is it?"

"Ma, stop with the questions." She obviously had been wracking her brain trying to figure this all out. "Come on, let's get in the shower. Aren't you ready to wash your husband up? I'm hot, sticky, and smelly. We will talk about this madness later." I kissed her forehead and let her go.

We went into the bathroom, and I turned on the water. A calm came over me. The shower was one of our favorite spots. My wife undressed me, and then I took my time and undressed her. She began to plant light kisses on my lips, my neck, and my chest. "I love you so much." She told me. "Baby, I was so scared that you wasn't coming back home to me."

I caressed her nipples and her ass. "Oh, I was coming back."

"I'm so glad. I needed you too. I missed you."

"I missed you even more. Tasha, you will always be mines. And there ain't much that can keep me away from you."

"I know, baby."

I walked her backward to the shower. As we stepped into the

hot and steamy water, we continued to hug and kiss. I loved the sight of the water glistening off of her smooth, chocolate skin. The sound of her moans mixed with the sound of the water turned me all the way up. When we finally came up for air, Tasha grabbed the sponge, lathered it up, and began to sensually soap up my body. By the time she finished, my dick was standing way past attention.

"I love him when he gets rocked up like this. Lets me know that I'm doing my job and that my husband can't get enough of me."

"Oh yeah? I can't get enough of you?" I was nibbling on her neck and playing with her nipples.

"Ummmmm. No you can't." she purred.

Taking the sponge from her, I took my time and gently massaged and lathered up her silky-smooth skin. Tasha took my dick into her hand and began to stroke him. The warm, soapy water caused her hand to slide effortlessly as she stared into my eyes. She wouldn't let go of my pipe, so he remained ready and at attention. After I rinsed her off, I bent her over, making sure we were in front of the full mirror so I could watch myself as I fucked her.

"That feels sooo good." She cooed as I entered her.

I took my time, getting thrills each time I pulled my dick out of her and chills each time it disappeared inside her. This was our time, and we loved taking advantage of it. I held back and made sure she came hard. "Traaeeee, ba . . .beeee!" she squealed. I was saving mine for the bed. I wanted to bang her head up against the headboard a few times and then turn over, lie back, and watch my baby ride. The king was home, and the queen was giving him some royal pussy.

By the time we finished trying to outfuck each other, she was no longer asking who I had murdered and when it had happened.

Two days later

"Hello." I answered the phone in the den.

"Hello, Mr. Macklin."

Aww, shit, here we go. Could my luck get any worse? I should have known she'd be crawling out from under her rock sooner or later. "Why are you calling my house? Why are you calling me, period?" I asked her.

"This is business, Mr. Macklin. You're still a businessman, aren't you?"

"What do you want, Charli?"

"I have something that will be of interest to you."

"You know I ain't fucking with you like that. So stop calling my house. Don't contact me, period." I was tired of telling this woman the same thing over and over. Fucking with her was like hustling in the streets. At the same time you are throwing bricks at the penitentiary. It was lucrative and fun while it was happening. But when the smoke cleared, you were sitting in the cell, asking, *was it all worth it?* I hung up, and she called right back. This time, I didn't answer; I let it ring. When she called the third time, I said, "Charli, don't—"

"My father wants to see you as soon as possible." She cut me off.

"Good-bye, Charli." I hung up again. That fuckin' bitch! She was a scheming and calculating ho and never ceased to amaze me! *Her father?* I thought about it, and it caused me to frown. What could her father, the infamous Mr. Charlie Li, want with me? Leave it to this thirsty bitch to pull out all the stops. She knew that mentioning her father would get my attention.

TASHA

I got suspicious and nervous when the phone rang back-to-back three times. I was thinking it was Kyron. And him calling with Trae back in the house had me panicking, so the next time the phone rang, I picked it up.

"Oh, so you decided to talk to me?"

"Who is this?" I knew the answer but didn't think she had the audacity to call my house.

"This is Ms. Li. With whom am I speaking?" Her voice dripped with sarcasm.

"Bitch, whose house did you call? You know damn well with whom you are speaking! You must want me to fuck you up again! Call here one more time and I'll come find you and bust you in your ass! Leave my husband the fuck alone." That's all I needed to hear was her voice to make me crazy. I hung up the phone and went to find Trae. He had me fucked up. With each step I took, the madder I got. By the time I reached the family room, it was on. I lunged for Trae, and he grabbed my arm, twisting it, pulling me down onto his lap.

"What is your problem?" He was frowned up.

"Get off me! Why the fuck is that bitch back to calling my house?" I was squirming, trying to get up. My heart or my pride could not take Trae fucking with that bitch again. "She's calling you at home now? Are you still fucking with her?" I got all choked up, not really wanting to know the answer to my question.

"What do you think? Are you still fucking with Kyron?" he yelled at me.

"No, and you know it. Why would you even ask me something like that?"

"The same damn reasons you are asking me!"

I was in tears now. "Because she's calling you." I grabbed his face between my hands. "Why is she calling you?"

"Kyron is calling you, so what? Yeah, when were you gonna tell me that?" When I didn't answer, he shouted, "When, Tasha? When? I've been waiting patiently. No more secrets, remember? No more lies."

"I was scared, Trae." I dropped most of the attitude that I had in my voice. I was busted.

"Scared of what? Scared that I would react the same way you reacted when that bitch called me?"

I thought about what he said and nodded.

"Tasha, baby, I need you to stay focused. You can't be getting all emotional like this. We are a team, and we know that we have these outside forces threatening our union. You not telling me that the nigga is calling you lets me know that I can't trust you. Do you feel me?"

"Why are they doing this to us?"

"Fuck them! We can't let them tear down what we've built. Do you hear me, Tasha?"

I nodded again. "What are we going to do?" *What am I going to do?* If that bitch thought it was going to be business as usual, she had another thing coming.

"No secrets. No lies. It's me and you. I will handle Kyron and Charli . . . she ain't even an issue."

Yeah, right. I wished I could believe some bullshit like that. I laid my head on Trae's chest as he held me tight. I wanted to believe that everything was going to be okay, but my gut was telling me a totally different story. We had fucked up. Fucked up bad, and the universe is not that forgiving. Hell, I wasn't that forgiving.

"Tasha, Tasha! Wake up!" I opened my eyes to find Aunt Marva and Kyra standing over my bed. I threw the blanket over my head. *Have they lost their minds?*

"Tasha, somebody is poking around the house outside," Kyra said as she snatched the cover from over my head.

I sat up. "What? Who is it? Outside our house? Trae is supposed to be in Atlanta."

"Well, it ain't Trae," Kyra said.

I jumped out of bed and headed for the stash spot where Trae hid his burners. I reached for my favorite, a Hi Point 9-milli. I was dying to use it. I grabbed my robe and tied it around me, slipping the milli into my robe pocket.

"I called the police already," Marva whispered. Actually, we all were whispering as they followed me down the stairs.

"Where is he now?" I asked.

"He was on the side of the house. He's a bold little something, too. The security lights came on, and he kept doing whatever it was that he was doing," Marva whispered.

We went through the house, peeking through all of the windows. It was a full moon, and the moonlight was the only light we had. I then decided to turn on every light that we had outside. When I peeked out again, our eyes met. We were face-to-face, and even though he had on a hoodie, I was able to make out his features. He was a man of Asian descent.

"Call the police again." The sound of me putting one in the chamber echoed through the room. "I'm getting ready to shoot to kill." Shit, anything of Asian persuasion reminded me of Charli. Hell, for all I knew, she was the one who sent him.

"Nooo!" they both said at the same time.

"Watch me." Then, just in that instant, *WHOOSH!* We heard a fizzle, and then flames rose up. We all screamed at the top of our lungs. "Fire!" I screeched.

"The kids! The kids!" I heard someone say, but I was already headed up the stairs. *My babies.* Kyra was on my heels, and Marva was right behind her. We rushed into the bedroom, waking up the kids and snatching them up.

"We gotta hurry! We gotta hurry!" Kyra kept saying. Then she started praying out loud.

"C'mon! C'mon! C'mon, Caliph!" I was yelling. He was moving the slowest. We were frantically trying to gather the children.

"Fire drill!" Marva yelled out. Those two words perked the kids right up, and they began to move faster. She had been practicing with them on many different occasions. We all filed out of the bedroom as the smoke detectors began to screech. Caliph covered his ears and began to cry.

"My eyes," Shaheem kept saying. The smoke was getting thick.

By the time we got downstairs, the sprinkler system had activated. We rushed through the smoke-filled living room right out the front door. My eyes were burning. Everyone was choking and coughing. We were wet but happy to have made it onto the front yard. We turned around and looked at the house. I was numb. And then Caliph collapsed. Everyone gathered around him. I held my breath as I felt his pulse.

"Caliph, baby, can you hear mommy? Are you—" He started choking.

"Mommy . . . I can't breathe."

"I'm here, baby." I picked him up and he hugged me around my neck as if he was planning on never letting go.

The police were rushing down the street, and I heard the fire engine in the distance. It was weird, but only the left side of the house was burning and smelling like burnt wood.

Our neighbors across the street came onto their porch. When they saw us, they came rushing to where we were.

"Madge, call the fire department!" Mr. Sinclair yelled out.

"I already did!" I heard his wife's piercing voice.

"You all are wet. Is everyone out? Where's your husband?" Mr. Sinclair took off his sweater and put it around the twins and huddled them together. Mrs. Sinclair used hers to cover Aisha.

"He's out of town. Our house is burning." I was mesmerized by the blaze.

"Please, come inside my home. You are all welcome." Mr. Sinclair tried to pull me away.

"Thank you, Mr. Sinclair. You can take the kids and Kyra. My aunt and I will talk to the police and the fire department." I had to yell over the sirens that were now blaring behind me as the truck pulled up in front of the house. "Y'all go with Mr. Sinclair. Mommy has to talk to the policemen and the firemen." I tried to reassure the children as they looked up at me with fear in their eyes. Caliph was still holding onto me.

"You calling Daddy?" Kareem asked.

"Yes, I'm calling your daddy." I rubbed his little head as he shivered.

"My nose is burning," Kareem whined.

I looked around at the fire engines, police cars, and firemen as they hustled to put out the blaze. It was as if we were in a movie; time moved slowly around me. My eyes settled on Kyra, Marva, and the children, who were all dripping wet, coughing, rubbing their eyes and noses. It seemed as if some sort of chemical was in the smoke. "Have the paramedics check everyone out. I think some gases or fumes were released." Mr. Sinclair started leading everyone to the ambulance.

The crisp California air brushed over my skin, but the rage that rose in my gut had me on fire. All I could think about was Charli and how I was going to make that bitch pay with her ass for this one.

TRAE

Benny was able to get me out on bond with no restrictions. I had to fly down to Atlanta to check on Faheem. I needed to find out exactly what happened and wanted to see how he was holding up and if he needed my help in any way. I knew that he would do the same for me. I couldn't imagine losing one of my sons. Then, to add injury to insult, his son's mother had the funeral while he was laid up in the hospital. That was crazy as hell. The other thing he was concerned with was that Jaz kept talking about taking Oni out. He told me that she was serious, but when talking to her he would nix her off. I tried to tell him that she was just talking out of emotion, but he didn't think so.

Jaz gave me a key to the house when I was at the hospital and told me to chill out at their spot. I left the hospital, and before turning in, I decided to ride out to Lithonia to check out Gladys Knight's Chicken and Waffles. I picked up my food and headed in for the rest of the evening. I had the house all to myself. I ate, showered, and decided to get some much needed rest.

Around dawn, my cell vibrated, sliding across the nightstand.

I grabbed it and saw that it was Tasha. Why was she calling at five in the morning? I figured that one of the kids must be sick.

"Babe, what's up?"

"I need you to come home." She was frantic.

I sat up. "What's going on?"

"We had a fire. The—"

"A fire?" My heart sank to my stomach. "Is everybody all right?"

"We're all fine. There were fumes, and everyone's eyes and noses are burning. The paramedics are checking everybody out now. We all are a little shook up, but we're okay. The fire didn't have the chance to spread through the whole house. The sprinklers kicked in on the first floor. I'm not sure if they went off on the second floor. If so, then everything is waterlogged. If they hadn't activated, I might not be out here talking to you, because the heat and fire blew the windows out on the first floor, and then the water hoses did the rest of the damage. So I'm sure the first floor is soaked." She exhalted.

"Slow down, baby, you are talking too fast. Breathe, please. We can replace all of that shit, but I can't replace all of you." I was already getting dressed. "I'm on my way back now."

"I have to give the police my statement, and then we are going to find a hotel. It's chilly out here. Mr. Sinclair came over, and the kids are at his house."

"Okay, when I get back I will thank him. But for now you need to go to our other house."

"I'm not going there. That's exactly where the bitch wants me to go."

"What? What bitch?" My wife was sounding crazy.

"Charli. Who else? Plus, I am not going to the same house and sleep in the same bed where you fucked another bitch!"

"Tasha, don't start that bullshit. I told you I did not fuck her in that house."

"We are checking into a hotel, Trae."

"Don't take my kids to no damn hotel. Now is not the time to be talking crazy, Tasha."

"Crazy? How come the guy we saw looking around the house looked Chinese? Who else do you know would want to burn us down to the ground? Our kids were in that house, Trae."

"Not Charli. Somebody else, for some other shit I did, but not her."

"Oh, that's right. She loves you too much. She wouldn't dare try to burn your ass down to the ground. Trae, you need to open your eyes. That bitch was behind this."

"You're trippin', Tasha. I don't think she would do that."

"I know you can't be that stupid. Who do you think you are talking to? You know what? I am not about to argue with you. We going to a hotel and I will call you when we get checked in."

"Tasha, I—Tasha!" She hung up on me. And shit was going from worst to extreme. I had to get the fuck home and deal with not only these pending charges, but now a fire. Who the fuck would be crazy enough to come for my family?

CHARLI

"I don't believe this! You idiotic imbecile! My instructions to you were to blow up the car with her and the children. Not the house!" Yao, who worked for our family, stood in my foyer, expecting to get some sympathy from me.

"No, Ms. Li. You didn't specify. House. Car. Boat. Your instructions were to handle it as I saw fit," Yao said.

"But did you handle it? Of course not! The house is still standing. The car is still there. The wife and kids are still breathing!"

"I don't know what happened. The C4 had to be defective."

"C4? C4? Yao, you used C4 to blow up a house? Why would you do that? You fool! No wonder everyone is still alive. Yao, please don't tell me you left the explosives? Defective explosives! What about your prints? Serial numbers? C4 can be traced."

"I wore gloves. No prints, Ms. Li."

I was beside myself. If some harm would have come to Mr. Macklin, I don't know what I would have done. What Yao had done over and over again, with precision, this time was a fiasco. He killed people for a living and rarely made mistakes. Why he would use C4 to blow up a house was beyond me. He was beginning to lose his touch. "Yao, you'd better hope that this does not come back to haunt us."

"Ms. Li, you know better than myself that things don't always go as planned. I can carry out and complete the assignment tomorrow."

"No. Please. Let me rethink this." I grabbed my head with both hands. "Excuse yourself, and see your way out."

10

NINA

Devastated. Betrayed. Torn to pieces. A few words that came close to how I was feeling. Shocked and appalled was how I felt when I pulled up into that driveway and saw my man fucking some bitch on the porch. But then, when I got close and saw it was her . . . my knees got weak, and I just knew I had died and gone to hell. My worst nightmare and fear had come to fruition. I wish I could have run that bitch over with my car. Our life was better when she was dead. It took me too long to get this nigga over her. Now I am back to square one.

Kyra "the dead bitch" Blackshear. She will wish she was dead if she doesn't fall back from fuckin' with my man.

But this shit is not going to go away. I could tell by the look on Rick's face. The nigga didn't even want to leave the bitch. And it was obvious that he felt obligated to me, not out of love but out of responsibility and that broke my heart. I really hit rock bottom when

I got back into my truck and waited for Rick to take off and leave her right then and there. But instead, he came to the car and tried to calm me down, along with some *it ain't what it seems* bullshit.

Niggas. You can catch them with the dick up in the pussy, and they will still say, "It ain't what it looks like." So when he didn't leave right then, I already knew I had lost him. And believe it or not, I accepted it, only because I knew that this would happen. Maybe subconsciously, I brought it on myself.

Now, two days later, he was back home, or I should say here with me. I couldn't stand the sight of him. As far as I was concerned, this was no longer his home, and I was hoping he'd pack his shit and leave. Hell, this wouldn't be the first time a nigga packed up and left me.

"Nina, can I talk to you for a minute?" He popped into the laundry room, where I was washing clothes. I acted like I didn't hear him.

"Nina, you gonna talk to me or what?"

"Go talk to the bitch who just returned from the dead. I'm still trying to figure out why you're here. I know you don't think you're going to have us both?"

"Nina, stop."

"Stop?" I turned around to face him. "Stop? Rick, do you realize that I am this close to telling you to pack your shit and get out of my life? This is so not fair! I loved you. You got me pregnant. You put a ring on my finger. My kids call you Daddy. This house here, we turned into a home, together. You fixed up the baby room, for God's sake. I trusted myself with you. I allowed myself to feel safe." I choked up. "I knew this was going to happen. Why did you lie to me?" I started sobbing as I slid down against the dryer onto the floor.

He came over to me and bent down. He held my face in his hands. "I didn't lie. She's been in the hospital in a coma."

"And you just popped up and found her?" I had to laugh at that one.

"Crazy as that may sound, that's exactly what happened. And that's the truth. Nina, you should know by now that I would never hurt you intentionally, and I never lied to you."

"You already did hurt me intentionally. You fucked her, Rick. The entire time we've been together I know you secretly wished she wasn't dead. You wished that bitch back to life. And that hurts. My heart use to have love in it for you but now I hate you. I hate you for what you did to my love for you. I trusted you. All of my trust for you went out the window. I have to face reality. There is nothing left."

"What do you mean there ain't nothing left?"

"Typical question from a nigga who wants the cake and the icing. Rick, your story is whack as fuck I don't give a damn if they posted that bitch on the side of the milk carton saying she was found alive, apparently our love was never shit. How could you do this to me, Rick?"

"Nina."

"Nina, Nina, what? '*It's not what it seems!*' Rick, you were fucking her, and then you spent the night with her. You didn't come home with me! How do you think that makes me feel, Rick? How am I supposed to compete with her?"

"No, I didn't."

"Now you're lying again! Go! Just get the fuck out of my life!"

CHARLI

It sent chills up my spine just to hear Mr. Macklin's voice. Don't act surprised. You read my diary excerpts, *50 Shades of Trae*. You know my feelings for him.

I can honestly say that I am at peace with myself. It took a while, but finally I'm here.

The loss of our baby was both bitter and sweet. Sweet because I was under the impression for years that I couldn't get pregnant. But I did. Bitter because my father would never approve of me having a baby out of wedlock. And definitely not by someone my father would consider a common thug. He wanted me to marry a leader of a country. Royalty.

I knew that when I was ready to reach out to Mr. Macklin again, it had to be worthwhile. I didn't know of anyone to use better than my father to get his attention. And it just so happened that my father was looking to expand one of his operations, and he needed someone. So I decided to suggest Mr. Macklin. Now all I had to do was persuade Father to bring him in.

I tapped on the door to my father's study.

"Come in, my little one."

I eased the door open. "Father, how did you know it was me?"

"I can always sense your presence." He got up from behind his desk and met me. We hugged, and he kissed my forehead. I stood back and bowed.

"Father, I have an idea that you may be interested in." I sat in one of the chairs in front of his desk.

"It's Sunday, little one. Your day off. This must be a grand idea!" He teased me.

I got right down to business. "I found someone to be trained for our operation in the Midwest. If we continue to keep things the way they are, we will continue to see our profits diminish. Obviously, no one is taking Kon Li seriously. My recommendation is already familiar with the work, he learns fast, he's hungry, and you wouldn't have to worry about him double-crossing the operation."

"Why *wouldn't* he double-cross the operation? What stakes in our organization would he have?"

"First off, he's not built like that. He has morals. He understands and lives by our code. Also, there's me. There is a small bond between him and me. Or should I say, more of an unspoken bond."

"Sounds as if you are pretty familiar with this candidate. And I must admit, you have me curious."

"I only ask that you give him a fair chance, Father. And don't hold his past against him."

"So, you are vouching for him?"

"I am, but I have some conditions."

"Who is he? Tell me."

"Trae Macklin."

My father swiveled in his chair, turning his back to me.

I stood up and went over to my father with my head and my voice low. "Yes, I do still have feelings for him. With him under your wing, you can make sure he is the man who is fit for your daughter. Father, I rarely ask you for anything. So you can grant me this one request."

He spun around to face me, with the look of disappointment evident on his face. "You can't be serious. You almost lost your life because of this man. We lost one of our most trusted soldiers, who was also my friend and most trusted confidant, because of him. And have you forgotten that the man is married? Charli, I'm going to ask you to rethink this. Not only is your suggestion absurd, but you are asking me to groom him so that you can marry him? Charli, he is already married. And if he wasn't, I still would never even consider such a thing. This man is beneath you."

"Father, have you forgotten that you owe me one? And you gave me your word, remember? Your honor is all that you have. Keep your word, Father, or disgrace the honor of this family."

My father laughed. "I owe you? And me bring disgrace to the honor of this family? Little one, have you forgotten that I built this family? You are only here because of the work of these hands." He held both of them up for emphasis. "And now you want me to honor a thug?"

"Father—"

"Your judgment is clouded, little one. And that explains the stunt that you assigned Yao to. Never do that again."

"Father, I can explain. It was supposed to be her car, with her and her kids in it. She killed my baby. Why do hers get to live?" I tried to assert myself.

"Charli, Charli, Charli. Leave me now."

I wanted to plead my case some more but decided against it. I obviously had bad timing. But I was not done with this. My father owed me, and this was how he was going to repay me. Whether he liked it or not. I was in love with Trae Macklin and I wanted him to be a permanent part of my world. And this was my way of getting one step closer. I stood, bowed, and walked out.

TRAE

It was seven thirty in the morning, and I had been out walking for an hour, trying to clear my head. I had left Jaz and Faheem in Atlanta. I told Faheem that he was hot, and he needed to wait a while before he made any moves. He agreed but admitted that it was going to be hard. I know that I wouldn't be able to just chill either and let none them muthafuckas breathe. But I know from past experience that when you move on emotions you fuck up. His head isn't clear and he needs to calm down and think this thing out. The police in the A is a lot different from the ones up north. They will crawl up your ass with a microscope until they get whatever they want to arrest and charge you with.

Tasha was mad at me because she lost the last argument. Marva and Kyra were still at the hotel, but I made Tasha and the kids go to the other house. She was walking around pissed. However, I really didn't give a fuck. I never fucked Charli in our bed. Maybe on the couch, but the bed? Never that!

As far as the house, the upstairs only had smoke damage and a little water damage. But downstairs, everywhere except for the kitchen was ruined. The furniture, carpets, walls—all ruined. I had the contractors working around the clock renovating and remodeling. We should be back in there in about two to three weeks. Actually, as far as the house was concerned, I was simply going through the motions. I already had a Realtor looking at something in Texas or maybe wherever Faheem was going. The safety of my family was first, and California was no longer appearing to be a safe haven.

I loved the early-morning California brisk air, and as I inhaled it deeply, it was at that moment that I made up my mind to make a run to New York. I needed to see Kay. It was time for me to handle Kyron. I'd allowed the nigga to breathe as long as I possibly could, and it was now eating at me to the point where I could hardly think about anything else.

I noticed the same black limo whiz by me for the second time as I decided it was time to head back to the house. I began walking faster, while thinking that I wasn't even strapped. I looked back, and the stretch was making a U-turn and coming back toward me. *Shit!* I was out in the open. There was nowhere to get cover except in someone's driveway behind their car. That's when it hit me. *Charli.* And then the ride slowed down, and the rear window went down. That's when I thought, *Here it comes.*

"Mr. Trae Macklin?" A male voice with an Asian accent resonated in my ears. I turned toward the voice but didn't respond.

"Mr. Macklin?" The back door popped open. "I'm Charles Li. Please get in. I need to talk to you. I only need a few minutes of your time."

Damn. So Charli wasn't bullshitting after all about her father. I should have known that she wasn't.

The front door opened, and a medium-built Asian guy got out as I got closer to the limo. He had on a chauffeur's hat, but I could tell by the cold, piercing look in his eyes that this was definitely a killer. He walked to the back of the limo, opened the door, and motioned for me to get in. It was obvious that I didn't have a choice in the matter. As soon as I eased in, the door was shut, and there I was, face-to-face with the infamous Mr. Li. He was undoubtedly the staunch man in the photo in Charli's office; in person, his presence was a little bit smaller yet unmistakably powerful. There was a young lady sitting in the corner. She poured two drinks and passed them both to Mr. Li.

"I won't keep you long, Mr. Macklin. My daughter, as you know, can be very persuasive and persistent. And you came highly recommended. She said I should bring you on board." He gave me the drink.

I started to ask at what cost but thought against it. I threw the smooth wine back and decided to cut through the formalities. "I'm out of the game, Mr. Li."

He smiled, a smile that I read to say, *You honestly don't think that, do you?* He then leaned closer to me and said, "Once in, you never get out. That I can assure you. Have you built a stable foundation for your family? And by stable, I mean, do you have at least twenty million put away? Because if you don't, you have not built a stable foundation. You have a family. A wife and three children, is it? Both of your parents are still alive. And let's examine your lifestyle and spending habits. In this economy, anything less than that will be gone before you know it."

He obviously wanted his words to sink in, because he was staring out the window. I thought about what he'd said. How did he know both of my parents were still alive? My stash was nowhere near the figure that he mentioned. And he had a point. In this economy, twenty mil was equivalent to five mil. I knew I couldn't do shit with five mil. In my current situation, I probably would end up spending most of that in legal fees.

It agitated me a bit to realize that Mr. Li had my undivided attention. I had sworn on my grandmother that I would never get back in . . . on any level.

As if on cue, he faced me. "Mr. Macklin, by joining my organization, you could make that amount in less than three years. What I'm proposing is nice, clean, suit-and-tie work. That is, unless you prefer the roll-up-your-sleeves-and-get-dirty kind of job. I also have those. And they pay equally as well. Let's face it, some of us prefer to stay in the trenches. But in my organization, one job is just as important as the next."

"Mr. Li, I've spent almost half of my life in the trenches, and

I'm not going back. I'm now like you, a suit-and-tie kind of guy." I leaned in and placed my glass on the bar.

Mr. Li let out a chuckle. "And what makes you think I'm a suit-and-tie guy?"

"You did your time out there in the trenches; that's why you have on a suit and a tie. You ain't tryna go back. But we both know that any successful organization needs both, and we do what we gotta do."

He laughed again, and this time, I joined him.

As I sat in silence, I bounced his words around in my head. Twenty mil in three years. And in a suit and tie? Those were my kind of numbers. Ballin'-out-of-control numbers. But what would Don Carlos say? Would he think it was a sign of disrespect? Me joining another organization when he had work for me that I wouldn't take?

"You're not jumping at my offer. Therefore, I assume that you're still not convinced. I'll tell you what. That little charge you just picked up along with the one that was pending—with one phone call, I could make them go away. But I will still give you a few days to think about my offer. Thank you for your time, Mr. Macklin."

How did he know about my charges? And as if the chauffeur could hear everything being said, the back door popped open.

"Thank you for your offer," I said before exiting the vehicle.

As I began to walk back to the house, Mr. Li leaned out the window and added, "I must inform you, my daughter does not come with my deal."

"Is that why she sent a man to my home with intentions of blowing it up?" I was full of doubt at the thought of Charli going that far. But Tasha was positive it was her behind it, so I took my chances and threw it out there. I wanted to gauge his reaction.

"That won't happen again. You and your family will be under my full protection." The window rolled up and the car sped off.

Ain't this some shit? I became more pissed with each step that I took. Mad at how vulnerable I'd made me and my family. Full protection? Make my case disappear? Did I need him? I was feeling as if he was boxing me into a corner. What would the next extreme be from the Li family to get me to join their organization? And how would Tasha take this? She probably would leave me. I couldn't allow the odds to stack up against me.

11

KAYLIN

I was in my boardroom participating in a meeting via video conference, more like a bidding war, trying to sign this up-and-coming rapper, Semaj. Semaj had some mixtapes that were doing some serious damage, and I wanted him. Mind you, I was going up against the majors, including Interscope and Def Jam, and it was pretty intense. When my assistant, Diedre, burst in on the video conference and motioned for me to step out, I looked at her as if she was crazy.

"Mr. Santos, this is urgent." I leaned over to Angel and said, "I'm the boss of this damn operation. You see them plaques on the wall? They say Kaylin Santos. Why is she annoying me and not you?"

Angel leaned over and whispered right back in my ear, "Apparently, you are not the boss. Who is the force behind you that put the team together to help you get those plaques? Angel Santos." She went back to shuffling papers and talking.

"Excuse me," I said, and got ready to hammer Diedre.

"Before you go off, Mr. Santos, I tried to tell Mr. Macklin that you were in a very important meeting, but he stated that this was urgent and he needed to talk to you right now. When I told him I couldn't interrupt you, he began to threaten me, so please, save the rants, he's on line four." She turned around and walked away.

I started to follow her and go all in but changed my mind, thinking that Trae must have finally killed Kyron. I made it to my office, closed my door, took a deep breath, and hit the speaker button.

"Trae, I'm trying to get this money, and you are threatening my flow! What's up, nigga? What is so urgent?"

"Are you going to be around for the next couple of days? I need to come see you. I'm scheduled to leave tonight."

"What happened?" I braced myself for the news, as I grabbed onto the edge of my desk. He chuckled. "Chill, nigga. It ain't nothing like that. Not yet. I'm talkin' about that paper, nigga. Real long paper! Man, fuck that rapping chump change you sweatin'. I just got an offer, but you know I can't talk like this. I want to leave tonight—that is, unless you want to come out here?"

"Nigga, did you hear what I just said? I'm in a bidding war right now, but you dragged me out here talking urgent."

"Kay, trust me. When I say urgent, that's putting it mildly. Money? I'm talking about some real bread. Scratch, scrilla. Bigger than anything we was seeing with Don Carlos."

Shit. I thought about what he said and immediately got nervous. "Trae, talk to me now."

"Not over the phone, bruh," he said.

"Well, I really need to get back into this meeting," I told him. "Let me hit you up later."

"Handle your business. I'm on my way up to you. I'll be at your house before noon tomorrow."

I got the dial tone. I headed back into my meeting, wondering what Trae was up to. Needless to say, my edge was no longer there. And with that little interruption, instead of me winning by a landslide, Semaj's agent left saying all offers would be considered and they would make a decision within twenty-four hours.

"Baby, what the hell happened to you in there?" Angel asked me. I could tell that she was trying her best to remain calm. But I blew it, and we both knew it. "What was it that Diedre wanted?"

"It was Trae. He's on his way up here." I stuck my head into Diedre's office. "See if Trae needs a car from the airport. Tell him I want him to meet me here at the studio."

"No problem, Mr. Santos."

Angel grabbed my hand. "What happened? Do I need to sit down? Is Tasha all right? What about Kyron?"

"He said he needed to discuss business with me. That's all I know."

"That's it?" Angel stopped dead in her tracks. "And that is what caused us to possibly lose the hottest underground artist out there? Babe, you gotta come better than that!"

"Red, it is what it is. But it's not only what he said, it was the urgency in how he said it. Something is up. He said something bigger than Don Carlos."

Don Carlos was just that: a Don. And had been that for almost twenty years. He had his hands in powder, heroin, and real estate. From what I knew, he had senators, congressman and judges in his pocket. He was big. So in my mind no one I knew was bigger. Needless to say, I was anxious to hear what Trae had to say.

"Oh, no, no, no, Kaylin. Don't you even think about it! Baby, you're out. Don't even think about it. I'm warning you, Kaylin. Let Trae lead you into some bullshit if you want to." She pushed me out of the way and stormed into her office.

RICK

Back home in Tucson, tension in the house was real thick. I got caught fucking Kyra and then had the audacity to spend the night after the fact. Wrong move. It was obvious that Nina was done with me. But I wasn't done with her. I had mad love for her and plus she was carrying my seed. Since Nina told me to pack my shit and leave, she'd been giving me the cold shoulder and, on top of that, the total silent treatment. I had to admit I felt like a total creep, and getting busted fucking someone by someone I care about is a first for me. While walking the kids to school, I felt like Wesley Snipes in the movie *Jungle Fever*. The kids were tugging at me and talking to me, while I was zoned out. Other parents and the crossing guards were speaking to me, and I could only stare. I dropped the kids off and decided to go home, change, and head over to Dave's Gym to shoot some hoops.

Kyra had been calling me, but I wouldn't answer, because if I did, I wasn't sure what I would say. All I knew was I wanted them both. So I was caught with my dick in my hand and didn't know where to put it. The thought had even occurred about going back to Georgia. But when I spoke to Trae, he told me that running wasn't gonna do shit but change the atmosphere. The problem was still going to be there. He asked me to do him a favor and call Kyra, because she was hurt, confused, and driving him nuts.

Just as I turned the corner from the school, a limo pulled up, and to my surprise, out she jumped.

TRAE

I walked into Kaylin's office building around lunchtime. The guard at the front desk was acting as if he didn't want to let me up. So I got Kaylin on the phone, and he told me to stay put, he'd be right down. He said he needed to take a break and wanted to go to the deli next door.

After about five minutes, he got off the elevator, came over to me, and gave me some dap. "You made it, huh? If you know like I know, you'll take ya Hollywood ass back out to Cali." He said the same thing to me every time he saw me.

"Whatever, nigga. Hurry up and order your shit. We got business. I'll wait here. I need to call Tasha."

"You don't want anything?"

"Get me the same thing you gettin' for yourself."

"Aiight bet." He turned and left the building.

I found a corner so I could call and speak to my wife. "Where are you?" That was the first thing she asked me.

"You know where I am."

"Kyra has been gone now for almost eighteen hours."

"Gone? What do you mean, gone?"

"Gone. No phone calls. No text messages. Not here. I even went to the Vons where I found her preaching with her Bible. Aunt Marva thought I was lying about that until she caught her going up and down the block knocking on doors. I can't do this, Trae. We might have to have her evaluated. She's fuckin' bananas right now."

"Have her evaluated for what?"

"I think she's fuckin' . . . nuts. I can't raise our children, babysit a crazy patient, and run this house at the same time."

I had to chuckle. "A crazy patient?"

"I'm serious, Trae. I'm worried about her."

"Well, don't go back combing the streets for her. She's grown, and when she's ready to come to the house or check in, she will." When Tasha didn't respond, I said, "She will, Tasha."

"Hurry back home, please. And you're coming back when?"

"As soon as I take care of this."

"How soon is that? A few hours? A day?"

"Tasha, I'll call you when I finish. Here comes Kaylin now."

"Whatever."

"Love you, too." I hung up and turned my attention to Kay. "So what you get me? A hot dog off the cart?"

"Hell, no! Them muthafuckas don't have toilets or sinks to wash their hands. I got you what's called 'get a nigga whatever you got, because as soon as they see yo shit, they want it.' Here." He handed me my bags, and I peeked inside the container, saw some lamb over yellow rice, and smiled. "I got this, nigga," he said, walking onto the elevator with me right on his heels. We rode in silence until we reached his floor. When the doors opened, he moved fast, and I was right behind him.

"C'mon. Let's go into the conference room." As soon as he shut the door, he asked me, "So what's up?"

I sat my food on the table and immediately started pacing back and forth, anxious to get it all out. "I get this call from Charli, saying that her father wants to meet with me. I hang up on her, thinking she on some bullshit, and toss her and her conversation out of my mind. But then a couple of days go by, and I'm out gettin' my walk on and trying to clear my head, when this limo pulls up. I'm thinking all kinds of shit. Mainly, the fact that I wasn't strapped. Bottom line, it was the man himself, Charlie Li. The rear window came down, just like in the movies. He asks if he can speak to me. I get in, and that's when he gives me an offer. To make a long story short, he said if I came on board, I can make twenty mil in three years."

Kay looked at me as if to say, *Nigga, have you lost your mind?* He opened his food container and fixed himself a plate. He then said, "That's all fine and dandy, *if* you live to spend it. How do you expect, just like that"—he snapped his fingers—"to go from one organization to its rival organization?"

"They aren't rivals, Kay. They both have different hustles, different territories."

"You told the Dons you wanted out. Now you're going to sign on with somebody different? Trae, I don't think you are thinking clearly."

"Just like before and always, to answer your question, I'll go to the Dons out of respect. Nobody owns me, Kay. Fuck all that! We're talkin' twenty mil in three years? Seven a year. Come on, son, that's a no-brainer."

"You gonna let him lock you in for three years? Nigga, you dumber than I thought." He looked at me, laughed, and then ate a little of his food.

"Whatever, nigga." I sat down in front of him to look him in the eye. "He's making my charges go away. And you know I ain't tryna go visit nobody's prison. Especially since California is a death-penalty state."

"Trae, he knew the perfect carrot to dangle in front of you. Can't you see that?"

"So are you in or what? You making the move with me? My mind is already made up."

Kay took a deep breath. "Let me be clear. He dangled that carrot because he needs you. Up that 20 mil a little. Make it worth your while. And if you make that move, ain't no turning back. You know you're claiming MOL."

"MOL? What the fuck is that?"

"Money Over Life, nigga."

I pushed my food away from me, stood up, and went over to the window to peer out over the Manhattan streets. Kaylin was right, and I knew it. If I made this move, there would be no turning back. If I took the offer I would be back in the game. I knew that was a huge risk. Death or prison. Either way I was rolling the dice. Then there was the matter of Don Carlos. What would he say? More important, what would he do? I knew that if I ever decided to get back in, it was supposed to be with the same team. Especially since I bitched so hard to get out. And then there's Tasha. But all I could see was twenty mil in three years. All I needed was those three.

Kay wasn't finished trying to make sure that I knew what I was going up against. "I'm telling you, Don Carlos ain't gonna want to hear this shit. And the wives? Whenever they find out, they gonna shit bricks."

I grinned, not at the truth of his statement but at the shitting of bricks part. And he'd said "wives." Meaning his, too. He was in. But ironically, I thought about what his punk-ass brother had said. "Yeah, your brother said we got soft."

"Man, fuck Kyron! He crazier than a muthafucka. We spent damn near twelve years in the game, walked away without a long sentence, still breathing, and legit. Sheeit. That ain't soft. That's genius! Now you at my door talking about going back in?" He looked at me. "That's not genius, that's fuckin' crazy."

"Kay, I'm telling you, this here game is on a whole 'notha level, though. You're telling me twenty mil in three don't excite you? Then cool. I can respect that. Maybe I will get him to up to thirty. You know I want my right arm to ride with me, but if you feel you gotta do your shit legit, I understand. But I gotta do me." I started for the door but stopped. "Do me one favor. I'ma need you to take it to Don Carlos. Coming from you, he'll more than likely go for it."

I also started to tell him out of respect that it was time for me to handle Kyron. But I thought better of it. I needed him to keep his mind on talking to Don Carlos for me. I'd deal with Kyron later.

12

JAZ

Oni had them dig up Lil' Faheem and bring his body back to the funeral home. I had never heard of such a thing, but Faheem wasn't having it any other way. We suspected that she had an insurance policy on his son, and that's why she was so in a hurry to lay him to rest.

On one hand, I was happy that Faheem was finally able to lay Lil' Fah to rest. On the other, it tore me up to see him bury his son. There was only me, him and the funeral director at the funeral. He cried like a baby. I didn't know what to do or say to console him, I was so so caught off guard. After all of these years, I had never seen that side of my husband before. I moved to the row behind him and left him alone. He kept mumbling why did this have to happen and if he could only have one more chance. He said he took full responsibility. He said some prayers in Arabic over and over. Finally, I heard him mumble, "Forgive me Allah for the lives I am about to take." He was ready to go after that statement.

Afterward I couldn't get him to eat, and sleeping had become his escape. When he wasn't sleeping, he just sat in his chair and stared out the window.

I hated her even more now, and the fact that Faheem was not being gung ho about splitting the bitch's wig only added more fuel to the fire. I knew he had a cast on his leg, but there was nothing wrong with his mouth or his will. So what I did was tell him I needed to take a trip to Cali to check on Kyra. Tasha had called and was talking some mess about admitting Kyra into a mental institution. To me, it sounded like she was the one who needed to be admitted. But on my way to Cali, I'd stop in Jersey, to check on my granny and recruit somebody to make the moves I needed to make down here in Georgia.

I checked on my granny, who was doing surprisingly well. She was glad to see me, because she wanted me to promise her that I wouldn't put her in a nursing home. She was adamant about staying in the house she'd lived in for more than thirty years. I tried not to promise that I wouldn't admit her, but she wouldn't let me leave without doing so. After I hung out with her for a while, Snell finally hit me back and said that I could come by and see him.

As I drove through the streets of Trenton, my spirit felt heavy because I saw how the quality of the city had gone down. I mean, don't get me wrong, it was the same as every other hood in America. It was just that my hood had gotten older, and the city that raised me was now rundown and raggedy. And it was around 2000 or 2001 that it became full of Crips and Bloods, something I would never have imagined. But I had family who were active members of both.

Faheem's cousin Snell still lived on Hoffman Ave. but in a different house. He had been living on this street since I was in the fourth grade. I remembered when the park, the basketball court, and the recreation center down the street were full of life. But now either the drug dealers had taken over or everything was abandoned. No more green grass. All I saw was broken bottles, beer cans, cigarette butts and empty crack vials. Where did the children play?

"Jaz, I know Faheem don't know nothing about you being here," he said as soon as I walked up onto the front porch. I zipped my jacket. It was brisk outside.

"He knows I'm in Trenton but not here, and you're not going to tell him."

"What makes you think that?"

"Because I have a nice proposition for you."

"Jaz, you better let Faheem handle his biz. You ain't mixing me up in your bullshit. I know what you want. But if he wouldn't allow me and G to do anything, he damn sure don't want you even thinking about it."

"Snell, Faheem has not gotten over losing his seed yet. He is immobile, and muthafuckas killed his only son, and you're talkin' about don't do anything? It will be our little secret, and if anything goes down, I'll take the weight. He will never know you was involved. Did I mention the pay is nice?" I looked him in his eyes. "If you're not down to help a family member out, then my money don't discriminate. I can easily get the next man. I need to use your bathroom." I said as I walked past him into the house.

I wanted him to marinate on my offer before he told me no. He was loyal to Faheem, but at the same time, he was loyal to that almighty green, and plus, I was family. Faheem told me years ago, if anything ever happened to him and I needed some muscle, to go see Snell first. As soon as I came out of the bathroom, I told him just that. So technically, I wasn't doing anything against Faheem's wishes.

"Jaz, I know you gonna go out there and do it anyway. And Fah would kill me if you went to someone else and shit went south. So it's obvious that I'm damned if I do and damned if I don't. But I still would feel at ease if I told him first."

"You can't do that. I'm telling you, Fah is not in his right state of mind right now. Think about it. His son died right there in his arms. It's like he's shell-shocked. We gotta do this for him and do it now. Are you in, or are you out?" I was done trying to convince him that I had a crisis on my hands. I had said all that I was going to say. Whether he was in or out, either way I was still going to do me. I know it was crazy for me to ask Snell to help me kill muthafuckas. Shit, if he was a real killer he should be about killing anybody if the price was right. Steele needed to be got. He didn't have to kidnap a child just because he had a beef with the mother. And as far as she was concerned the bitch exposed her son to the madness, so it would be justice done.

KYRA

I woke up the other morning and had made up my mind that I was going to see Rick. He would have to face me since he didn't take any of the hundreds of calls I made to him. I snuck away and got the first thing smoking out to Tucson, Arizona, to see him. I got the address from snooping around in Trae's man cave in the basement. When I jumped out of the tinted vehicle, Rick looked as if he wanted to jump out of his skin. I couldn't blame him; there I was right down the street from his house. He was the one who told me that he walked the kids to school every day, and then he would head back home to change and go shoot some hoops. I had perfect timing.

"Kyra? What are you doing out here? How did you know where—"

"Shut up! Stop right there. You couldn't answer my calls nigga! What—" I had to stop myself. Seeing him had me on a whole nother level.

"Return them and say what, Kyra? That I want to be with the both of you?" He grabbed my arm and began walking me in the opposite direction of his house.

"Is that what you would have said?"

"At this moment, yes. I have feelings for Nina, and she's carrying my baby."

"So what about me?"

"I never stopped loving you Kyra. Even Nina knows that."

I had to stop him right there. "That's all bullshit, Rick. You have feelings for her, but you love me? That's some bullshit! I'll tell you what. You need to go to her and tell her what you just told me. And you know what she's going to say? Pack your shit, Rick! That's what she's going to say. So go do that now, and I'll wait for you. Let's settle this shit once and for all."

"Kyra, you ain't gonna do shit but get in that car and take your ass back to Tasha's. Let me handle the situation the way I see fit."

"You need to handle your business right now. If you don't, I will. I got your address, Rick. You don't want me to come to your house with my bullshit because it won't be pretty. I will see you later." I snatched my arm away and headed back to my limo. The chauffeur jumped out, ran around to the back passenger side, and opened the door. As soon as I got in, Rick was getting in behind me. It was just me and him in the back and I was ready to cuss him out.

"Rick, go handle your business or—"

"Or what, Kyra?" He had grabbed me around my neck and pushed me back. "Or what?"

I couldn't breathe. He was pulling away at my shorts. I was stunned. No, this nigga wasn't getting ready to take my pussy. While I was trying to get his hand from around my throat, he was pulling my shorts down over my feet.

"Or what? Kyra?"

My nails dug into his arms. But now he was opening my legs with his knee, and he was pulling his dick from his sweats. I dug my nails deeper. His dick was now at my opening. He squeezed my throat tighter. His dick tore through me as he took his other hand, placed it under my ass, and grabbed it, pulling me closer, making his dick go deeper. He fucked me hard. In and out, he pounded furiously. I felt as if I was floating.

When I came to, Rick was kissing my breast. He was still hard inside me, grinding nice and slow. I wrapped my legs around his waist and began to fuck him back. He began to moan. I dug my nails into his ass cheeks, forcing him to go deeper. I couldn't get enough of his dick.

"Fuck me, Rick! Fuck me, Rick!" I screamed. I felt as if I was on a Ferris wheel that was speeding. Then I felt the tingle, the waves, and then contractions. I started coming. The way Rick was banging my back out, I guessed he was coming, too. He gave me a bliss filled mind-altering orgasm. And he thinks I could let him go.

After what felt like an eternity, Rick rose up off me, handed me my shorts, and fixed his clothes. Then he leaned over and kissed me passionately.

"You know I love you more than anything, right?" I nodded. "Then let me do this my way."

He got out of the limo. I rolled the window down and said, "Rick, I love you, too. But don't keep me waiting."

JAZ

I was dog-tired but had finally made it to Tasha's. I'd thought I was going to be able to jump into a hot bubble bath and get under the covers. But instead, I was greeted by the drama queen looking discombobulated wearing bright pink Victoria's Secret PJs. Her eyes were red and puffy.

"Tasha, what happened? Why are you crying?" I set my bags down.

"I'm not crying. I'm just upset." Oh shit. This was going to be a long night. I went to hug her.

"Let me call Faheem to let him know I'm here. Do you have any herbal tea?" She nodded. "Can I get a slice of lemon with that? Please?" I saw that smart-ass look on her face. "I said please." She waved me off and headed for the kitchen.

I pulled out a White Owl wrap from my $2,500 Michael Kors snake tote. I had hid a small case holdin' that loud and went to rolling me a blunt while dialing Faheem.

"Hey." Faheem answered the phone.

"Hey, babe, just wanted to let you know that I'm at Tasha's. Are y'all all right?"

"We good."

"You sound good, but why are you still up?" It was almost two-thirty in the morning East Coast time.

"Why are you so nosy?"

"Whatever."

"I was waiting on your call. That's why I'm still up," he said.

"How sweet. You got my call, now take your ass to bed. Love you." I kissed into the phone. "Give that to Kaeerah for me."

"Whatever," Faheem had the nerve to say, and then hung up on me.

I smiled, tucked the phone into my bag, and headed for the kitchen, glad that he was sounding a little more like himself.

"So, Miss Thing, what the hell is going on, and why are you talking about committing Kyra to some institution?"

"Kyra has been gone for almost two days. No phone calls, no texts, no note, nothing. I don't have time to babysit her. I have three kids, Aisha and Trae. And you know that bitch Charli has been calling here. And he's been to see her father a couple of times."

"Her father?" Now, that was a shocker. "Why has he been going to see her father?" I passed her the blunt. She took a pull and passed it back.

"He said it's business. They are working on this big business deal." Tears were streaming down her cheeks. "He's not home. He's there now. I swear, Jaz, I'ma do something to that bitch. I just haven't figured it out yet."

I passed it back to her. She obviously needed it. She got up and fixed my tea. *But shit. She's beginning to sound like me.* And it appeared that we both had the same problem. A bitch. But my problem I was going to kill. I wasn't sure whether Tasha was thinking about taking such drastic measures. I was just hoping that she was just letting go of some steam. She set my cup of tea on the table. I took a sip. "Ewwwww. You got any honey?"

"Jaz, where do you think you're at?" She went to the cabinet and came back with a honey bear.

"Thank you. Now, tell me about the fire. For real, I can't even tell that y'all had one. Look at these beautiful floors! And that sofa . . . I love it."

"Well, it wasn't really a fire on the inside, that's why. Just smoke and water damage. Because of the sprinkler system and fire-resistant insulation, the fire was contained to the outside for the most part."

"For the most part my ass! You got all new stuff. I like new stuff." I tried to look at the bright side. They had a new red leather sectional that was to die for. It could seat at least fourteen people comfortably. A huge, dumb ass flat screen on the wall. The kitchen was painted a bright blue with stainless steel appliances and decorated with black granite counter tops. The floors were a beautiful light gray wood that was very different. The house had a new look with the same drama. I snickered at the thought. Tasha looked at me as if to say, "What the fuck is so funny?" I switched up and asked, "Were you scared?"

"Girl . . ."

I listened intently and smoked away as Tasha told me what had happened that night. I was grateful that no one was hurt. That was a blessing. Thank goodness Aunt Marva was as nosy as she was. If she hadn't spotted the guy lurking around outside, they would have been stuck inside and possibly sucked up into a flaming fire. We then sat in silence, each of us momentarily lost in thought, the only sounds were her occasional sniffs, me stirring my tea, and the faint hum of the freezer. The blunt was gone. I was fucked up.

We heard someone at the door, and we looked at each other.

Tasha started wiping her eyes and fixing herself up. I assumed she thought it was her husband coming in. I had a front-row seat for the fight. "Too late. You look like you were crying," I told her. I thought she was going to get up and go running to the door, but she didn't. She just sat there, and to our surprise, it wasn't Trae. In walked Kyra. I looked her over and she had on this short ass Versace aqua dress that said easy access.

"Jaz! What are you doing here?" She kissed Tasha on the cheek and then came around the table to give me a hug.

"I came to check on you. You got Tasha worried half to death. You leave, don't tell anyone where you are going. You don't call nobody, no text, no nothing. Kyra, that ain't right. Where were you?" I scolded her as if I was her mother.

"Awww. Tasha, I'm sorry." She went back around the table to hug Tasha.

"Kyra, where were you? Why didn't you call?" Tasha pushed her away. She was clearly agitated with our girl.

Kyra grabbed a chair and sat down next to Tasha. "I went to go see Rick."

"Rick!" We both yelled at the same time.

Then Tasha said, "Bitch, you could have called, left a note or something. How could you up and leave your daughter like that?"

"Stop it! Stop yelling at me!" Kyra put both hands over her ears. "I know. I know. And I'm sorry, Tasha. He wasn't returning my calls. I was trying to be patient, but my patience ran out. I had to go see him. I'm sorry." She paused. "But shit, I'm grown. Y'all don't ring my phone before you go see your man." She looked at us sideways.

I threw up my hands and backed off, thinking that was the flip-personality shit Tasha was talking about. I knew Tasha was getting ready to dig into that ass.

"Kyra, you have a child here! Have you forgotten? A parent does not just up and leave to go to another state without making sure her responsibility is safe and secure. I'm thinking something happened to you. And when your daughter asked me where you were, I couldn't even answer her. How hard is it to pick up your cell? Send a text? You don't fuckin' get up and leave for days without telling anybody! You just don't do that!"

"I didn't say anything because I knew you would try to talk me out of it, Tasha."

"Kyra, you don't know that. Your dumb ass could easily have said, 'I'm going anyway.' At least, then I wouldn't be out looking for you and worried sick about you. That was so stupid of you, Kyra."

"I know, I know." Kyra started kissing her all over her face. "Can you forgive me? I won't do that again."

"Stop it, Kyra!" Tasha yelled while trying to push her away. But Kyra wouldn't stop.

I couldn't help but laugh, and then we all started laughing.

"So what happened? What did he say? Why did you go out there?" Tasha asked her.

"I needed some of that dick," Kyra said nonchalantly.

"You what?" I had to be sure I'd heard her right.

"I needed some dick. Y'all forget, it's been a long time for me."

"You bitch! I'ma fuck your ass up!" Tasha said, laughing as she jumped out of her chair and dived on top of Kyra.

13

TRAE

You talkin' about Mr. Li opening my eyes to a whole new level of being in the game? I'd have to call that an understatement. In five days, I'd traveled on private jets to Mexico and Texas, and in two weeks, I'd be going to Singapore. I made a mental note to cross Texas off my relocation list.

Why? Because you don't shit where you eat, and the Li organization had the state of Texas on lock. My job was to handle any business with the organization's black clientele. I was now the black poster child for the Li organization. Wherever there was black clientele, they had to deal with me. My job was simply to collect money. And since it appeared to be all business people, and no block niggas, everything was cut clear and dry. I was told how much I was picking up, they would turn it over, no questions asked, no excuses. And I was picking up money by the shitload.

Throughout Mexico and Houston, the Li's owned a string of

banks called the People's Bank. What they were running through them wasn't shared with me. I was overly anxious to find out what was happening in Singapore. They had me open.

I was assigned to a mentor named Kon Li, who I found out later was Charli's cousin. After a few short hours, I saw how the whole situation was going to be to my advantage. One, I had Charli in my pocket. The bitch would do anything I asked. Two, Kon Li had loose lips. Three, he was fascinated with black people. The black that was portrayed in the rap industry, hood movies, and the media. Hell, he was the blackest Chinese dude I knew next to TV Johnny the Jeweler. But best believe he didn't act or speak that way when he was around Mr. Li.

But from what I could gather, Kon was fucking up with the black people. At first, I didn't know why. But when I saw how he thought he was Nino Brown from *New Jack City*, I knew that was where the trouble was. He was dealing with these black professionals as if they were niggas on the block. I saw exactly why they were replacing him.

"Dude," Kon said through slurred speech. "I'm not stupid, you know. I can teach you a lot. I know they want you to replace me. But it's okay. You know why? Because I will be getting a promotion. The Big boss is about to be even bigger. He's about to fuck up the whole banking system. And I'm going to help him. We about to get paid, dawg!"

Banking system? I poured him another drink. "So, I can come to you and get a loan or get some side work or what?"

"No doubt, bro!"

"School me. What I got to do?"

"Hold up. Let me holla at that chick over there. I'll be right back."

We were at one Li's private clubs in Houston. There were only two other black brothers there besides myself and they were security. Needless to say, I didn't see Kon for the rest of the night.

The last thing that blew my mind was that the Li organization had a ritual that consisted of having your finger cut and mixing your blood with that of your assigned mentor. That ritual was performed in front of two witnesses. My witnesses were Charli and an old head named Wong. They made a small slit at the tip of my finger and one on Kon Li's. We pressed our fingers together, and the drops of blood dripped onto the document. The same document that I had to sign.

Right before that, Wong, who was not generous with words pulled me aside and said, "Sun Tzu's *The Art of War* says, you never let your enemy know your strengths or your weaknesses." And he walked away.

TASHA

This was my sixth night in a row sitting up in the dark, in the family room, waiting for Trae to come home. For the last three days, our conversation was the same, him saying to me, "I'll be home tonight." But he would never show up. I didn't know what the fuck he was doing or with whom, but I had a strong feeling it was that eggroll bitch. Hell, I didn't even know where he was. But I did know that it was stressing the shit out of me.

My mind began to drift as I thought about everybody. Kyron was too quiet, which meant that he was up to something. Trina had been laying low. I still hadn't reached my brother. I didn't know if he was dead or alive. Angel was doing her thing running her husband's record label. Kyra had lost her damned mind chasing after Rick. It was as if in her mind, Marvin had never existed, which was scary. Jaz's sneaky ass was up to something, even though I couldn't put my finger on it.

I was getting sleepy, so I turned on the television. The house alarm chirped, and I hit the mute button. My heart began to race. My husband was home. Finally. I got up and headed for the front of the house. When I reached the living room, I stood still and focused to make sure it was him.

"Baby, why is it so dark in here? Come here!" He walked over to me and gave me a big hug and a fat kiss. "I missed you, girl."

I missed you, too. Of course, I didn't tell him that, because I wanted him to know that I had an attitude. I looked him over for any signs or clues of infidelity. He was clean, smelling good, and dressed to the nines. He was suited and booted as if he had just stepped off a photo shoot for Armani.

"You waited up for Daddy?" He took off his suit jacket and placed it neatly over the back of the couch.

"I've been waiting up for six days. Do you even realize how long you've been gone?"

"Of course I do. I've been counting, too. And now Daddy is home. But I don't feel the love. Where's it at?"

He eased his hands down and palmed my ass cheeks. I tried to pry his fingers free.

"Tasha, you better stop acting crazy and act like you know. Where the love at?" He leaned in and sank his teeth into my jaw.

"Trae, no!"

"Aiight, then you better act like you know. Where the love at? A nigga been away for days from his pussy, and you're trying to act crazy. You're supposed to be all over me. Give me a kiss." His hands were all over me.

177

I gave him a peck on the lips, and he went back for my jaw. "Okay, Trae. Damn." I kissed him for real this time.

"That's what I'm talking about. Now give me another one."

I did. But this time, I melted in his arms.

"I love you, girl."

I didn't say anything as he backed me onto the couch. I held on to him as we fell backward.

"I missed you," he kept saying as he passionately kissed my cheeks, lips, and neck. His fingers slid between my thighs, where two fingers entered me, came out, and went up to my clit. He tickled it lightly, slowly heightening the good feeling and taking me to . . . "Oh, baby, wait." Trae stopped pleasuring me in mid-action and began to rise up off me.

"What?" I asked with slight panic in my voice as I grabbed at his shirt.

"Hold up now! Hold up! I got you."

He went to two, big, shiny red shopping bags. He turned on the lamp. When he opened the first one, he reached in and pulled out a fly ass coal black, Crocodile Birkin handbag. That had to run him at least 50gs. I tried to act as if I wasn't impressed but inside I was jumping up and down for joy. But when he opened the second bag and pulled out a heart-shaped box, I couldn't help but blush. He set it on the coffee table and opened it. He took out what I knew was my favorite, a box of chocolate-covered strawberries. *Awwwww. So he* was *thinking about me.*

"That's right. I was thinking about my baby the whole time," he said as if he'd read my mind. He came over to the couch and sat next to me.

"They're probably melting." I finally spoke, whispering.

"Perfect." He placed a strawberry on my lips, smearing the

chocolate on them, then on my cheeks and neck. He put the strawberry in my mouth, and I nibbled it slowly. "Dayuum, baby, that's what I'm talkin' about."

He pulled my nightshirt off and got another strawberry out of the box, and this time, he spread chocolate on the insides of my thighs and all over my breasts and nipples. He then placed the strawberry in my mouth, and as I ate it, he seductively licked and sucked the chocolate off. The sucking noise he made was making my pussy dripping wet. The next thing I knew, Trae was coming out of his pants as I lay there, legs spread wide open. His dick was so hard it was rising up and down, damn near jumping. As his body began to cover mine, I lifted one leg and put it on his shoulder. That's right. I was ready to feel my husband's big dick as far up in me as he could get it.

"Why are you so quiet?" he asked with concern in his voice.

I was quiet because I was confused. I was skeptical. He had been away from me for days, and all of sudden, he showed up showing a side of himself I hadn't seen in a while. I didn't know what the fuck he was out there doing, and I was scared to death. It reminded me too much of his hustling days. The days when I would sit up waiting and praying that he would come home to me at least one more time.

He entered me slowly, and I moaned. "That's right, talk to me. Talk to Daddy," he said as he stroked in and out. All I could do was hold him tight, pant, and moan. "You missed Daddy, didn't you?" He fucked me harder and like the champ that he was. It always felt so right when my husband was up in me. He was stroking me faster, and then he immediately pulled out. "Fuck! I was about to come." He jumped up. "Get on top." He pulled me up and lay down on his back.

I climbed on top of him, slid down on the dick, and rode and rode and rode until I started coming while screaming and hollering. I didn't care if I woke up the dead or the living. I came so hard I didn't even know if Trae came or not. I only knew that when I collapsed on top of him, his dick slid out. I lay on his chest, wrapped in his arms, as he planted soft kisses on my face.

I started to have him eat my pussy, but instead, I waited for my breathing to get back to normal and was then ready to get some shit out in the open. I had a million and one questions.

"So where were you?"

"A little bit of everywhere."

"What does that mean?"

My husband took his time, and I could tell he was going to answer the questions very carefully. "That means a little bit of everywhere and chill on the questions." He kissed my forehead again.

I sat up and grabbed my nightshirt off the coffee table and put it on. "Trae, you know what this feels like?"

"What?" He looked at me.

"It feels like when we first got together. It feels like you are back in the game. Why, Trae? Why does it feel like that?"

"Tasha, I told you I was taking care of business. That's exactly what I'm doing."

"The bitch is back to calling our house, Trae. What kind of business is that?"

"Tasha, don't start the insecure bullshit." He sat up.

"Insecure? You said it's business with her father. She works for him. So you're telling me that you don't have any dealings with this ho?"

"Ma, lower your voice."

"Then answer me, Trae. You've been gone for six whole days, and you are going to sit here and tell me you didn't see her, not once?"

He jumped up off the sofa, dick swinging, and went behind the easy chair. He came back with two briefcases and slammed them onto the coffee table. He popped one open and then the other. They both were full to the brim with evenly stacked bills.

"This is what I've been doing, Tasha, gettin' money! Are you meaning to tell me you got a problem with that?"

"How you gonna get money with the enemy, Trae?"

"Enemy? I'm getting money with the muthafucka that made my murder charges go away, and you got a problem with that too? The man fuckin' called the governor of California, while I was sitting right there and told him to expunge my record Tasha."

"That's all well and good. So he has political clout. Big fuckin' deal! But I still have a problem with how you're gettin' it and who you are gettin' it with, yes."

"It's only a problem if you make it a problem." He gritted his teeth while slamming the briefcases shut. And then he snatched up his clothes and headed for the stairs.

"I only have a problem with that bitch. I should have taken care of her when I had the chance."

"Taken care of her? What the fuck? So, you killin' hos now? Get the fuck out her with all this dramatized bullshit."

"You're going to wish I was bullshittin'."

"Tasha!" He turned around and came back to where I was and stood in front of me. "I am not going to tell you a—"

"Trae, this shit don't feel right. Fuck that money! I'd rather be broke than not have you."

"Tasha!" The walls felt as if they shook. "I don't want to hear shit else about Charli. What I'm doing out there is for us. This conversation is over. And I mean that shit."

"Fine, you won't hear shit else about Charli." *But you just signed the bitch's death certificate. Soon you gonna be at her funeral.*

JAZ

Almost ten days had gone by since I came back from seeing Snell. I was getting impatient and anxious at the same time. I had to put the money together to pay him while at the same time covering my tracks in case Faheem went to sniffing around. But Steele was still alive. Snell said that when he called me and said he was home, that would mean that the deed was done. I was walking around like a nervous fool. To make matters worse, I couldn't focus on my plan to handle Oni until Steele was done. I couldn't wait to get that bitch.

"Jaz! Where you at?" Faheem interrupted my chain of thought. I was busted. He was sitting in a chair, and I was straddling his lap. He was dicking me down, and I was zoning out.

"I'm right here, big daddy," I cooed.

"The hell you are. Your pussy is drying up." He stopped. "Here we ain't fucked in months, and you drying up. Now, tell me, where the fuck are you?"

"Baby, don't make me do that."

"What the fuck you mean, don't make you do that? Get off of me, Jaz."

"Baby—"

"Get off me," he barked.

I slowly got up, careful not to bump his leg. Then, as fate would have it, my cell rang. I knew who it was as I rushed to answer it. I took the call, which lasted about thirty seconds. "We good babygirl," the voice on the other end said.

"Are we?" I wanted to jump up and down. I wanted to hear every little detail. "So what was the look—" He hung up on me which was the smart thing to do. But I still couldn't help myself. I was geeked. The first half of my plan was done.

"Jaz, you got five seconds to start talking."

I stood there naked, thinking long and hard. I had so much to say, but nothing would come out. All I could say was, "Steele," as I tried to contain my smile.

"Steele. Steele? What the fuck he got to do with your pussy drying up, Jaz?"

Faheem instantly transformed from a loving husband to a roaring lion. And I knew right then and there that if I didn't start talking fast, my naked ass was going to be grass.

"Steele. He's dead. The deed is done, Faheem. That was the call. You can thank me later."

Faheem just sat there staring at me coldly. I swear, I now know firsthand what it meant when they said, "If looks could kill." I snatched up my robe from the bottom of the bed, threw it on, sat down, and braced myself for the worst. But at this juncture, the deed was already done, and there was no turning back.

"What the fuck is wrong with you, Jaz? Didn't I tell you I wanted to handle that situation myself?" His voice shook the walls.

"Yes, you did," I mumbled.

"Then why the fuck are you sitting here telling me that you handled it? What? Just because I'm banged the fuck up, you think I'm pussy, Jaz?" He got up and came hopping on one leg at me. Before I could dodge out of the way, he had the front of my robe balled up in his hand.

I grabbed his wrist. "Faheem, get your hands off me." I didn't know what he was getting ready to do to me.

"Why, Jaz?" His eyes were dark, and his pupils were dilated.

"Get your hands off me." I was petrified. "Baby, please. At least, hear me out."

He turned me loose. "Why would you go behind my back and put yourself and our family in harm's way like that? And after I told you not to? That was fuckin' stupid!"

"How could you say it was stupid? It got done, didn't it?"

"Who did you get to do it, Jaz?"

"That's not important, Faheem. I can't tell you that. It's done."

"Ain't this some shit." Faheem laughed.

It was a *ha ha she told a joke* laugh, coupled with an *ain't this some bullshit* smirk, which pissed me off. "You can laugh all you want, because the deed is done, and I took care of it. You always want me to honor your thug, but you need to recognize and honor mines."

He released that same annoying laugh again. "Jaz, I already told you, you ain't no thug. You got someone else to do it. You know why? 'Cause you ain't no killer."

"Whatever. But like I already told you, the deed is done." Yes, it was. And I felt liberated. I set my sight on a desired result and got it. It was exhilarating, and I was ready to do it again.

I got up and stormed out of our bedroom with my head held high. Hell, I was calling the shots, and I was feelin' myself. *He thinks he's shittin' bricks because of Steele; wait until I do Oni.*

14

KYRA

It had been been exactly sixteen days, three hours, and seven minutes since I snuck up on Rick in Arizona, and I hadn't received one call or text message. Nothing from him at all, and I was sick about it.

Tonight Trae was hosting a fight party, Chavez Jr. versus Martinez, and Tasha damn near dragged me out of my room and made me come join the festivities down in the basement. Trae must have been in an extra-good mood, because Trina was there with some dude named Jameer, along with the couple down the street, Elisa and Paul, the Sinclairs who came to our aid the night of the fire, and two other dudes that I didn't know, all hanging out. I wasn't up for it, so I found me a seat on top of a stool behind the bar in the corner. One of the dudes kept looking back at me, but I was sure he picked up on my body language, which I made sure screamed, *Stay the fuck away.*

In the middle of the first undercard fight, I started looking at the clock. There was no way I was going to sit down there for the next three to four hours. I didn't know why Trae didn't just take his ass to Vegas and watch it ringside like he can afford to. That way, I wouldn't have had to get up, get dressed, and make believe that I was okay, because I wasn't. That was until I looked back and noticed who was gliding down the basement stairs. It was none other than Rick. *Oh, my God!* I could have died and gone to heaven. I perked right up. I was so glad that Tasha made me throw on something decent and lose the funky sweats that I had been moping around in all week that I could have done a back flip.

"Look who's here," Tasha said, looking over at me. She got up to give Rick a hug.

"Nigga, you late!" I heard Trae say.

"It's not like I still live down the street, lil' bruh."

So, Mr. Trae knew all along that Rick was coming and didn't even tell me. I guessed that was his way of getting me back for snooping around in his man cave and getting that address. I couldn't take my eyes off of my man as I watched on while Trae introduced him to everyone in the room. He already knew Elisa and Paul and, of course, the Sinclairs, who went crazy when they realized it was him.

When he looked over my way, we locked gazes. I felt as if I was sweating bullets as he smiled at me and came my way. "Hey, pretty lady," he said, walking up in front of me and then leaning over and kissing me on the lips. I obliged him by accepting his tongue, and it taste so sweet. "You know what I'm here for, right? It damn sure ain't no fight," he said in between kisses that were sending chills all up and down my spine.

"Nigga, please. Two weeks? You obviously don't know me very well if you think you ain't got some begging, groveling, and explaining to do," I hissed.

"Kyra, don't be like that. I was working on some things. But your man is here now."

"I'm sure you were *working on some things*. But I hope you've been tying up some loose ends and getting your paper right, because I missed my period, Mr. Family Man." Rick froze and then stood straight up. I'd single-handedly crushed his cocky little attitude.

"You what?"

"You heard me. I missed my period." I had been dying to say those words to him. "You're about to be a daddy."

He looked shocked. He was about to say something but didn't. Then he looked like he was going to pass out.

"Shit, Kyra. Not now. You can't—"

"I can't what? Oh, so I'm not good enough to have your baby? But she is? Fuck you!" I jumped up off the stool, kicking it over, and left the family room. He had me fucked up.

TASHA

Fight night at the Macklin Palace, and I got to play hostess with the mostest. Trae was in a real good mood, and since he hadn't taken any unexpected trips recently, I was in good spirits, too. I was surprised to see Rick walk through the door, and I could tell that Kyra was even more so. However, Rick was now looking quite perturbed. I didn't know what Kyra said to him. She must have cursed his ass out, which I didn't know why, since she had been so down in the dumps and crying because he hadn't been in touch with her. But then she up and stormed out of the party. I couldn't wait to get all of the nasty little details.

I still was in shock that Trae had allowed Trina to come over. And you can best believe that she was on her best behavior, offering to get drinks, serving snacks and shit . . . just kissing Trae's ass. I had to find out about this dude she came with. Because she'd never told me about him, and they seemed to be into each other.

Other than Rick looking crazy and Kyra storming out, everybody else was sitting around having a good time. Blunts were being passed around, and of course, there was plenty of liquor and beer. Well, a minute ago there was plenty. I had just noticed that the beer was just about gone. Between Elisa, her husband, and Trina's date, they were downing the Heinekens as if they were cans of Pepsi. Everybody was talking, laughing, getting drunk and having a good time.

"Damn, they're goin' in, aren't they?" Trae joked.

"My thoughts exactly. I'll go get some more."

"Tasha, baby, while you're at it, can you fix me a sandwich?"

Leave it to Trae to be on some different shit. Now, mind you, I was looking at all of the food and sandwiches down there, and he wanted something different. "Sure, baby, what do you want?"

"I got a special stash in the red foil."

"What is it?"

"A chef's cut of Grade A turkey pastrami. And a half-pound of extra-spicy pepper jack cheese. I want that on a wheat roll with all the trimmings." I got up, and he pulled me down onto his lap and whispered in my ear, "If you make my sandwich real good, as soon as the fight is over, I'ma eat this pussy like I ain't never ate it before."

"Are you?"

"You damned right. Then I'ma dick you down until you faint."

I whispered in his ear, "Well, if you fuck me like that, then when I wake up, I just might deep-throat your dick so good you'll start sucking your thumb."

"You gonna fuck around and make me put these niggas up outta here," he teased.

I giggled that *I'ma get dicked down tonight* giggle, got up off his lap, and headed upstairs for the kitchen with a smile on my face. I couldn't wait for the main event to be over. I was singing to myself as I got the beer out and started making my baby his sandwiches. The phone rang and "Unknown" flashed across the caller ID. I picked it up.

"Helloooo."

They hung up.

I went back to doing what I was doing, and a couple of minutes later, the phone rang again.

"Hello?"

"Is Mr. Macklin available?" I took a deep breath and counted to three. *This bitch!* "Well, is he? This is a business call." Her voice dripped with sarcasm.

I hung up the phone. I was tired of talking. She called right back, but this time, I allowed it to ring. After about seven times— yes I counted—it stopped. A few minutes later, it rang again. After ring number seven, I picked it up, and so did Trae.

"Yeah."

"Mr. Macklin, thank you for answering. We need to have a meeting this coming Tuesday per my father's instructions."

"Why are you calling my home? You know the rules. And what do I look like meeting with you?"

"Something urgent has come up."

"I don't get my instructions from you, Charli." He hung up, and so did I.

And then the doorbell rang. Who else did Trae invite? Pissed, I made my way to the front of the house, opened the door and there stood a messenger.

"I have a delivery for Mr. Trae Macklin."

I looked at the letter pack in his hand before opening the screen door.

"You need to sign for this."

I cracked the screen door and took the package from him, refusing to sign and slammed the door in his face. I knew who it was from. I tore the envelope open as I headed back into the kitchen.

> *Mr. Macklin,*
>
> *My father is out of the country, and I have instructions for you. We can meet Tuesday, one o'clock, at Joe's. I know you prefer to meet on your turf, or shall I say the seedy part of town? You can confirm it with him, if you wish. After all, this is simply business. Nothing else."*
>
> *Charli Li*

A couple of minutes later, Trae came into the kitchen carrying the phone. He eased up behind me and kissed me on the neck. "You aiight in here?"

"I'm good." I lifted the top half of the roll and showed him his sandwich. "How does this look?" It took everything I had to hold onto my composure and act as if I was cool.

"It looks good." He eyed his sandwich and licked his lips. He kissed my cheek. "Thanks, baby."

"Here, take this downstairs, and I'll be right behind you." I shoved his plate into his hand along with the envelope and grabbed the beer. I took them downstairs, then came back up and rushed outside onto the front porch. I had to get some fresh air. I sat down, and it felt as if I was suffocating. I was so furious all I could do was cry. I felt helpless, and it took me damn near forever to pull myself together. The only thing that calmed me down was swinging back and forth on the porch swing. Finally, my mind, my spirit and my breathing became steady. I hadn't even noticed the two pit bulls in the truck in my driveway. They were barking and scratching at the windows.

"Tasha, why are you out here?" Trina appeared in the doorway. "Your husband is looking for you and he said, don't sweat the small bullshit."

"I needed some fresh air and fuck him!" I told her as I kept staring straight ahead. I could feel her looking at me.

"I could shoot those albino-looking muthafuckas!" she snapped.

"Who do they belong to?" I asked her.

"Jameer. Those are his damn dogs."

"You rode over here with him in the truck with those stinking beasts?" My sister was nastier than I thought.

"Hell, no! Don't you see my car over there? I can't stand those dogs. I told him he better put them muthafuckas to sleep if he think he's gonna be gettin' some of this."

"What did he say?"

"What do you think he said? He's putting them to sleep."

"Yeah, right, bitch, you ain't that good." I had to smile at my own sarcasm.

"How much you wanna bet?" she challenged.

"Why does he need two of them?"

"Two? He has one more."

"They look vicious as hell."

"And believe me, they are. He be on some grimy shit with them beasts. Robbing people and shit. I watched them eat a cat. I told him he done got all he could out of them. He needed to stop before shit goes south. Girl, you making me miss the fight! Come on inside and see what your husband wants." She turned around and left me sitting there. I needed a few more minutes. I looked at the two albino pit bulls and had to agree with her. Those muthafuckas should be put to sleep. At one point they started fighting each other and they wouldn't stop growling and gnashing at the teeth. After about ten minutes, I got up to go join the party in the basement.

To me, the fight didn't get good until the last round, when Chavez, Jr., who I was rooting for, finally knocked Martinez down. I jumped up screaming. But it was too late. Martinez had already won all of the other rounds. I watched as Trae and the other men talked shit and then money changed hands. Finally, around one thirty, the last of the guests left. Kyra and I started cleaning up the basement while Rick and Trae went out onto the front porch.

"You sure are happy right about now," Kyra said to me.

"That's because Trae said he was going to eat my pussy and fuck me until I fainted. So hell, yeah, I am very happy."

"Ewwww, save me all of the gory details, please, ma'am."

"Well, you asked. Now, hurry up and help me clean up, and then go and get your man. Because I am assuming that there is going to be some serious fucking in your room tonight. Or are you gonna use my front porch again?"

"Whatever, bitch!"

"Umm-hmm. What did you say to him? Why is he looking so discombobulated?"

"Damn, you don't miss a thing, do you?"

"It's my house, I'm not supposed to. Plus, you stormed out of the party. So what happened?"

"I dropped a bomb on that ass."

"What bomb? What happened?"

"I told him I missed my period."

The serving bowl I held, dropped right out of my hands. "No fucking way, Kyra!" The bitch had the nerve to leave me standing there and go over and plug in the vacuum. I went over to her and cut it off.

"What, Tasha? You told me to hurry up." She turned the vacuum back on. I reached over and turned it back off.

"Bitch, you better stop playing with me. Were you just fucking with him, or were you serious? What did he say?"

"Yes, I was very serious. That's what his ass gets. A fuckin' dose of reality. But I think he was getting ready to say I can't keep it. But I cut him off and left him standing there."

"What? No, he didn't! That creep."

"I said the same thing." She turned the vacuum on and went over the carpet.

When she finished, I asked, "So what's going through your mind?"

"All kinds of shit. But mainly how I now have the focus on me and this will show me where his heart is at, because I damn sure ain't gettin' rid of it."

Well, I'll be damned.

15

JAZ

"Faheem, we don't have to move. Anybody could have taken Steele out. You are in a wheelchair, baby."

We had been having this same argument for the last week, and I was tired of it. At the same time, it looked like it was an argument that I was losing. I was still in school, Kaeerah loved her school, I loved my house, and the bottom line was, I didn't want to move. Moving hadn't even crossed my mind.

"Jaz, I'ma say it one more time. And it will be my last and final time. We are moving. Start looking, and start packing."

"So you mean to say I gotta quit school? I can still be traced, Faheem. If someone wants to find us, they can."

"We will pay to get the records sealed or some shit like that. I don't know. Find you another school. You should have thought about that before you went out playing vigilante. You the one made it hot for us around here. You made your bed, now you

194

gotta lay in it. And if you fuck with Oni, I swear I'm leaving you, Jaz."

It felt as if someone stuck a pin inside me and sucked out all of my air. I was obsessed with taking this bitch out personally and now this? I knew Faheem and he was not one to issue false threats. I had to go to my plan B, which was Rock. I was now crushed.

I stormed out of the bedroom and went into the backyard and started pacing. Kaeerah came outside and started pacing with me.

"Mommy, are we moving?" I detected the excitement in her voice.

"Not now, Eerah. As a matter of fact, go back in the house while Mommy figures this out."

"One last question."

"What is it?"

"Are we moving because of what happened to my brother?"

"That has something to do with it, yes."

"What about Miss Oni?"

"What about her?"

"Is she moving?"

"I don't know, baby. You said one question. That was three. Now, go back into the house."

It looked like I was in a no-win situation. To my disappointment, I wasn't going to get the experience of killing Oni. But she was getting done, regardless.

CHARLI

I was looking forward to meeting and conducting business with Mr. Macklin. Actually, this would be my second time in his presence since all of the unfortunate circumstances. I had strategically arranged for him to work directly with my father, and he was already witnessing the fruits of his labor. I was confident that Mr. Macklin would be feeling pretty generous.

I took extra time with my makeup and hair. My choice of dress was impeccable. I had on this cute black Vera Wang skirt and blouse that showed just the right amount of cleavage, and of course, I didn't have on any panties. I was tingling at the thought of him entering me. And I was even more turned on at the thought of us meeting in a public place that wasn't too seedy but not far from it. I was hoping that he would take me right then and there.

My first order of business was to have him speak to that wife of his. She should not hang up at the sound of my voice. When I requested to speak to him, she should have obediently called him to the phone. Simple as that. No need for the theatrics every time I phoned there. I could only imagine what sort of chaos she caused the moment he hung up with me.

My stomach fluttered and my pulse raced as I pulled into the parking lot of Joe's. It was bar in La Jolla. I pulled my hand mirror and makeup case from my handbag and gave myself a once-over. After I was satisfied, I placed everything back in my bag and popped a breath mint. It was show time. I looked out my rearview and side-view mirrors before opening my car door. I tried not to be too flashy, so I drove my BMW 650LI. After looking around the parking lot and not sensing anything out of the ordinary, I stepped out of the car and locked the doors. It was a beautiful day. As I proceeded to walk around to the front entrance, I heard barking. I stepped up my pace and turned around; a gentleman was walking two big albino pit bulls only a few feet away from me. Those were the most disgusting pit bulls I had ever seen. The gentleman smiled at me and made a noise with his tongue. Then the two beasts began to growl at me. I was getting nervous wondering what on earth was the matter with those dogs. And to my horror, the guy stopped and disengaged the leashes. He said, "Get her boys!" He made a clicking sound with his mouth, and the two dogs began to charge towards me. On instinct, I took off running in the opposite direction, and the animals gave chase. My heart was racing as I ran as fast as I could, kicking my heels off in the process.

A vehicle stopped right before me. I banged on the car. "Let me in!" I grabbed the door handle, but it was locked. "Help me! Let me in, please!" The woman just sat there. There was nowhere to run. The dogs were almost to the car. They were determined to get me. "Don't you move this fucking car!" I jumped on top of it, and the two beasts circled it as they barked, growled, and scratched at the car. "Don't you move this car!" I slid my hand to retrieve the blade held by my garter belt and grabbed it tight. One pit bull jumped onto the hood of the car, and the other was on the trunk, causing me to jump off of the hood. I twisted my ankle as I landed on the ground. I aimed the knife at the first pit bulls throat. I had perfect aim, but it didn't stop the beast in its tracks. I raised my arm, and the monster's teeth latched on to it. My screams were stifled when the second albino pit bull came to join the party. I quickly grabbed it by its throat. They growled and bit into my clothing and began to shake me like an old rag. I gave the animals a fight, but I was no match for the two beasts at the same time. I could feel my bones being broken into pieces.

TRAE

I kept trying to get through to Mr. Li to find out why he had insisted on sending Charli to handle this business when we had an agreement. In my book, that was a breach of trust. I left several messages. And now Charli was late.

I had a seat at the bar so that I could see everyone who came in. By one thirty, I had waited long enough and decided that it was time for me to bounce. I had my doubts about meeting with her in the first place and was relieved that she hadn't shown up.

"You out, big Bruh?" Scat, the bartender asked me.

"I'm out."

I stepped outside into the bright sunlight and headed for the parking lot. There was a crowd of people and two ambulances. I couldn't have cared less as I made my way around the excited crowd. Everyone was chattering.

"Dang, them dogs ate that bitch up."

"What was she doing around here, anyway?"

"Probably delivering somebody's lo mein."

"Hell, nah, that Chinese ho had a real Gucci bag. She wasn't no delivery woman. "

"That's a shame that ol' hag wouldn't open the car door for her."

I had heard the bits and pieces of conversation but didn't put it all together until I saw Charli's car. I stopped dead in my tracks and peeked inside the candy-apple-red Beamer. It was empty. I rushed back over to the ambulance as it was pulling off. I went over to the first police officer I saw and asked what happened.

"Who are you?" the officer, whose name was Gilliard, asked.

198

"I was here to meet a young lady, Ms. Li, but she never showed up."

"Hey, Paulson! Paulson! This guy says he was here to meet the lady," Gilliard yelled to one of the other officers. "Who is she to you?" He turned back to me.

"My attorney. She's an attorney."

"Well, she was attacked by pit bulls. We are not done putting the report together yet." He handed me a card.

Whoa. "Attacked by pit bulls? Is she all right?"

"You'll have to call the hospital for that, sir," Gilliard told me.

I headed for my truck, wondering how fast I could get word to Charlie Li.

"Mr. Macklin, good of you to call," Mr. Li said. "I've been away on travel, but Kon told me of your progress and how confident you've been in handling yourself on all of your assignments. You'll be hearing from Kon again. If you have any problems, he's your point of contact."

"No questions, Mr. Li. I'm calling because of your daughter. Were you aware that she set up a meeting with me for today? Per your instructions and our agreement I would not have to communicate with her. However, she called and said you had an assignment for me, and since you were out of the country, you gave it to her. I tried to confirm her story with you and could only leave several messages. She was supposed to meet me at one o'clock. By one thirty, when she hadn't showed, I left. That's when I found out that she was bitten by a dog and was taken away by ambulance. I was calling to see if you were aware of that and if the hospital had reached out to you."

"This is the first that I've heard of this. Are you sure it was my daughter who was bitten by a dog?"

"I am. The police officer gave me a card with his contact info as well as an incident report number. I have it right here."

"Give it to me."

I did.

"Mr. Macklin, my orders to you were that under no circumstances were you to have contact with my daughter outside of my presence. But I will deal with our problem at another time. For now, I must check on my daughter."

Before I could part my lips, the big man hung up. Didn't he hear what I just said? *I tried to reach out to his ass.*

JAZ

Faheem's cousin Rock was easy to work with. He even had a role for me to play being that he wasn't going to allow me to do Oni myself.

"Rock, at least let me meet with him," I said full of excitement.

"Jaz, I gotta make the initial contact. All you are doing is paying him off with a package, and trust me, that will be the last time you see him, because the package is a bad package." Rock was killing two birds with one stone.

"Rock, I can handle this. Just set up the meeting. That's what I'm paying you for."

"Naw, babygirl. He ain't gonna meet with you. The plan is, I set it up. He handles the chick. Then all you do is pay him by giving him the package. That's all I will allow you to do. Nothing more, nothing less."

"That's some bullshit!" I was still obsessed with doing Oni, but Faheem deaded that issue. I even danced with the thought about finding someone else other than Rock, scrapping his plan, and coming up with another one. But Rock said he didn't want anything to be able to be traced back to him or me. He told me to take his offer or leave it. So I took it.

FAHEEM

Thanks to Jaz getting her thug on, my gut instinct was telling me to move. And it never led me wrong. For real, I didn't want to be anywhere near Georgia. Georgia rekindled memories. I was thinking Miami, Nevada, even Charlotte. But since Jaz wanted to stay in school, I'd let her decide. I would give her that.

However, I had to admit, but not to her, that it was a boss move for Jaz to make sure that Steele got handled, and it turned me on. I looked down at my dick, and it was standing straight up. I knew how to remedy that.

"Jaz, Jaz! You ain't asleep, because I can hear your breathing. I want you to come and say hello to my big friend." I reached over and patted her ass. She slid my hand off of her. "Jaz."

"Nope."

"Jaz."

"You're mad at me, remember?"

"I am. But thinking about what you did turned me the fuck on. See? Look at him."

She turned over on her other side and looked. "So you are lying over here at four in the morning thinking about how I, little ol' helpless me, took out your enemy, and now you want to fuck me?"

I liked the way she said that. My dick jumped. "No, I want you to put him down your throat, and then I want to fuck you."

"Hell, no. Not until you apologize."

"Apologize?"

"Yes, apologize," she said.

I began stroking myself. "Jaz, look at him. I can beat him into submission my own damn self, but if you sit on him, I think we both would like that a hell of a lot more."

That got her. She tossed the sheet aside, crawled over to him, and began to tease the head with her tongue. I placed my hand behind my head and closed my eyes. She moaned and then stopped. "I want my apology first." She rose up, straddled me, grabbed a hold of him, and put him to her opening. Sliding down onto my pole, she said, "I ain't sucking shit until I get my apology."

"Stop talking and handle your business. It's four in the morning."

"I don't care what time it is. Apologize."

I was all the way up in her, and the shit was feeling magnificent. She began rocking back and forth at a medium pace. "You need to be apologizing to me." She wound her hips while gazing into my eyes. The pussy was wet and hot. My dick was soaking it all up.

"Apologize, baby. Tell me that you honor my thug," she seductively said.

"Nope." I reached down grabbed an ass cheek and pulled her further onto my dick.

"Ummmmm," she moaned.

"Now, you apologize to *me*. Tell me what I want to hear." I told her.

She rode my dick a little faster. "Wh-wh-why?"

I tried to match her rhythm. "You know why."

"But . . . oh, this is good. I'm not . . . Faheem, there, baby." She leaned up, placing her petite hands on my chest. She was taking the dick all in, riding it like a true jock. "Ssss . . . sorry."

"You should be," I told her. *Damn, the pussy was feeling good.*

"Fah. . ." She was rockin' and ridin' hard and fast. I felt that G-spot and could tell that her clit was getting the stimulation it needed. My baby was going all in.

"Apologize, Jaz. Again."

"I . . . sorr . . . oh, shit . . . oh . . . shit!" When she started coming, I kept going as I held onto her ass so she couldn't get away.

She must have woken up the neighbors, because somebody was banging on the door and ringing the bell.

JAZ

Oh, you talking about a good fuck? Faheem had some good dick! Over the years, I've learned to master that monsta and subjugate him to my command. In certain positions, I could get my clit and my G-spot freaked at the same time. And Faheem let me go in. It didn't get any better than that. I came so long and hard I thought I was going to go into shock. I knew I was dragging my juices up his stomach as I seductively slid up to kiss my baby's sweet lips.

"I love you," I told him.

"You woke up the neighbors. You didn't hear the knocking?"

"Umh. Umh."

"You hear it now?"

There was banging. And whoever was there was also ringing the doorbell.

"Shit." I climbed off of Faheem and snatched my robe off the bed. I peeked out the bedroom window and saw the squad cars. I caught a lump in my throat.

"Fuck! It's the police!" I yelled out.

"See? I told you to let me handle shit. Put some clothes on, and I will call Steve."

"Wait, maybe they just want to ask some questions."

"Not at five in the morning. You know how they roll. Put some clothes on, Jaz."

I did and headed downstairs to see what they wanted. They were there to take Faheem in for questioning. His baby mama was found dead.

16

TASHA

Trae came back from his so-called meeting with Charli wearing his poker face—and it was driving me insane. I hadn't heard from Jameer, so I didn't know if I should panic or not.

Trae was standing on the front porch, waiting for his ride. I was standing inside the doorway, watching him. I didn't know where he was going, and according to his body language, I shouldn't even think about asking.

"Do you mind me inquiring as to how long you are going to be away?"

"Not sure, but you know I'ma call you. So no need to even trip, Tasha." His back was still turned away from me.

"I'm not tripping. I'm just wondering how long you plan on being away." I opened the screen door. "For real, it's no sense in going, because your side bitch is done. So I'm trying to understand why you have to go." *Fuck*. That slipped out, and I hoped like hell that Trae didn't catch it. But when he turned around and cocked his head to the side, I knew it was on.

"Tasha, what do you mean, she's done? Who is—fuck, Tasha! Do not tell me you did what I think you did!" He gritted, turning slowly in my direction.

His mood and his face turned dark. When I saw that, I eased the screen door shut and locked it. He lunged at it and tried to snatch it open.

"Tasha! Open the fucking door." He threatened.

"No. Go be by the bitch's bedside. You think I didn't know where you were going?" I yelled.

"Open the goddamned door!" He looked as if he was trying to yank it off its hinges.

I walked away. Then I heard a crash and turned around, and Trae's arm was inside, unlocking the door. My vase that I had made all by myself in pottery class was now broken up in big chunks.

Trae caught up to me, snatched me by the shoulder, and turned me to him. "Tell me you didn't do what I think you did." He shook me. "Tell me!"

When I didn't say anything, he looked as if he wanted to cry, and that's when I lost it. I hauled back and slapped the shit out of him. "Fuck that bitch!"

He grabbed the front of my shirt, lifted me up, and slammed me into the wall, pressing me and holding me there.

"How many times have I told you it ain't about her? This was business, Tasha. Money, security, knowledge, business, not pussy! You fucked with the wrong bitch, Tasha. And why? 'Cause you're scared that she's gettin' your dick?"

Marva came bursting through the door. "There's a limo parked in the driveway. And put that girl down. What's the matter with y'all? Trae, you better get your hands off of that girl. Now!" Marva warned him.

Trae let me go, and I almost tumbled to the floor.

"If I don't come back, make sure you tell my sons why. I can't believe how stupid you allow some bitch to make you act. Now I don't know what the fuck I'm walking into. You told me you trusted me, Tasha."

"I do. It's her that I didn't trust!" I screamed as he walked out the front door. "She sends someone to blow up our home, and it's fine. I sick some dogs on her, and I'm a dumb, jealous, insecure bitch. Fuck you and her, Trae! Y'all deserve each other." He didn't even bother to look back.

I thought about what he'd said, the reality of his words sunk to the pit of my stomach. And what if he didn't come back? I had promised myself that I wasn't doing any more bids with another nigga. Trae promised me that he was never going back to jail, that he was going to stay clean. The game was over for him. That's what he said. Now this.

TRAE

Walking to the limo felt more like treading through quicksand. I had my doubts about it being known that someone in my camp was responsible for Charli's mishap, so at least I had a little time. I put my game face on as I got into the back of the limo and was thankful that I was back there alone. I didn't know what I was walking into. My instincts were telling me that this trip wasn't business . . . it was personal.

After about an hour, I knew it was personal when we

pulled up in front of Ronald Reagan UCLA Medical Center. My door came open, and a gentleman I never saw before greeted me.

They know.

"Mr. Macklin, I am Pu Chang. Mr. Li asked me to assist you this evening."

"Assist me with what?"

"I will be taking you up to visit Miss Charli Li. Come, follow me."

We went inside, bypassing security, and stepped onto the elevator. As we took the short ride up, I imagined Mr. Li at his daughter's bedside and also trying to figure out his reasoning for wanting me to see her.

We walked past the nurses' station, down to the room where one of Li's henchmen stood. I recognized him from riding with us on the private jet. He nodded at me as I followed Pu Chang into the room.

Flowers were everywhere, on the floor, against the wall, in the window. Hell, I saw the flowers before I saw her. I walked closer to the bed. She had tubes coming out of her mouth and going through her nose, an IV in her left arm, and her right arm, foot and head were bandaged up.

"Is she unconscious?" I asked in a low tone.

"Yes, she is," Pu Chang answered. "Luckily, they found four inches of Miss Li's scalp on the ground and gave it to one of the EMS workers. We are hopeful that her scalp can be reattached. She has severe bites on her right hand and arm and on her left leg. There were two dogs, and we are not sure if they had been vaccinated or tested for rabies." He stood looking down at Charli and then back at me.

I immediately turned and walked out, thinking the worst. Mr. Li was blaming me for what happened to his daughter.

Pu Chang was on my heels. "I will take you back to the car."

"I can show myself out, but I do need to speak to Mr. Li."

"There's a phone in the limo. It's already being arranged for you to speak to him."

I left him standing there and decided to take the stairs. Charli was fucked up, so I could only imagine the magnitude of the repercussions I would have to face. Tasha really had my back up against the wall with this one.

As soon as I got situated in the limo, the phone rang. I picked it up.

"Yes."

"Mr. Macklin, did you see my daughter?"

"Of course, and I offer my deepest condolences. She had called me and told me that she had new and urgent instructions from you. I called you several times to confirm but was unable to reach you. So I decided on meeting her in a public place, just to be on the safe side. Actually, she was the one who suggested the meeting place," I found myself explaining once again.

"My instructions to you were under no circumstances to be in my daughter's presence. If you would have followed those instructions, my daughter would not be lying in some hospital bed fighting for her life. Because of your betrayal of my trust, I can no longer offer you my protection. This concludes our business, Mr. Macklin. And my daughter was right. You would have been a great asset to the Li organization. Kon Li told me all of our people immediately showed respect to you and took you seriously." He hung up.

And just like that, I was left out there.

TASHA

I had been sitting on the porch for the last two hours. When I saw what looked like a limo coming down the street, I jumped and practically ran off the porch. It didn't pull up into the driveway but stopped at the entrance. My imagination was running wild. I envisioned a shot-up Trae being tossed out of the vehicle onto the ground. So I was extremely relieved when he stepped out of the car, shut the door, and began to trudge up the walkway. I ran and practically jumped into his arms.

"I'm so sorry, baby. I really messed up this time, didn't I?"

He didn't answer me. He pushed me away, and we went up the front steps and sat down. I sat next to him and waited as he called his attorney. I listened in as he told him that he might be picked back up on the murder charges and that Benny needed to be prepared for that. He rubbed across his bald head, while listening intently to whatever it was that Benny was saying.

When he finally hung up, all I could say was, "Baby, I really fucked up, didn't I?"

"You have no idea! Your shit was not thought out, and now everything will eventually point at me."

"You really think you are going to jail?"

"What the fuck do you think, Tasha? Mr. Li said all of the protection and connections have been revoked."

"What protection? What connections?"

"Tasha, do you have any idea who you are fucking with? I had an agreement with these people. Charlie Li is a made man, Tasha. He can wipe out me, you, and our entire family right now."

"That ain't right, Trae. It wasn't your fault. Anybody could have done her."

"We better hope that he doesn't find out who did. Tasha,

210

what—" He got up and started pacing back and forth. He was so angry he couldn't even finish his sentence. "And you didn't even check with me!"

"Check with you for what? So you could tell me not to do it?"

"Fuck, yeah! And if I was going to approve of it, I would have told you how to do it! Tasha, baby. You ain't no gangster. What's gotten into y'all? First Jaz, now you. You have to think things through. Calculate shit. When you don't, serious shit like this happens. Now, look. If he somehow finds out that you are responsible for this, you best believe some serious harm is going to come to this family." He let out a deep sigh. "The dogs? Whose are they?"

"That dude who came over on fight night with Trina." I saw the gleam in his eyes and the light bulbs go off. "No, Trae. Oh, my god."

"What the fuck you mean, no, Trae? Nine times out of ten, they are going to trace the dogs to him. And what do you think he's going to do when put under pressure? He's going to rat your ass out. This was so sloppy, Tasha. Damn!"

I thought about what Trae said. What if they did find out Jameer sent the dogs? They would kill him. I didn't even know if Jameer had a family. Kids? A wife? What if Trina was with him? They would probably kill her, too.

Because of my insecurities, I had just signed Jameer's death certificate as well. And that bitch was still laying up there breathing.

17

ANGEL

When Jaz called, Kaylin and I came as fast as we could. She refused to say anything over the phone, so we didn't know what to expect. So there we were in her living room, on the couch, with her seated across from us.

"I just needed to talk to my family. Sorry y'all had to travel so far just to hear me vent, so I'll reimburse you guys for the expenses."

"Girl, please," I said. "Now you talkin' crazy."

"Jaz, Faheem would look after my wife the same way. So don't insult me like that. Now, tell me what's happening with you," Kaylin said. "And where's Faheem?"

Jaz took a deep breath. "I know that having this all bottled up inside me can't be good." She got up and came over to the sofa and sat next to Kaylin. "I told Faheem I would handle everything. Y'all know that he's in no condition to put in any work. Hell, he is still not right mentally. He had lost little Faheem, so I felt that he should not have to be bothered with this bullshit. What was I here for? He always underestimates me."

"Jaz, what do you mean by 'he's in no condition to put in any work' and to let you 'handle everything'?" Kaylin asked her.

I was already reading between the lines. I knew Jaz. And I knew that she was getting ready to tell us about some outlandish shit that she had done. She didn't call us way down there to "vent," as she called it.

"All I'm saying is, I stepped up to the plate and helped him."

"Helped him do what?" Kaylin asked.

"So where is he now?" I wanted to know.

"He's locked up."

"Locked up for what?" I asked. Jaz was beating around the bush, and it was starting to irritate me. *And the plot thickens*, I thought to myself.

Kaylin had eased up to the edge of the sofa. "You helped him do what, Jaz?"

"It's me that they should be questioning. But Steve said they should be releasing him today. They are questioning him about Oni's murder." She glared at us.

"Jaz, she got murdered? Are you saying that is why they should be questioning you?" I asked.

"Shit," Kaylin mumbled. He then leaned over and whispered into my ear, "Her ass took her out or had something to do with it."

I looked over at little ol' Jaz and couldn't wrap my mind around her killing somebody. So now that made two of us in the clique who'd committed the deed. But did she really actually do it?

"Angel, I see the wheels in your head turning. Chill out. I didn't do it, I got someone else to do it. That's how I know that they are going to have to let Faheem go. They don't have anything on him."

"What's Faheem saying about all of this?" I asked, but I already knew the answer.

"You know Faheem. He's livid. That's why I called y'all down here. Kaylin, I need you to talk to him. He already knew about the first one but just found out about Oni when they came and picked him up."

"Oh, my God, Jaz! Who was the first one?"

"Who do you think? That nigga responsible for lil' Faheem, Steele. He was the first one, and he deserved to die, just like she did. Don't judge me, Angel." She looked at me with one eyebrow up and one down.

"Jaz, cut the bullshit. You know I'm not judging you. But if you think I can just sit here while you tell me you had your hand in bodying two people and me not be stuck on stupid, you must be crazy."

"Angel, please." Kaylin raised his hand, putting it in my face. Translation: *Shut the fuck up.* "Jaz, so what do you expect me to say to Faheem?" Kaylin asked her. I knew that he was just as surprised as I was.

Her eyes got big, and she began to frown. I could tell that she was shaken at the thought of dealing with Faheem on this. "I'm not sure. I just need you to talk to him before he talks to me. I only did what I did because it needed to be done. What else was I supposed to do?" Jaz popped up off the couch and started pacing back and forth.

"I'ma be straight up with you," Kaylin began. "You acting like what you did ain't no big thing. Have you thought about the moves your opponent would make? I can tell you right now, that's gonna be Faheem's beef. You can't do what you did and not overthink your opponent. You can never plan for the worst, let alone the unexpected. I mean, it is what it is. And I'm sure Steele had people. You don't think they comin' after you?"

"Are you done? Can I talk now?" Jaz asked in a condescending tone.

"Go ahead. I'm just keeping it real with you. That's why you called me down here, ain't it? I'm anxious to hear your logic." Kaylin was talking to Jaz as if she rode the small yellow bus.

"Kay, what the fuck was I supposed to do? The nigga needed to be got. The bitch did, too. So what? As far as I'm concerned, I did the right thing."

"But it wasn't the right thing, Jaz," I cut in.

"Red!" Kaylin motioned for me to shut up once again. I turned my head and began to rub my hands together. I was ready to slap the shit out of both of them.

"Angel, I know you ain't talking! You forgot that you did a nigga before? You felt as if it was the right thing to do. And Kaylin, you were down with her. You had her back."

"So what, you think Faheem ain't gonna have yours? Is that what this is all about?" I asked her. "Why would you even think that?"

When she got all choked up, I knew that's what the whole thing was about. Faheem had such a temper. And whenever Jaz did anything he didn't like, he would punish her as if she was a child. And now it looked as if she was petrified. She was more worried about Faheem when she should have been worried about some drug dealer shooting up her house and coming after her whole family.

"Angel." Jaz started crying. "He is going to flip. If I could do it over, I would have let him handle it, but I can't. It's done. Please don't leave until you talk to him, Kay."

I got up and hugged Jaz. I could feel her body trembling. I knew that she was scared shitless. "I'm here for you, Jaz. And I'll be here for as long as you need me."

TASHA

My sister had been blowing up my phone. This was her third time calling me tonight.

"Tasha, something's up. Why would he leave his truck in front of the house? His neighbors say it hasn't moved in days. And where are those damned dogs?"

"Trina, chill out. You said yourself that he was getting rid of them."

"But he would have told me first. Tasha, he's not even answering his phone."

I tried to put her mind at ease before I hung up. I didn't have to be a rocket scientist to figure that one out. Trae got to him already. But for now, I was on a mission. I had to do this. This would complete the deed. I concentrated on the click of my stilettos against the shiny hospital floors. As I got closer to Room 311, the gentleman sitting outside of the room became more attentive. He finally stood up.

"Can I help you?"

"Hello. I'm Rosalind, a friend of Charli's. I just wanted to drop these flowers off and to see how she was doing." I tried to get a peek to see if anyone else was in the room with her.

He stepped in front of the door and pulled out a phone. I

began to get nervous. This was exactly what Trae meant when he said you were supposed to think things through. *What if they take me away and kill me?* Trae would never know. I was out here all willy-nilly, walking right into the hands of the enemy. And why? Because of my emotions. I understood why a bitch shouldn't run the country. Just because I was feeling catty, there I was, jeopardizing my life and the possibility of my children and husband never seeing me again.

Right when I was about to turn my ass back around and leave, he hung up. "You can visit, Mrs. Macklin, but please be respectful, and stay no more than ten minutes."

When he called me by my last name I could have shit myself. He knew who I was. I should have hauled ass out of there right then, but noooo. I had to go and see this bitch. I needed to see my handiwork. But why would he allow me to visit?

"Thank you," I told him.

He bowed his head slightly and moved from in front of the door. I stepped inside the flower and gift-filled room. The curtains were drawn, allowing the glaring sun to shine in. The television was on, but there was no sound coming out. I laid the bouquet of flowers with the card attached across the foot of the bed.

I stood there for a minute looking down at my nemesis. I felt a sense of empowerment. Here I was alive and healthy. There she was head, face and arms bandaged up, breathing through tubes, hanging on for her life. Life was sweet.

I leaned over and whispered in her ear, "Oh, poor little Charli. Can you hear me? You fuckin' ho ass bitch! I told you time and time again to leave what's mine alone. I know that dick is good but is it worth what you are feeling now? I am so glad you can't speak. I don't ever want to hear your irritating voice again. Ever.

And if by some fluke you wake up and survive, then you better not open that nasty mouth of yours to call my house, speak to me or my husband. Trust me you won't even survive my next attack. Most flea bag bitches have nine lives but yours will be cut at the third. So play with me if you want to. And you had the nerve to try to burn down my house? With my kids in it? Stay in your fuckin' lane, you nasty bitch."

I wanted to spit on her. I stood tall, turned around, and walked out. As I hit the hallway, her heart monitor began beeping really fast.

JAZ

I had just finished fixing a plate for Angel and Kaylin when I heard Kaeerah yell, "Here comes Daddy and Mr. Steve!"

I looked at Kaylin preparing to eat. "Don't get up. I will bring him in here." I took off for the front of the house. Kaeerah was already outside at Steve's car, helping her dad with his crutches.

"Jaz," Steve called out to me.

"Steve, thanks for bringing him home."

"Hey, it's what I do," he bragged.

"Dad, where were you?"

"I had to talk to the police."

"Were you scared to talk to the police?"

"Not at all."

"Good."

They came up onto the porch, and I held the door open. Faheem leaned over and kissed me on the cheek. "We have company," I told him.

"Who?"

"Kaylin and Angel. They're in the kitchen eating."

"Cool. What a surprise. What did you cook?"

"Lasagna, asparagus, and salad."

"What brings them down here?"

"I called for backup."

"Why do you need backup?"

"Because I know you, Faheem. Like you're being real cool and calm right now. I know that this is just the lull before the storm."

"You think you know me, Jaz."

"I know you, Faheem."

"Did you know that I spoke to Snell and Rock and told them exactly how to handle my situation? Did you know that they were doing everything I told them to do, not what you wanted? Did you know that I knew every move that you were making? Every phone call? Every dollar you paid out? Now, what did you say was for dinner?"

I was stunned. I didn't want to believe what Faheem had just told me. Anger slowly heated up my entire body. I balled up my fist and punched the wall. "Fuck this!" I needed to take a walk. I stormed out of the house. That nigga just pissed all over my parade.

TRAE

I was still trying to figure out how my training and time under the wing of the one and only Charlie Li lasted only a measly two months. Everything was going smoothly. They were feeling me and how I handled things, and they told me so. I was feeling them and how they kept their word and never came with any bullshit. But then, *boom*! It was all over. And Tasha was walking around as if she was on cloud nine, tickled about the whole damn thing, and I didn't like it.

She was sucking my dick real nice like she always did, when I finally dumped my seed down her throat. I came real hard, and it took me a minute to get my head clear.

"Baby, what's the matter?" she asked as she began planting gentle kisses up my abs and on my chest.

"I'm just thinking, that's all."

"Thinking? About what? And right in the middle of my fabulous head game? I'm down here puttin' in all this hard work, and you're someplace else."

"Just trying to figure out my next move."

"While I'm giving you head? Are you serious?" She got up off the bed and disappeared into the bathroom.

When she came out, she sat at the bottom of the bed. I patted the spot next to me. "Tasha, come here."

"Not until you tell me what's on your mind." She grabbed my nightshirt off of the floor and put it on.

"Business."

"What business?"

"I was able to get a meeting with Mr. Li. But I still haven't figured out how I'ma distance myself from this whole dog incident but at the same time use it to my advantage."

"Use it to your advantage? What does that mean? I don't like the sound of that. I'm going with you to the meeting."

I looked at Tasha as if she was crazy. "No, you're not."

"Yes, I am."

"Okay, go with me and do what?"

"I don't know. I just need to be there."

"Why are you so threatened by this chick? Why are you

allowing your jealousy of this chick to make you block me from taking care of my business? That is not a good look, Tasha."

"She's no longer a threat to me, Trae. I made sure of that."

"She should have never been one in the first place. I still can't figure that out."

"Why can't you? You sure lost your mind when Kyron came into the picture."

"That's different."

"No, it's not. You're gonna sit here and tell me that you didn't feel threatened? C'mon, Trae."

"I'm not talking about me. I'm talking about you. You know that I belong to you and that I'll always be yours. So why did *you* feel so threatened?"

"You want to know why?"

"Yeah, tell me."

"You want to know why?" She jumped up off the bed, stomped over to her nightstand, pulled open the bottom drawer and took out some papers. "This is why! You allow the bitch to call my house, and then she sends me this!" She threw a stack of pages at me.

"What is this?" I turned on the lamp.

"The bitch sent me some of her diary pages!"

I snatched the pages up, and sure enough, there were copies of Charli's handwritten diary pages titled *50 Shades of Trae*. "So what is this supposed to prove, Tasha? I don't care about this bullshit."

"She talks about the *several* times that y'all fucked, Trae."

"Bullshit. Anybody can write some shit down on some paper. Who are you going to believe, me or her? Tell me that you don't know that bitch is delusional. Tell me, Tasha!"

"I told myself that. But she talks about shit that she just couldn't make up."

"Tasha—"

"Don't Tasha me! What about the flowers you brought her? Or you going to her house? That may be delusional, yes. But what about that little trick she did on you? The trick that you taught me to do on your dick. She made that up, too? Is that delusional? Nigga, I don't think so. I hope that bitch dies up there in that hospital room, and if she isn't dead, I hope those dogs ate her beyond recognition."

"Tasha, I told you time and time again, that was business, nothing personal. You are my wife, my world, and that will never change."

"Translation, *but I'ma fuck other bitches if the business calls for it*? Fuck you, Trae!" She went into the bathroom and shut the door. Here we were back at square one.

"Tasha!" I called out to her, but she didn't answer. I picked up the stapled pages. *50 Shades of Trae*. That bitch was crazy. I began to read . . . page after page. I didn't know if I should laugh or be scared of the bitch. She had shit in there that I never did. Ate her pussy? That shit never happened. Spent the night at her crib? Hell to the no! That ho was more than delusional. She was deranged.

Of course, the next two days, all I got was the silent treatment. I had been staying close to the house, keeping an eye on my crazy wife, but I finally got the call, and it was time for that meeting. I needed to know where I stood and if my family was in danger. Even though deep down inside, I knew there was no running and hiding. If Charlie Li wanted to get me, no matter where I was, I was got. Over the phone, I wouldn't be able to know, but with a face-to-face, I didn't care what came out of a man's mouth. The eyes revealed it all.

"Trae, Marva and your parents are taking the kids to SeaWorld." Tasha said interrupting my thoughts.

"When?"

"Tomorrow."

"Nobody said—"

"Don't even try it. We told you several times. Nana wants you to call her. She wants one of us to come with them. I nominated you."

"You know I can't go. I gotta make this meeting and don't know how long I'll be gone."

"Okay, but I can't, either. And I won't be here when you get back."

"What are you talking about?"

"For my cousin Stephon's birthday, Trina and I are going to his favorite hotel in Vegas to celebrate him."

"Vegas? When were you planning on telling me about this?"

Tasha was sitting at her vanity table, playing with her hair, looking at me in the mirror. "I'm telling you now."

"Unh-uh. No. I got important business to take care of, and I don't need to be worrying about you in Vegas somewhere with your sister. I want you here when I get back."

"People in hell want ice water but everybody can't get what they want." I went over to the vanity, leaned over, and sank my teeth into her shoulder. "Trae, please, that hurts."

Her eyes were getting watery. I released her shoulder and kissed her on the very spot that I just bit. "No Vegas. And be here when I get back."

18

TASHA

As soon as Trae left, I pulled out my bags, got to packing, and was headed for the door. Trina had booked us suites at the Bellagio in Vegas, my late cousin Stephon's favorite spot, may he rest in peace. She'd also put together an itinerary that included a day of pampering, a night of clubbing, and a night of gambling. We were only going to be gone for three days. I figured I would go have my fun and beat him back. But if not, oh, well. Fuck Trae!

"Rosalind Tasha Macklin, I am tired of hearing you bash Trae. I know you are angry at him for fucking other bitches, but trust me, you don't want to let that destroy your marriage. He loves the hell out of you, Tasha. You know how many women, including myself, wish they had that? And how soon we forget, you fucked a nigga, so now y'all even. You done put the dogs on the little Chinese bitch, so let it go. Once we step foot off this plane, I don't want to hear Trae's name. It's all about Stephon. We are here to celebrate him."

"Trina, that's easy for you to say. You didn't read those diary pages, but I did. He was fucking that ho and throwing rose petals down and shit. My stomach churns at the thought. I hate him right about now."

"Tasha, dead that shit and burn it. You don't even know if that shit is true. And bitch, you was pregnant by his mans! Not some ole regular nigga. His fam, that he has been trying to kill. So shit, the score is even! You gotta let this shit go. I'm telling you, you're gonna run him away."

"Run him away? He's running his own self away by maintaining a relationship with a bitch he was fuckin'. That bitch worships him, and believe me, he gets off on that bullshit."

"Tasha, the bitch is on life support, fighting for her life. How is she going to worship some nigga? You're allowing that ho to get all in your head. The minute we step off of this plane, I don't want you to say the word *Trae*. I want you to unwind . . . relax. It's only for three days. Damn! Three days!"

"I heard you, Trina."

"Good. Now, let me do a little ranting." She lowered her voice. "Jameer is still missing. Tasha, don't lie to me. Do you think this has something to do with the dogs? I mean, why all of a sudden, now? I knew I shouldn't have hooked y'all up."

"Now you're sounding stupid. How the hell is this going to have something to do with the dogs? Did he know the Chinese bitch? Did he know any of her people? Hell, no! You don't even really know him! You said he was into all types of shit. Does he have another girl?"

"He's got a baby mama . . ."

I began to tune my sister out. Needless to say, she kept talking about Jameer until we got off the plane, all the way until we walked into the Bellagio. *Whoaaaa!* We stepped into the spacious marble foyer with the prettiest glass chandelier I ever saw. The shit was bling-blinging so hard I could hardly see. We were welcomed with fresh fruit, flowers, nuts, and assorted chocolates. *Nice touch.* She'd booked us a villa at the hotel, and we checked in at the front desk. We were escorted to a European-designed three-bedroom, five-bath, heavenly domain. Our suite had a workout room, a massage room, a dry sauna, a full kitchen, a dining room, a full bar, and dual fireplaces, topped off with a gorgeous private terrace and garden with a pool and whirlpool.

It is about to go down! I saw why Stephon loved this spot and treated himself often. Trae who? I was getting ready to enjoy some me time, right there in the villa all by myself. Trina was ready to hit the casino before she even unpacked her bags. I told her to go ahead. I was one who could do without the casino. I was calling the masseuse to bring me some vanilla-scented candles and to arrange for my full-body massage. It was about to be on right there in the next room.

"I feel lucky, sis! You sure you don't want to go?" Trina was standing at the front door, ready to get her gamble on, and was trying one more time to get me to hang out with her.

"I'm sure," I told her as I waved her out the door. I was anxious to enjoy some solitude. No kids, no Kyra, and No Trae.

By ten thirty, Trina was back and all gambled out. I had ordered a birthday cake and took the bubbly from our bar, and she'd managed to get some weed from somewhere. We celebrated Stephon as if he was there. We danced, we laughed, we cried, we drank, and we even prayed. We celebrated our cousin's birthday until two in the morning. I didn't even think about Trae or start to miss him until I woke up the next day around noon.

I felt around for my phone to see if I'd missed anything and saw my text messages. The first was, of course, from Trae: *I'll be in tonight u better have ur ass home.* Kyra's said: *Marva called the kids r fine.* I sent Marva a text: *Keep an eye on Caliph.*

I pinned my hair up and ran me a nice bathtub of bubbly water. The hot tub was big enough for four. Before I got in, I called room service and ordered myself some blueberry pancakes, a vegetable omelet, and fried potatoes.

I didn't know where Trina was, but again, she left me all alone, and I had no problems with that. She was acting like a kid who had just arrived at Disney World. Silly ho!

I stepped into my pool of bubbles and actually relaxed and got my weed on. The water was nice and hot, and my vanilla-scented candles made the atmosphere just right. I was feeling real nice, and my muscles were relaxed. The massage I had was just what the doctor ordered. I closed my eyes and began to erase everything. I soaked until my fingertips began to wrinkle up, which was my cue to get out. Before I could oil my skin down, our personal butler was at the door.

"Perfect timing!" I mumbled as I tightened the towel on my head, wrapped and tied a knot in the towel around my body. I went to the door, stood behind it, and opened it.

"Room service!" the slim butler in full uniform announced as he pushed the cart inside, handing me the slip to sign.

"Thank you," I told him. "Your tip will be on here, too."

"Will there be anything else, madam?"

"No, thank you."

"I'm just a call away," he reminded me as he took the slip and disappeared out the door.

As I went to close the door all the way and lock it, I was stopped. Trina had finally decided to bring her ass in. "Where have you been?" I asked, walking over to the food cart and noticing the bottle of wine and two glasses on the cart, items that I didn't order.

"I was wondering the same thing about you." His voice was a whisper, but there was no mistaking who it belonged to. I damn near snapped my neck as I turned around and stood face-to-face with Kyron. Here I was standing naked except for a towel wrapped around the top half of my body. I didn't know whether to run or scream. As if he was reading my mind, Kyron said, "Relax, Shorty. I've seen you naked before."

"What are you doing here, Kyron? I want you to leave." I went to the door, and he moved in front of it. I was trying my best not to panic.

"Not before you have a drink with me," he whispered. He turned around and put the lock on the door. He took off his jacket that went with a three-piece Armani suit. There was a burner tucked down in the front of his pants. He folded the jacket and laid it across the back of the sofa.

"Kyron, please. I need you to leave." I started trying to figure out why he was here. How he knew I was here, how he got here, the whole nine.

"Not before you have a drink with me. Have a seat."

"Let me put some clothes on."

"Sit down, Shorty. The sooner you have this drink, the sooner I can leave. We fucked before, remember? I've seen all you have to offer." He was being a little too laid-back for me.

I hated this nigga and was a glad to see the burner in his waist. I thought maybe I could take it from him and blow his fucking brains out. I looked him over. He had lost a little weight, and I noticed that his voice was raspy, and he had a large scar at the base of his throat. I couldn't help but crack on him. "So it looks like you wear your scars well."

KYRON

I smiled. Shorty still had a sense of humor. However, through the tough exterior, I could see that she was nervous. She was puzzled about how I found her or why I was there. I'd let her figure it out, since she had so many jokes. I went over and popped the wine bottle.

"Can I at least have my breakfast before it gets cold?"

"Sure." I waited as she got up, picked up her trays, and set them on the table. Then I filled both of our glasses with wine.

"You know what? Forget it. You messed up my appetite. As a matter of fact, you messed up my day, my marriage, you name it. Let's drink to that, muthafucka! Since you want to drink to something." She came charging at me. I grabbed our drinks and set them on the table before she could get to me. I turned around, lifted her up, and to her surprise, set her on top of the table, too.

I stood between her legs and stared into her eyes. I was excited to finally have this time with Shorty. "Relax," I said as I sat in the chair in front of her. I pulled my burner from my waist and set it on the chair next to me and slid it under the table. If she had plans on snatching it out of my waist, she had to come up with another one.

"Kyron, why are you here?"

I passed her the glass that I'd poured for her, and I picked up the other one and tapped it against her glass. It was time for a toast. "To life." I sipped my drink.

"To death. Specifically, yours," Tasha said, and she took several sips of her wine. "Okay, we had our drink, so now can you leave?"

"Not until you drink up." I took another sip and then placed my hand on the bottom of her glass, easing it toward her lips.

"I swear, you fucked up my day, my whole vacation." She drank the last of what was in her glass. "Does your girl know that you're here fuckin' with me?"

"She knows what she needs to know."

"What is she saying about you constantly fuckin' with me?"

I removed the blunt and the lighter from inside my vest.

"Why are you getting comfortable? You said a drink, not a smoke. And how do you expect to smoke with a hole in your neck?" She chuckled. "Seriously, you need to be seeing your way out, Kyron."

"I thought you wanted to know what my girl had to say about me fuckin' with you?"

"I've changed my mind. I really don't give a fuck what she thinks. Can you leave now?" Tasha asked.

I saw sweat beads beginning to form on her shoulders. It was about to be on.

TASHA

When he had took the gun out of his waist, I thought it was over for me. I just knew that this crazy nigga had come to kill me once and for all. But when he set the gun on the chair, I exhaled. I was still scared, so I kept running my mouth. But now there I was, sitting on top of the table with only a towel wrapped around me.

"Can I turn up the air? It is getting warm in here." I unwrapped the towel from around my head and began fanning myself with my hand.

"You'll be all right."

"What is that supposed to mean?" He lit his blunt. "I'm not smoking with you, Kyron. I had the drink, and now I would like for you to leave. You are making me very uncomfortable."

He took a pull, held it in, and then released the smoke. "How uncomfortable do you think I felt laying up in that hospital bed?" He took another pull and blew some smoke in my face.

I was beginning to feel light-headed. My pussy was tingling, and I was sweating, ready to come out of the towel. "I gotta turn the air up, Kyron." I went to get off the table, but when I rose up, I felt dizzy. Then it hit me. "Kyron, you put something in my drink, didn't you? Where is my sister?" I was beginning to panic.

"Chill. Take a pull of this. This will level you out."

"What did you give me, Kyron?" It had to be something, because my vision was a little blurry.

"Take a pull."

"Why are you doing this? Why can't you leave me the fuck alone?"

"Take a pull, Tasha, or else you gonna start trippin'." He put the blunt to my lips; I inhaled, held the haze in, and felt as if I was floating and my pussy was smoking hot. Kyron leaned over and put the blunt out. He sat up and kissed my knee and the inside of my thigh. I began to tremble.

"Why can't you leave me alone?" I was confused. I honestly wondered why.

He shrugged. "I keep asking myself the same damn thing."

231

I could feel the tears streaming down my cheeks. I knew he wouldn't do it, but I asked anyway. "Kyron, please leave now."

"You know you don't want me to leave, not right now, anyway. Things are about to get heated." He kissed my knee and thigh again. It felt like this nigga might be right. My clit was throbbing. I placed my hand on his head and found myself running my fingers through his curly hair. The tears were still flowing. "Shorty, stop crying. Eatin' ain't cheatin', and you know I ain't got nothing but love for you," he said as he spread my legs and planted kisses up and down the insides of my thighs. "I thought I'd never be able to do this again." He spoke as if this was what he lived for as he parted my lips and went to licking on my clit. I now had both hands on his head, encouraging him on.

"Kyron . . . " I moaned. "You've got a girl."

"She ain't you."

"This has to . . . ssstop . . . oh, this feels good." I spread my legs wider as he ate my pussy as if he hadn't eaten a meal in months. I came real quick. My towel came open, and now there I was, butt naked lying on the table in front of Kyron. He stopped eating my pussy to admire my nakedness. I was ready to fuck. I felt high. I felt dizzy. I was on fire.

I leaned forward and began unbuttoning his vest. He smirked. "You ready to fuck big daddy now, huh." He placed one of my nipples in his mouth and sucked it just the way I liked it.

"You gotta drug a bitch to get the pussy? What's wrong with this picture?" I asked him. "I thought you were more of a boss than that."

"I wanted you bad. But would you have given it up willingly?"

"Hell, no . . ."

"Well, you answered your own question." He unzipped his

pants, and I swear, the biggest dick I'd ever seen popped out. It looked as long as my arm. It had to be the drugs. I felt his strong hands grab my ass; as he lifted me up, I grabbed that big monster and put it at my opening, and he eased me down onto the hardest dick I'd ever felt in my life. Again, it had to be the drugs.

We both moaned out loud.

"Fuck me, Kyron! Fuck this pussy real good, and make me know who this pussy belongs to." But in reality, I was doing all the work. He leaned back and stretched his legs out, and I was riding that big dick. I couldn't get enough. "Kyron, fuck me, damn it!" I gritted. He sat up, held me up and still inside, set me on the table. He raised both my legs up and went to fucking me. Fucking me good and hard. I was taking the dick like a champ, but still, I couldn't get enough.

He pulled out. "I'm about to nut."

"I don't care, nigga. You came here to fuck me, so fuck me!" He sat down and went to eating my pussy. I couldn't come for shit, and it was driving me insane. "Give me the dick, Kyron, I need the dick." He stopped and looked up at me, mouth glazed with my juices. He yanked me up, turned me around, and he went deep into my pussy from the rear. I heard the food tray hit the floor as I grabbed onto the table. Finally, he had found my spot. "That's it, nigga! My spot! Punish my spot!"

"Like this?"

"Just give me the dick, nigga! Punish this pussy."

He was going all in, and it was good as fuck. I was loving every stroke, trying not to climb across the table.

Finally, I felt that first wave. My orgasm was coming on good and strong. Kyron kept stroking until he couldn't stroke any more. He pulled out and squirted all over my ass and my back as if I was some ho in the strip club, who had just finished fucking him for twenty dollars. He snatched me up by my hair and stood me up. He was trying to kiss me and went to sucking on my neck.

"You hate me, remember?" I reminded him. My head was spinning.

"I love you, too."

"A bitch like me thinks my clit is made of gold, remember? I'm a ho, remember that?" I reminded him of the shit he had put in his letter to me as he passionately planted kisses on my neck and shoulders. "You'll die over this pussy, won't you?"

He turned me around roughly and set me back on top of the table. He went to kiss my lips, but I turned away. "I want to fuck some more," I heard myself say. I didn't care that his dick was limp. I was still on fire. He picked me up and carried me to the bedroom. As soon as he laid me across the bed, he stripped. The last thing I remembered was him spreading my thighs and telling me how good it felt to be fucking his Shorty again.

I was crouched in the corner, wrapped in a sheet and shivering. I was freezing cold. I wondered why the police and all of these strangers, along with Trae, were standing over me. My ears were popping as if I was up in high altitude or as if I was under water. I could barely hear.

Someone had a blanket and was hovering over me, trying to get me to stand up. I was fighting him off me. "Who do you think you are? Get away from me! I hate you! I'm a ho, remember?" I heard someone say, but it didn't sound like me. I felt a needle pierce my arm, and then everything faded to black.

19

TRAE

My meeting with Mr. Li was bittersweet. Bitter because he said he was standing firm on the fact that he was going to hold me responsible for what happened to his daughter, despite what I told him about her telling me he wanted the meeting. Our business deal was off the table. I thought it was some bullshit, but what could I say? It was sweet for two reasons: first, he hadn't linked the dogs to me, and second, he gave me his word that there was not going to be any retribution against me or my family. That was the number one reason I'd wanted a face-to-face. I needed to look into his eyes.

When I went home and Tasha wasn't there, I checked with my aunt, and she had Tasha's travel itinerary. "So she's not coming back until tomorrow?" I asked her, not wanting to believe that Tasha had taken her ass to Vegas anyway.

"That's what the travel plans say. Don't tell me you're going out there? She's only on a relaxing trip, boy. Damn. Let her be."

"No. She's with her sister, and I haven't heard from her. Something's not right. I can feel it."

"Okay, then. Suit yourself."

I showered, dressed, and headed to Vegas.

As we drove to the hotel, I could only think about how Tasha always had to try me. It was like she got off on that shit.

When the driver pulled up in front of the Bellagio, I spotted Trina strutting in her stilettos going inside. I barely gave the limo time to stop. I jumped out and rushed to reach her. You talking about perfect timing? I had it today.

"Trina!" I called out. When she turned around and saw me, it looked as if she shit on herself and the color drained from her face.

"Trae?"

"That's my name. Why are you looking at me as if you just saw a ghost? What did you do with my wife?"

"I left her in the room. What brings you out here?" She asked me that shit as if I'd bumped into her at the park or the mall.

"My wife. What do you think?" Placing my hand on her shoulder, I led her to get on the elevator. "Take me to Tasha."

"We are not in the main hotel, we are in the villas. Follow me."

"Lead the way." I released her so she could do just that.

Trina was walking, but the bitch wasn't moving fast enough for me. It was if she was stalling. "I know Tasha told you that I didn't want her ass out here. However, once again, I see that you managed to get her tied up in some bullshit. So what y'all been doing?"

"Trae, for your information, it was Stephon's birthday, and your wife hasn't even been out of the room. She's been gettin' her chill on. Me? I've indulged in a little bit of gambling, shopping, and partying. You know how I do."

I didn't respond, because I knew the bitch was lying. I followed Trina, and she stopped at villa number 1711. She fumbled around in her purse for a few seconds and then pulled out her key card and opened the door. "I'll let y'all have a few minutes. I'ma go and check out this little shop that I saw."

Whatever, I thought to myself as I stepped into what looked like a town house. My Berluti's sank into the plush carpet. My eyes darted around as I made my way toward the kitchen. I saw the two empty wine glasses lying on the table. There was a tray of food on the floor, towels on the table. *What the fuck is going on in here?*

I pulled out my hammer as I inspected the rest of the suite. No one seemed to be there. One bedroom door was open, and the other one was closed. I put my ear to the door and didn't hear anything. I eased it open inch by inch as I peered in. The bed was unmade, covers on the floor. I heard sniffling. *Tasha?* The drapes were closed, so I reached for the light switch. What I saw caused my heart to sink and made my knees weak. I slid my hammer back into my waist. Tasha was crouched in a corner, naked. She was twisting her hair with her finger and was mumbling incoherently. She acted as if I wasn't standing there.

"Tasha, why are you down there?" She didn't say anything. I looked closely at the bed, and it was obvious that somebody had been fucking. My stomach flipped.

"Tasha!" I yelled. "Why are you down there?"

"No. No, I didn't." She kept mumbling as her eyes opened and closed.

I opened the closet, and there was fresh linen on the top shelf.

I didn't want to touch anything in the room. I grabbed a blanket and snapped it open. I went over to Tasha, who was shivering, and went to put the blanket around her. She started swinging at me.

"I said no, Kyron! I want you to leave, you said you would leave. Who do you think you are? Get away from me! I hate you! I'm a ho, remember?"

I grabbed her hand and then went for my phone. I dialed 911; I told them where I was, what room, and that my wife had been . . . raped. I dropped the phone and bent down in front of Tasha.

"Tasha, it's me, Trae. Look at me." I tried to hold her face as her head kept falling to the side. "I love you, baby. You're shivering. Let me wrap this blanket around you. It's okay, baby. It's me, Trae."

"Trae?" She cocked her head and looked at me as if it finally registered who I was.

"It's me, Trae. Your husband. I'm here, baby."

"Trae?" She started to cry. "You gotta keep loving me. I didn't do anything," she said as she started to drift. She closed her eyes and then reopened them. "I didn't. I didn't let him kiss me. I told him . . . no."

"It's okay, baby. I love you. I love you more than anything. Stay with me, baby." I patted her face, and her eyes began to flutter.

"I didn't. I swear to God. Do you believe me?"

"I believe you, baby."

"I want to go home," she said as the tears streamed down her face.

"I'ma take you home. Let me get you off the floor, baby." I wrapped the blanket around her and pulled her onto my lap, but she wouldn't stop crying. I held her in my arms, and we sat in the corner until I heard the knock at the door. *That muthafucka is going to feel my wrath.* I couldn't get it through my thick skull that the nigga would stoop this low.

TRINA

As soon as I left Trae, I called Kendrick. I had been hanging out with him ever since I left Kyron in the room. I didn't know and didn't want to know if Kyron was in there, and I definitely wasn't going to stick around to find out.

"Kendrick!"

"What's up?"

"Trae just got here."

"Trae just got where?"

"Here at the hotel. Is Kyron with you, or is he still with Tasha?" I held my breath.

"Nah, he went back to get Mari from the hotel room."

I breathed a sigh of relief. "Mari? You mean he had his bitch with him the whole time? Then what did he want with Tasha?" When he didn't say anything, I said, "Y'all niggas ain't shit!" I hung up. I had lost my appetite and decided to head back to the villa and face the music. If I was lucky enough, they would be in the room with the door shut, fucking, and I could pack my shit and sneak off to the airport.

When I saw the EMS workers, a stretcher, and then Five-O rush through the lobby, I knew something had gone down. I waited for everybody to pass me before I trudged over to the villa.

When I turned the corner, all of the workers were by my door. As I got closer, I saw that they were, in fact, at our spot. "What happened?" I asked no one in particular. I pushed my way through the workers but was stopped by one of the police officers.

"You can't come in here, ma'am."

"I'm staying here. My sister is in there!" I proceeded to move forward.

"Parker, this is the other guest right here," he yelled out.

"Let her in," Parker said.

"Oh, my God! What happened? Tasha?" They were laying my sister on a stretcher.

I looked at Trae, and he mouthed the words, *You are going to pay*. I knew at that moment I was fucked.

"Ma'am, we need to talk to you," one of the officers said. I was immediately whisked into the extra bedroom.

TASHA

The past few days, weeks, months . . . I didn't know time anymore. Everything was a blur. I swear, if it wasn't for Trae being the man I fell in love with, I would be in the loony bin. He got me through this. Kyron had put a date-rape drug into my glass of wine. The after effects seemed more harmful than anything. I could hardly remember shit. I was having cold and hot flashes and constant headaches. I did know that they issued a warrant for Kyron's arrest. Trae wouldn't allow me to press charges against Trina, because he said he had plans for her. Just the thought of him doing something to my sister sank my stomach.

Back at home, when the limo turned onto our street, Trae and I both noticed the unmarked black-tinted Chevys. I snuggled up closer to Trae, not wanting to get out of the car. "They must be here to question me about Vegas," I remarked.

"Nah, that's not Vegas police. And Cali police don't have jurisdiction over Vegas. I believe they are here for me. Remember, I lost the protection of the Li organization."

I leaned away from him and shot him daggers. "I know you're not saying what I think you're saying?"

"I'm sure that they're not here for a social visit."

"Baby, don't let them take you away. Can't you call the Dons? Somebody? Trae, I need you here with me." I felt as if I was having a panic attack, and I grabbed onto him.

"I'll be home as soon as I can." He tried to reassure me, but I wasn't going for it. I held him tighter.

I broke down and cried. "Please, baby. Do something. Don't let them take you." I pleaded with him. This couldn't be happening.

"Tasha, I wish I had that power." We pulled into the driveway, and Angel was coming down the stairs, followed by Kyra and then Kay. "See, you won't be by yourself. Angel and Kyra will be here with you. Tasha, pull yourself together. You know I can't do what I've got to do if I'm worrying about you."

I swear, I was trying to get myself together, but I couldn't. I did not want Trae to leave me. He rolled down the window, and Angel stuck her hand out.

"Tasha, come on. The kids are out back, and Kaylin needs to talk to Trae."

This was real. I fucked up. If I lose Trae, Charli will have gotten the last laugh.

ANGEL

My girls' lives seemed to be crumbling all around me. Kaylin and I traveled from New York to Georgia, Georgia to Cali, back to

New York, back to Cali, handling one crisis after the next. Trae called, and I was thankful that Kaylin and I could be there to offer support. The only bright spot was my excitement for Kyra, who was now pregnant by Rick. She actually seemed happy. And no one has seen her out preaching with her Bible. But now this.

In regards to Jaz and Faheem, since Jaz went out on some rah-rah shit killing spree, they now had to up and move. Faheem said that she had to find a new house, a new school, the whole nine. But come to find out, she wasn't the hitman she thought she was. Faheem was like the puppet master, handling his business, using Jaz to set it all up. She was high up there with her drama, but I still thought Tasha and Trae outdid everyone else. Tasha putting the pit bulls on Trae's Chinese mistress. Now that shit was . . . priceless. And those unmarked cars that were out there all day parked in front of Trae's house, they were for him. I believed that he was about to do some real time. From what I was able to gather, he wanted Don Carlos to step in, but since he switched teams, I didn't know if that was going to happen.

And Kyron committing rape? He had lost his fuckin' mind. But I could say this, it was good that they were picking Trae up, because according to Kaylin, he was at the point of no return. He was going to get Kyron. Hell, I wanted to get him my damn self.

"Baby, we're gonna be all right. Trust me," Trae was telling Tasha. I had to make her get out of the car, because Trae and Kaylin still had to talk while they had the chance. Even though it was almost eighty degrees, she was shivering.

After about twenty minutes, the detectives were getting out of their cars, with their guns and badges drawn.

20

KAYLIN

We finally were back home in New York after spending almost a week out there in Cali making sure that Tasha was all right. We knew all of the particulars in regards to them holding Trae without a bond. He really pissed off the Li organization and now wanted me to go talk to Don Carlos. I had no idea how that would go, because I didn't know the relationship between the two organizations, the Li organization being Asian and Don Carlos being Latino. For real, I couldn't imagine them having anything in common or anything to beef about for that matter. However, Trae was my nigga, and we went hard for each other all of the time. But for now, he was going to have to sit tight.

My first order of business was to catch up with my brother Kyron. Of course, I went to his apartment, and he wasn't there. I slid by Kendrick's; no one was there, either. En route to Kendra's, I changed my mind. I knew he wouldn't be there, and she would only alert him that I was looking for him. Then it hit me. *Swing by Mari's.* She lived all the way up near Poughkeepsie, New York, in this suburb called Cooperstown. I didn't care. My gut was telling me that's where he was. Plus, I needed the drive so that I could clear my head.

I drove for about an hour and a half before pulling into Mari's driveway. I didn't see Kyron's car, but that didn't mean anything. She had a four-car garage in the back of her beautiful two-story brick home perched up on a hill. A perfect place to hide.

I deaded the engine and got out. Even the air was different up top. I made my way up the winding cement stairs and rang the doorbell. When I rang it again, the curtains moved, and then I heard the locks being opened.

"Kaylin! What a surprise." Mari gleamed as she opened the screen door. Then she frowned. "Is everything all right?"

"I'm looking for my brother. Is he here?"

"Yeah, we've been here since we arrived back from our trip to Vegas."

"Oh, you went to Vegas? What y'all do, elope without telling anybody?"

She started laughing. "Yeah, right. You know your brother isn't trying to elope with anybody but some money and the streets. Follow me, we are just chilling in the den, watching the game."

It smelled like she was cooking enchiladas. I followed her through the house. The Spanish artwork and décor were dominant. The ceilings were high, and they matched the marble floors. That was kinda dope. I had never seen that before.

"Looks like you remodeled it since the last time I was here."

"Yes, that was a long, long, long time ago, brother."

"Yeah, you forget that you are always out of the country. What I'ma do? Come over to an empty house?"

She laughed. "Do you like it?" She spun around slowly on her tippy-toes.

"It's nice. Real nice."

"Kay, don't just say that to be nice. I want the truth." Her hands were on her hips as she glared at me.

"Seriously, I like it. After I talk to my brother, can I get the grand tour?"

"Definitely." She beamed.

We walked down the stairs into the den. No marble there, only plush white carpet. "I guess you want me to strip now."

"Ha ha ha. No, just lose the boots," Mari told me. And she stood there until I took them off.

Kyron was sitting in a big leather recliner. "Uh-oh! Look who took the drive way out here. Something tells me this ain't a social call. Can Mari get you something to eat? Something to drink?"

"Nah, I'm good." I watched as Mari disappeared up the steps.

My brother didn't even bother to get up and greet me. "Have a seat. What's up?" He got straight to it.

"That's what I'm trying to find out. You know you have an arrest warrant for rape?"

"Rape?" He started laughing. "I know you ain't falling for that bullshit."

"Not if Tasha wasn't involved."

"Here you go. Whose side are you on, bruh?"

"When it comes to family, I'm on the right side, and Tasha is family."

"Man, get outta here with that bullshit. Tasha ain't blood, nigga.

You keep forgetting who I am, Kay. I got work to do. Nigga, I'm untouchable. You better talk to Don Carlos."

"Does Don Carlos know that you are going around raping the wife of one of the family members?"

"What I do is my business. Not the Don's and definitely not yours. And Trae is a traitor. He jumped ship, remember? Don Carlos ain't tryna hear that shit."

"Rape, Kyron. What about the rape?"

"I didn't rape her."

"What do you call it, then?"

"You got me fucked up, bruh."

"What do you call slippin' a date rape drug into somebody's drink and fucking her?" I stood up, ready to punch my brother in the face.

"You can see yourself out. And as long as you stay faithful to that traitor-ass nigga, we ain't got shit between us," Kyron said, not even bothering to look up. "Whatever we had between us, we lost it a long time ago. From this day forward, you are dead to me."

"Fine, nigga. Just know that I ain't through dealing with you."

"See yourself out."

I put my boots back on and looked over at my brother. His eyes were glued to the game. I was not finished with him. I reached the top of the stairs, and Mari was standing there with tears in her eyes. Apparently, she hadn't made it too far and was eavesdropping. I tried to force a smile. "I'm outta here, Ma. I'll take that tour another time. I'll let myself out." She didn't say a word to me. Instead, she headed for Kyron.

"Kyron, what the fuck is your brother talking about?"

"He ain't talking about nothing," I heard Kyron say.

I made it to the car already knowing what needed to be done.

TASHA

I was trying my damndest to block out my time with Kyron. But I couldn't. I remembered every detail vividly up to him laying me across the bed. Afterward everything faded to black. After that, I recall lying in a hospital bed, looking up at Trae and a nurse who started explaining to me what was in a rape kit.

I felt guilt. Betrayal. More guilt. More guilt. More guilt. I remembered fucking Kyron and enjoying it. I could have stopped him, but I didn't.

"Tasha." Kyra was right up in my face. We were in the waiting area at the private jail called CCA, waiting to get called in to see Trae.

"What?"

"You're doing it again," Kyra said to me in a sing-songy voice.

"Doing what?" I snapped

"Blacking out. Spacing out."

I looked around, embarrassed, wondering if anyone else was watching me the way Kyra was.

"What's the matter with you? You want to talk about it?"

"No, I don't want to talk about it. But since you want to talk about something, what was the matter with you? You were going around toting your Bible, banging on doors, standing in front of shopping centers, preaching hellfire to anyone who would listen."

"Bitch, please. You're taking shit all out of proportion."

"Ask Marva. I kid you not. You don't recall any of that? Look at you now. One minute you're calling me a bitch, the next you're preaching to me from the good book."

Kyra thought about it for a minute and then said, "I do, but not to that extreme. Having been in a coma, I know my head is a little fucked up. I probably do a lot of shit that I don't understand why I'm doing it."

"Isn't that scary?" I asked her.

"Scary? Yeah, it's scary. But I guess it is even scarier watching me do that shit."

"Very. I started to commit you to an institution."

"You what?" She looked at me with squinted eyes and a wrinkled brow.

"You heard me. I was getting ready to put your ass away."

"That's fucked up, Tasha. I wouldn't do you like that." She shook her head, looking at me with disappointment. I started to say something, but before I could, we heard keys and laughter.

"Macklin!" the guard yelled out. I still couldn't believe that Trae was in custody. Thank God we had money. Benny was able to get him moved from the county jail to a private holding facility in Santa Barbara. The only thing I didn't like was the two-hour drive there and the two-hour drive back. That was too much driving for me. Especially taking the kids. They were talking about a speedy trial, but Benny was fighting hard and was trying to make sure it didn't get that far.

"Come on, trick," I said to Kyra. She wanted to come with me so she could talk to Trae. Ever since she seemed to be back to her old self, she was saying that she needed to talk to him.

We went through the usual searching procedures and then were led into the visiting area, which was outside. The weather was simply beautiful. Trae was standing there waiting for us, wearing a pair of jeans and a white tee. This was definitely a country club. I promised myself I would be strong and not break down and act like a spoiled brat.

"Babeee," I cooed as I pulled him in for my hug. I missed him so much.

"I miss you," he whispered.

"I miss you more."

"Everybody all right? The kids? Marva?"

"Waiting on you to walk through the front door. How about you?"

"Missing y'all." He hugged me tighter.

"I feel so bad that you're in here."

"Hey, stop that. You promised me, remember? We're in this together. You felt that you had to do what you had to do, so did I, and now we have to deal with it. Am I right?"

I nodded, but my heart wasn't in it. I wanted my husband and king home where he could rule his castle. But that was looking like it wasn't going to happen.

KYRA

This wasn't a jail. It was a country club. We were seated right behind the tennis court. The grounds were neatly manicured, they had the grills going, a playground for the children. Hell, I was ready to kick off my sandals and take me a nice stroll.

I had to laugh when Tasha told me how weird I was acting. I laughed on the outside, but on the inside, I was crying. It was embarrassing and frightening. What if it happened again? What if when I was having one of my episodes and something happened to me? It was scary, because I didn't even remember being in front of the supermarket with my Bible or going from door to door preaching. And preaching what? What the fuck? I didn't want to tell my doctor; hell, she might commit me her damn self. I couldn't take the meds that she prescribed because of the baby. It was the baby, Aisha, and Rick who made me smile on the inside.

My attention went back to Trae and Tasha standing there hugging. Talking about a couple determined to weather the storm? No, fuck that, those two would survive a tsunami. I was convinced.

But shit was crazy in all of our lives. I was worried about Tasha. Tasha was worried about me. We were worried about Jaz. Angel was worried about all of us. What happened to our picture-perfect relationships? When we got involved with our men, we thought they were leaving all of their baggage in the streets and they were starting over with a clean slate, two kids, and a house with a white picket fence. That was simply not our reality. We were obviously looking through rose-colored glasses. Life was subject to change at any given moment. Obviously there was no such thing as perfection in life. We had to learn to enjoy and love our imperfect loves and lives while we had them. We couldn't know how long it would all last.

"So what's up with you, Kyra?" I was so lost in thought that I didn't even know how long Trae was standing there in front of me. "What's up? How are you doing?"

I smiled. "How are *you* doing? I miss you around the house, runnin' thangs."

He laughed. "I miss being there."

"Can we take a walk?" I asked, and stood up.

"Sure. What's up?" We started walking around the yard.

"I need to talk to you. Get some answers to some questions that won't leave my mind. But . . . at the same time, I'm not sure if I want the answers."

"Well, if you don't want the answers, don't ask," he told me.

"Maybe I will. Maybe I won't. But if I ask, promise me you will tell me the truth. Okay?"

"All right. What's on your mind?"

"Is that a promise?"

"I promise."

I took a deep breath. *Do I really want to know this?* Lately, I had been thinking about him a lot. A whole lot. "Marvin. Did you kill him?" There. I got it out. My eyes were glued to Trae's facial expression. I was looking for any signs to confirm his answer. He didn't look at me. He kept looking straight ahead.

"Does it matter?" he finally answered.

"Yes, Trae, it does."

"Why?"

I thought about it. My *why*. But I couldn't come up with an answer.

Sensing that I wasn't going to say anything, Trae started talking. "It killed me to see how bad Tasha was hurting. We hadn't heard from you or Aisha. And then, when we did hear from Aisha and she said that you were dead, I knew he had something to do with it. I went for him, but he was already got."

Trae is lying.

We continued to walk in circles around the yard in silence. I was trying to figure out if I wanted to dig deeper by pressing the issue a little more or let it go. I didn't know.

"You aiight?" Trae asked me.

"I guess so. But I do need to thank you, Trae, for being there for Aisha. I know that you and Tasha have been going through your own problems, but still, you provided her with a stable family. She is so happy, and I will always love y'all for that." We stopped walking, and I gave him a big hug.

"No thanks needed. I would do it all over again," he said, releasing me so we could continue our walk.

"Next question. What did you think about me when you found out I was pregnant?"

"Is that what you wanted?"

I laughed. "I wanted Rick."

"Do you have him?"

"I don't know. Not really. I hope so. I feel like I should be the one to have him. I do know that I'm not going to walk away without putting up a damned good fight."

Trae was quiet. It made me wonder if I sounded stupid to him. My thoughts went back to Marvin. "Marvin. He loved me, Trae."

"I know he did."

"He loved his family."

"There is no doubt in my mind."

"But I was falling out of love with him, and that's what started all of this madness between us."

"You stopped loving him because of Rick? Or because of him being other than himself, on drugs?"

I didn't want to answer that question. "He loved me, but he left me for dead. How did he die?" That question flew out of my mouth but I wasn't sure if I really wanted the answer.

"Gunshot. I thought that you knew."

"I don't think I wanted to know."

Trae nodded slightly and continued to walk.

"So . . . did you stop loving Marv because of Rick? Or because of him strung out on dope?"

"It was both." The words left my mouth, and the reality of them sank into my heart. I began to feel like I had betrayed Marvin. My emotions were beginning to take over, so I figured I didn't need to say anything else about that subject. "Trae, it appears that we are all crumbling to pieces and at the same time. I don't understand it. Why do things have to go downhill? Why can't life keep getting better?"

He smiled. "Hard trials purify. It may appear that we are going downhill, but if we all stick it out, we will be all right. Only the strong survive. I know that sounds like bullshit, but it is what it is. We either hold up or fold up."

"Simple as that?" I asked him.

"Simple as that."

TASHA

That was a much-needed visit, for all three of us. I was glad to see Trae, and he was ecstatic to see me. Kyra seemed totally revitalized. I didn't know what all she and Trae talked about, but it was obviously what she needed. She seemed whole again and ready to be able to withstand anything. I just had to see how she'd hold up if Rick decided to stay with Nina. That would be the real test.

I had a doctor's appointment the next day which I was not looking forward to. I took a home pregnancy test, and it was positive. I was petrified at the thought of having to tell Trae. I was with him the night before my trip to Vegas. And then with Kyron two days later. Whose baby was I carrying this time?

21

ANGEL

"Baby, it's almost three thirty, are you ready yet?" I stuck my head into Kaylin's office. We had been there in the studio since six thirty that morning, and I was ready to go home.

"Come in, I want you to listen to this." I reluctantly went in and sat down in the chair in front of his desk. I was ready to go, not to listen to another guy trying to rap. He hit the speaker button, and it went into his voice mail. "Listen to this."

"Dad, it's me, Jahara. I got a proposition for you. Can you buy me the new iPhone 5? Ummm, you can cancel my piano lessons or my gymnastics lessons. Whichever one equals to the iPhone 5, but don't answer right now. We can discuss it when we go to the mall this Saturday. Love you. And oh, Daddy, don't tell Mommy about this. This is our business."

Kaylin thought it was cute. I thought otherwise.

"I'ma beat her ass! What is she talking about, don't tell Mommy?

254

And she's not quitting piano or gymnastics! And an iPhone 5? She's only six! What—oh, my God! She's growing up so fast. She's making me feel like I'm getting old."

Kaylin burst out laughing. "You may be getting old, but not me, I'm getting younger and better."

"Baby, our daughter is talking about an iPhone 5 and making propositions. Soon she'll be asking to borrow the car. I was just changing her Pampers, Kaylin."

"I know how to remedy that!"

"Don't even think about it! I am not having another one anytime soon. So get that out of your big little head."

"Think about it, Angel. Don't you think you need to get it out of the way?"

"Oh, like Tasha?" *Damn.* I'd let that one slip. I had just spoken with her, and she told me she was pregnant again, and just her luck, she didn't know who it belonged to.

"Really? She's pregnant again? I think that you need to follow her example. She's getting 'em all over and done with."

"Don't say anything, Kaylin! She is scared to death to tell Trae."

"She hasn't told him?"

"No, she hasn't. She just found out. Plus, she doesn't know if it's Trae's or Kyron's. So can you blame her? Mentally, she has to be a total wreck. I can't even imagine what's going through her head right now. So you and me, we need to stay out of it. Let her and Trae deal with this the best way they can. This is too delicate for us to pry."

"Damn," Kaylin mumbled.

"That was really fucked up what Kyron did. What he slipped into her drink could have killed my girl." I looked at Kaylin, waiting on a response. Lately, I'd noticed that whenever I mentioned Kyron's name, Kay would shut down. Which could only mean that he was up to something. I just didn't know what. On the one hand, I wanted to know, but on the other, I didn't, because I knew Kaylin, and brother or not, it was going to be ugly.

"Come on, let's get out of here." Kaylin stood up and grabbed his keys.

See what I mean? He shut down at the mention of Kyron's name.

"I've been ready since noon. Let's bounce. I haven't been out of the building at all today." I reminded him.

I followed Kaylin as he performed his end-of-the-day ritual, which was making his final rounds of the office, with the studio his last stop.

"Yo, Kay, I need to holla at you," his new producer, Heart Throb, yelled out.

"I'm outta here, man, you should've hollered at me earlier. I've been here in the office since the break of dawn. How long you here for? I may swing through later on tonight."

"I'm waiting on E. She's on her way."

Kaylin looked at his watch. "She's late."

"Ayyy, I'm just the producer." He picked up his drink and made a toast to the air.

I grabbed Kaylin's hand, ready to go. He got the hint. "So you coming back later?" I wanted to know. Because I wasn't. I dragged him towards the elevators.

"I might, depends on how I feel. Why? You got something for me to get into?" He licked his lips looking me up and down.

"Always."

"Well, that ain't gonna take all night," he teased, throwing his arm around my neck and kissing me on the neck.

"You don't know that." I wrapped my arm around his waist, and we stepped onto the elevators and rode down, locked in a kiss. When it stopped, we stepped out onto the bottom level of the garage.

"Don't make a scene, just walk with us," a voice barked. At first, I was thinking that he wasn't talking to us. But when I turned around to see three dudes in what looked like janitor uniforms, I tried to remain calm. These niggas had rolled up on us with guns. We were about to get jacked.

"Yo, son, tell your wife to keep going. You have to come with us," the light-skinned one ordered.

What the fuck? How does he know I'm the wife? I thought as I held Kaylin tighter. I studied their faces and was glad that they were dumb enough not to have them covered up.

"What? Y'all here to rob me?" Kaylin calmly asked them.

"Nah, homey. We just need you to go with us." They kept the guns pointed at us.

"Aiight. But just make sure you let my wife go."

"Let your wife go? I already told you we are here for you, not her."

I held Kaylin that much tighter. He looked at the two goons standing in front of him, and I peeked at the one who was directly behind us.

"Baby, go ahead home. I'll be there later."

I panicked. "No!" I blurted out. "If they take you, they gotta take me, too." I balled up a fistful of his shirt. If they wanted me to turn him loose, they were going to have to cut my arm off.

"Babe, go ahead." He was stern, and his whole demeanor changed, but I didn't care.

"Yeah, babe." One of the goons in front mocked him as he went to grab me. Kaylin blocked him.

Wahida Clark

"Don't touch my wife!" Kaylin hissed. *Splat!* The goon smacked Kaylin, slammed him in the face with his gun. I was now scared to death but even more determined not to leave.

"Man, the next time you use your hands for anything, I'm releasing one in you," the one with the YMCMB fitted cap threatened.

"That's what you're going to have to do, because I don't let muthafuckas put their hands on my wife."

"I'm not leaving my husband."

"Red!" Kaylin gritted at me.

"Kaylin, I'm not leaving you."

The goon in front of me got in my face. "Lady, don't be stupid. Turn your man loose. I'm not gonna say it again."

"I'm not saying it again, either. I'm not turning him loose."

"Red, c'mon, now." Kay was trying to get me to turn him loose.

"Baby, no. Please don't make me go." I was more petrified of leaving Kaylin's side than of the three guns.

Then the goon in the front grabbed me by my arm, and all hell broke loose. We started scrappin'. The three of them against us, with Kaylin trying to use his body to block me. We were having a good run until we both ended up on the ground with cocked barrels pressed up against our temples and another one pressed up against our foreheads. But guess what? I was still holding onto Kaylin's shirt.

"Y'all muthafuckas gonna have to shoot me!" I yelled out, all out of breath, hoping that someone around would hear me.

"Man, fuck this, look how much time we wasted! Rock this bitch to sleep," the angriest out of all three of them said. "Boss man ain't say nothing about no bitch, so we can get two for one since she ride or die."

"Shit, let her go, because we need to get the fuck outta here. Look how much time we already wasted! Get him in the car, and pop the trunk," the one wearing the YMCMB cap said.

The goon in back of me punched my arm, causing me to let go of Kaylin. The other two forced him into the backseat, and YMCMB dragged me to the back of the car. He popped the trunk. "You wanted to go, right?" He picked my ass up as if I only weighed five pounds and threw me into the trunk, slamming it shut. I smelled gas, and it felt like I was lying on top of shovels and brooms.

"Why the fuck y'all gotta take her?" I heard Kaylin ask. His voice was muffled, and I strained to hear whatever else I could. I felt something crawl on me.

Damn, what the hell was I thinking?

LIL' E

I was on my way to the studio, hoping to put the finishing touches on this new song. I was anxious for my boss, Kay to hear it. "Yo—" I was bent down in my car, peeking over the dashboard with the phone glued to my ear, not wanting to believe what I was seeing. It was some shit that I only rapped about.

"Where you at? Time is money!" Heart Throb, who was producing about half of my next album, yelled out.

"Yo, I just left the garage—"

"You just left? You need to get your ass up here in the studio."

"Throb, they got Boss Man. I saw them, and they threw Boss Lady in the trunk. I saw it!"

"Who? What the fuck are you talking about?"

"Throb, they're in a black sedan! They gotta be New Yorkers

because they got New York plates. I'm following them. I'm about to call the police, so I gotta go." I hung up and dialed 911 as I followed the black sedan. They were flying. I had to speed to keep up.

"Nine-one-one, is this an emergency?"

"Yes, it is! I just saw my boss get shoved into a black sedan and his wife thrown into the trunk. The kidnappers had guns!"

"Where are they now?"

"In the car! Didn't you hear what I just said? I'm following them!"

"Ma'am, can you see the license plates?"

"Yes. They have New York tags, H47-2499."

"I have that, ma'am. Thank you. Now, you said a black sedan?"

"Yes, a black sedan! I'm looking right at it. Hurry up! It looks like they are headed for the George Washington Bridge."

"Ma'am, we have it from here. It is too dangerous for you to be following them. We will take it from here."

"How can you take it from here? Where's the police? I don't see any police around, and yes, we're headed for the bridge! If something happens to my bosses . . . I'ma make sure you lose this job. They record these calls," I threatened the operator.

"Ma'am!"

I hung up and dialed 911 again. We were going over the George Washington Bridge heading for Jersey. Fuck the NYPD! I needed to get the Jersey police on the line. "Damn it!" I found myself experiencing road rage. A car jumped in front of me, and I dropped my cell phone. I was weaving in and out of traffic.

"Nine-one-one. Nine-one-one, hello."

"Hello! Don't hang up!" I yelled. "I dropped my phone! Please don't hang up. Give me a minute. It's an emergency. There has been a kidnapping, and they had guns."

I was feeling all down the sides of the seats for my phone while trying to watch the road. I was way beyond frustrated. I slammed on the brakes, almost ramming into the car in front of me. The traffic slowed a little bit. I damn near did gymnastics reaching on the floor for my cell while driving.

"I got it! I got it! Are you still there?"

"Ma'am, I'm here." This time, it was a man.

"My name is Lily Penzera, and my bosses where kidnapped by gunpoint. They are in a black sedan, license plate H47-2499 NY. We are on the George Washington Bridge. This is my second time calling."

"How many suspects in the sedan, ma'am?"

"Three gunmen, my boss Kaylin Santos, and his wife Angel Santos."

"Are you on the bridge going to New Jersey or into New York?"

"New Jersey. Hurry! I'm trying not to lose them."

"You are not supposed to be following them, ma'am. We will take it from here."

I lost it. "I am not fucking hanging up or stopping following until I see a police car. What if I lose them—"

"Ma'am. Please."

"What if I lose them?"

"You are not supposed to be following them."

"Fuck you!" I would die if I lost them. I had to keep up. I owed it to Bossman. He saved my life literally and to took me off of the streets. He was like a father to me. I could pull out my strap and shoot at them but what if they crashed? What if I fucked it up? It was a chance I had to take.

KAYLIN

I couldn't believe what had just happened. There I was in the backseat with two guns on me, and Angel was back there in the trunk. I was kicking myself for not being strapped. Sometimes, I allowed this legit shit to take me off of my square. From listening and watching these lames, I thought their motive was robbery, but then I got the impression that they were going to kill me. But when the one named Herb was on the phone, I got the impression that he was talking to my brother, Kyron.

"Yo, it's me, Herb. Yeah, I got him. We picked them up as they stepped into the garage. Yeah. I checked his waist. He didn't have his hammer on him. His wife wouldn't leave him. We had to bring her. Huh, I ain't saying too much. Hello. Hello?"

"Nigga, he hung up on you because you *was* saying too much," YMCMB cap said. His name was Knowledge.

My guess was that Kyron was mad because I checked him about raping Tasha and put him on blast in front of Mari, so now he was in retaliation mode. The nigga was officially crazy. I knew one thing for sure, I was taking a burner from one of these muthafuckas. I wasn't going out without taking at least one of these niggas with me.

"So where we going? Let me speak to my brother right quick. Get him back on the phone," I said to Herb, just to see if I could get him to confirm my hunch.

"Too late for that."

"Why? I need to talk to him."

"Shut up, fool!" Knowledge said.

Damn. So Kyron was gettin' grimy with it. Then my thoughts went to Red back there in the trunk. "Y'all can do whatever with me, but I'ma need y'all to let my wife go. I know my brother didn't say anything about my wife." Nobody responded to me.

After we came off the GW going into Jersey, we took the exit that said *The Ridgefields* and drove for miles until we came up on a graveyard. *I'll be damned.* We pulled into the graveyard and drove around a circle and made a left. The car came to a stop. Herb, who was in the front, got out of the car. The two goons in the back with me made me get out with my hands behind my head. I seized the opportunity and swung around, trying to grab a burner. Both of the fools pounced on me as if I had stolen something.

"Chill! Chill!" Herb barked. "Keep him alive, niggas!"

They laid me face down on the ground and tied my wrists behind my back. I felt helpless. I looked up, and when the trunk came open, Angel popped up, swinging a crow bar. The dude slammed the trunk on her head. She screamed out. I was hoping that they hadn't killed my baby.

"Fuckin' bitch!" He spat.

They dragged me over to a grave. "You see what this tombstone says? 'Betrayal is worse than slaughter.' Think about that, son."

I looked close, and it damn sure said those words. My brother actually went through the trouble of getting a headstone made. They pushed me down into the already-dug hole. I fell head-first into a wooden coffin. I groaned. It was fucked up for me both physically and mentally. My own brother wanted to bury me alive.

"Kaylin! Where are you? Kaylin! Kaylin!" I heard Angel yelling out. They finally brought her over to the hole that I was in, and she was kicking and screaming. The angry nigga was trying to throw her in, but she wasn't having it. Finally, he succeeded, and she came crashing on top of me, damn near crushing my ribs. There we were, looking at each other face-to-face.

"Owww," she screamed out in pain.

"Red, hurry up. Untie me! These niggas are getting ready to bury us alive! We gotta get out of here." As soon as I said that, the muthafuckas had the nerve to take the top of the coffin and lower it on top of us. We were crammed together, barely able to move. Angel was feeling under me, struggling to untie me.

"This is some bullshit! Who dug this deep-ass hole? We gonna be in here all night tryna fill this bitch up," I heard Knowledge say. "Just shoot 'em, and let's bounce."

"If we shoot 'em, we still gotta cover them up, you dummy. And the instructions were to bury him alive," Herb said. "And fool, you was supposed to fill up the coffin!"

"With what? Two bodies and dirt can't fit in that little box." Knowledge spat.

"This is still some bullshit," the high-yellow brother said. I never got his name. "Just throw the dirt on it. The dirt will weigh it down. Them niggas ain't going anywhere if they tied up. I'm hungry, shit."

With the sound of every thump hitting the wood coffin, a knot formed in my throat. It was nauseating. Red began to sob quietly as the weight of the dirt heightened the pressure of the closed coffin. Her body began to shake with fear but she was still struggling to untie me. She was having a hard time working under my body weight. I could feel her beginning to panic.

"Stay focused baby. You can do this."

"I can't."

"Yes, you can. I can feel it loosening up."

"But I can't."

"Red, focus!" She was finally able to loosen up the rope, and I wiggled my wrists free.

"Babe, stop crying. I told you to take your stubborn ass back inside. But no! You said, 'I love my man! I'ma ride or die!'" I tried to make light of the situation.

"Forget you, Kaylin!" She released a slight chuckle but kept on crying. "What are we going to do, now?" She whispered.

"I'm thinking, babe. I'm thinking." I got serious and the only thing I could do was say what I was feeling. "I love you more than life itself. And you made mines worth living. Baby, I have no regrets."

I could feel her beginning to shake again. She began to panic. "No, not like this! We can't die like this!" She was raising her voice.

"Red, calm down, baby. I need you to stay calm," I said, trying not to panic my damn self. Because the reality of the situation was beginning to set in. You could hear the dirt being tossed on top of the coffin.

"I can't . . . I'm scared, Kay. Not like this! We can't go out like this!" She started squirming around.

"Red! Stop that!"

"Tell me we are gonna make it out of this. Just tell me we are gonna make it!" she cried.

I wanted to say, *I got this. We are going to be okay. I'll get us out of this*. But I couldn't. I couldn't bring myself to utter those words, and it was killing me. I felt like I had died already, realizing that I had no way of getting us out of this situation.

Red had stopped sobbing, anticipating my response. My mind went blank. The only thing I could blurt out was, "I love you, baby. If this is the way we are gonna go, I'll rest in peace knowing that I'm lying here with you. Sorry, baby, that's all your man got."

Once again, her tears began to wet my face as she kissed my lips. "I love you, too."

Silently, I began to pray.

"You hear that?" Red asked. "I hear sirens."

"Babe, I don't hear shit but them niggas up there and dirt slamming down on top and around us."

"I hear them!" Red was starting to get delusional.

The dirt stopped coming.

Those niggas must have heard the sirens, too. "Yo, Herb, you think they coming here? They sound like they mighty close." I heard those words vaguely.

"I'm not going to stay here and find out. We can come back and finish this later. They can't climb out. Let's bounce."

The sirens were getting closer. But were they coming for us? We heard car doors slam, the engine crank up, and tires screech away.

22

TASHA

I was gaining weight and experiencing morning sickness, which was, in my warped mind, confirmation that this was Trae's baby. With his babies, the morning sickness damn near killed me. When I was pregnant by Kyron, I had no problems. My stomach was getting pudgy, but I had decided it would be best to hide it as long as I could. The hardest part was hiding it from Aunt Marva, since she was always around the house. Kyra was so caught up in her little world, I could be ready to deliver, and she would never know the difference. When I would go visit Trae, I would throw on a pair of Spanks and tight jeans.

The last visit, I had brought a cell phone for Trae. I left it exactly where this guard they called Dirty Harry told me to.

Now I was sitting in the waiting room ready to go in, when Benny came and sat down beside me. He startled me. "Benny? What are you doing here?"

"I've been here since seven this morning. Come walk with me. I need some fresh air."

"They are getting ready to call my name, Benny!"

"No, I don't think so. Come on, and take a walk with me."

Oookay. Something wasn't right. I stood and began walking to catch up with Benny. "Is something going on that I should know about?"

He waited until we got outside away from everybody before he spoke. "They are getting ready to transfer Trae out of this country club and send him to the county lockup."

"Why? What did he do?"

"He allegedly killed a guy."

"He did what? Why? Is he okay?"

"The guard Dirty Harry, who everybody uses for their contraband, got busted. So this guy was talking shit to Trae, telling him it was his fault and that his woman was the cause, yadda yadda yadda. They exchanged words, he threatened Trae, they got into it, and Trae allegedly strangled him with his bare hands."

This was a little bit too much for me to handle. "Benny. So what does this mean?"

"It means that he has a brand-new murder charge, but of course, he argues self-defense."

"I gotta go talk to Trae." I turned around to leave.

"I doubt they will let you in," he called out.

I kept walking. I needed to see my husband. Another murder charge? He had me fucked up! Here I was, pregnant with three kids at home. I needed his ass out here. We both fucked up, yes. But he didn't need to go and fuck up some more.

KAYLIN

What a night! Red and I didn't leave the police station until about seven thirty that next morning. Once we left there, we had to get Angel's head looked at. Thank god it was just bruised. After the doctor cleaned and wrapped it, we were on our way home.

While driving, I couldn't help but reflect on how if E, our artist, hadn't seen them put us in that car, we would have been fucked. Hell, as far as we were concerned, we were gone. As I lay in that fuckin' box, pitch-black, with Red on top of me, there was no doubt in my mind that it was over. I couldn't see her face but could feel the tears rolling down her cheeks. The sound of her voice cracking as she said, "I love you." The way she said it was as if it was the last time those words would ever leave those sweet lips. I couldn't even give her a comforting hug, because my hands were tied. That was the moment when, as a man, my pride kicked in. Hell, my ego was totally crushed as I lay helpless, not able to do shit to rescue my wife. I had failed. I had failed as a husband and a father, and I got mad as fuck. All I could do at that point was pray. "Lord, if you get me out of this situation . . . I don't know how you can do it, but if you get me out, I'm gonna kill that nigga, and that's my word on my seed." That was a hell of a prayer to pray, but that's what was in my heart.

Jahara spent the night at my moms', and we decided it would be best to let her stay over there for now. Plus, I didn't want to be around Mama Santos. Once she started asking questions, it would be hard to sit there and be in her face. It was very hard to lie to Mama Santos. I couldn't tell her that her own son, our flesh and blood, had tried to bury me alive.

As soon as we got into the house, we both rushed to hit the water. I scrubbed from head to toe. I had dirt in my eyes, ears, nose, fingernails . . . everywhere. After we cleaned up, we jumped into the bed. Angel curled up under me, and I could hear her sniffling. I didn't say anything. That was an experience that we would never forget. I didn't even think anyone would believe what happened to us. In a weird way, I was glad that we experienced that together. It made our bond that much tighter.

"We almost lost our lives today, Kaylin."

"Yeah, but you could have avoided the whole situation. That was some dumb shit that you did out there. You should have left when the opportunity presented itself. Jahara could have lost both of her parents. What were you thinking?"

"What do you think I was thinking? I wasn't going to leave you. I wouldn't be able to live with myself, remembering how I left you and remembering the last time I saw you. You were being shoved into the backseat of a car. Either way, I was damned."

"Angel, don't you ever do that shit again. The only thing I'll allow you to do is get into a car and follow me. I couldn't have been able to rest in peace, knowing that I was the cause of your death. Plus, our daughter needs you."

"Allow me? Allow me?" She sat up.

"Yes, allow. I'm thinking about our daughter, Angel."

"Well, our daughter needs her father, and I need my husband." She started bawling. "Why are you making me choose? Our vows said 'till death do us part.' I can't live without you, Kaylin. There is no way in that situation I would have been able to choose."

I didn't know what to say. All I could do was hold her tight. I tried to look at it from her point of view, but I wasn't seeing it.

"They're gonna come after us again, aren't they?" she asked me.

"Not if I go after them first."

"Baby, what have you been hiding from me? Who are they?"

"Nobody. Don't worry about it. I'm just venting, that's all."

"No, you're not, Kaylin. I know you better than that. You know exactly who was behind this. And you're going to tell me. Kaylin, you can't be around me twenty-four/seven. If the enemy is coming my way, I need to be able to identify him. Don't leave me out here like this."

She was right, but I didn't want to tell her just yet. "Red, you're worrying about the wrong shit."

"Oh, am I? You know what? Forget it."

My wife jumped up, snatching all of the covers off of the bed, and stormed out of the bedroom. I couldn't bring myself to tell her that my own brother was the one who had sentenced us to death.

TRAE

"Macklin! You have a visitor."

I turned away from the small window that allowed me to see the sunlight and walked over to the steel door. "Do I have to get cuffed up?"

"Just leg irons. In case you haven't noticed, you are in the hole now. So they are mandatory."

"Aiight, Officer Smart Ass." The door popped open, and Officer Smart Ass motioned for me to turn around. I didn't understand why I needed cuffs on my legs and not on my wrists. Where the fuck was I going to run? To the other end of the tier? He put them on and motioned for me to step out of the cell. I walked down the hall to the small room that housed the window visits and sat in the first booth. Tasha was heading toward me. I picked up the black phone, wiped it against my jumper, and placed it to my ear. Tasha picked up hers and wiped it down with a Clorox wipe.

"From the look on your face, I gather that Benny filled you in."

"You gathered right, mister. Seriously, Trae, a new murder charge? And the county jail? You know what? It doesn't even matter, because I'm not bringing your sons to see you at some damn, filthy county jail. I made sure Benny found you someplace decent where you could be comfortable and you wouldn't have to get into trouble," Tasha ranted.

"Get into trouble? Tasha, this shit ain't grade school. And even though that spot was laid-back, it was still a jail, and it still had niggas in it. And niggas are gonna try you. If I got put in that same situation again, I would do it again."

"Then you know what? You're gonna do this shit by yourself. Call me at the house!"

"What do you mean, call you at the house?"

"Just what I said." She stood up. "You think this shit is fuckin' cute? I told you, I'm not doing county time. Call me at the house." She slammed the phone down and walked out. Spoiled bitch.

KAYLIN

Almost two weeks since the graveyard incident, but here I was. I was alive. Edgy, but I was alive.

It took me a few days to get in touch with Don Carlos, but obviously, I had perfect timing. He was vacationing out in Santa Barbara at the Bacara Resort and invited me to come out. I saw this as the perfect opportunity to snatch up my ten-year-old son, Malik, Jahara and Red. I had to admit, that near-death incident was a wakeup call. Life can be cut short at any time. So enjoy it while you can. Make it count. Relish every moment with those you care about the most.

Angel and the kids were somewhere on the beach. Don Carlos and I were strolling past the flower-filled gardens on our way to the 12,000-bottle wine cellar. Don Carlos was one Latino boss who loved his wines and knew them well.

The Santa Ynez Mountains were breathtaking. Seventy-two degrees in October got no complaints from me. This was perfect weather. The crystal-clean air had me feeling like a brand-new man.

I looked over at Don Carlos. Mama Santos said he reminded her of the actor, Danny Trejo, just taller.

"Kaylin, you gentlemen are like sons to me. You know that, don't you?"

"Yes, I do."

"You were always the most level-headed out of everybody, and for you to come bringing me this news lets me know that no one is no longer in control."

"That's not true, Don Carlos, that's why I'm here. I wanted to let you know what moves I wanted to make before I made them. If you give me your blessings and your guidance, you will see that everything will remain under control. I just need you to hear me out." The warm breeze was blowing the scent of a salty Pacific Ocean, tickling my nostrils. I made a mental note to bring Mama Santos out here for a little rest and relaxation, even if I had to drag her.

"I'm listening," Don Carlos said, interrupting my thoughts.

"Let me start with my brother Kyron. He was recently charged with rape."

"Rape?" Don Carlos retorted. "You know that is against the rules."

"Of course, I do. But he told me that because of you, he was untouchable. He slipped something into a drink that belonged to Trae's wife and did whatever he wanted to do to her. When I confronted him about it, he felt I was betraying him by taking sides with Trae. He then sent his men after me, took my wife and me to a graveyard to have us buried alive."

"He touched another man's wife?" Don Carlos raised his voice slightly. I could tell that he didn't like the sound of that, even though I thought Trae had told him when it first happened. He paused for a moment, then asked. "And bury you and your wife alive? Why are you still here?"

"One of my artists saw us being taken away, followed us, and called the police. They found us right as the dirt was being tossed on top of us."

"Ay-yi-yi, Kaylin, if I didn't know that you were an honest and loyal man, I would think that you were making this up."

"I wish I was making this up, Don Carlos. Now back to Trae."

"Trae! Trae! My hardest-working hot-headed one. He really disappointed me, going over to the Li organization after he kept telling me he wanted out."

"Let me explain."

"He should be here explaining on his own behalf."

"He's incarcerated right now."

"Kaylin Santos, you bring me more problems in one day than I have had to deal with all year."

"Yes, but when I find a solution to a problem, it always is to your benefit, Don Carlos."

"Thank heavens for that, Kaylin. My old heart can only take but so much."

"I must admit, Trae went over to the Li organization because of greed, yes. But Mr. Li's daughter, who has a thing for Trae, made it all possible. Without her, he wouldn't have been able to penetrate their walls. Trae was working on something to benefit us all. But he has a situation where his fingerprints showed up at the wrong place, and he was charged with murder. Mr. Li offered to have those charges removed in exchange for him working for the organization. Trae agreed, but when Mr. Li's daughter got hurt, he blamed Trae and dismissed him from the organization."

"And let me guess. He takes back everything that he offered."

"Yes, Don Carlos."

"He should have come to me."

"I know. But Trae is now back in jail, and while he was in, he got into a scuffle and killed a man. Hear me out, Don Carlos." I raised my hand to stop him from speaking. I knew that he was getting ready to go in on Trae. "A new murder charge that I'm sure we can beat using self-defense, so I'm not worried about that. And I can handle my brother, but I need you to talk to Mr. Li. Get him to lift that figure up off Trae's head."

Even though Mr. Li had told Trae that no harm would come to him and his family, he still sent someone to take Trae out, right there behind the wall. He was not a man of his word. And I had a big problem with that. It was now personal to me.

"Don Carlos, I need you to stop the hit now. Trae shared some info with me. You get him to lift the hit, and we can put a dent in the Li organization."

"A dent? What do you mean?"

"Trae was able to gather some very pertinent intelligence. Again, it would be to your benefit and also mine and my family's. Trae is sure that if you go to him, it's going to come with a price, and that price is putting his team to work. Li likes how Trae gets down. And that's when he can put the intelligence he has to use, using me."

I stopped Don Carlos in his tracks and faced him. I'd known this man for almost half of my lifetime. Kyron introduced Trae and me to Don Carlos after we had been coppin' weight from one of his people, Freddie Pinta. When Freddie got busted, we stepped in and took over, and we never looked back.

Don Carlos had always granted me everything I asked of him, but to my surprise, he said, "I'll get back with you. This news you brought me has worked my brain to the point of fatigue. Come, let us enjoy some wine."

"But Don Carlos, we obviously don't have much time. It may already be too late."

"Then there is nothing we can do about it, is there? Come. Let us enjoy."

KYRON

"I can't do this anymore, Papi." Mari sighed as she slid off my dick and climbed up off of me.

"What's your problem?"

"You're fucking me but thinking about her, aren't you?"

"What?"

"Get out, Kyron. When I come out of the bathroom, I want you gone. The disrespect is never going to stop as long as I allow it. You took me to Vegas, Kyron, but when you came back into the room, I could smell her all over you. But this here . . . this is the last straw. Get out!" She stormed off to the bathroom and slammed the door.

Bitches always gotta find a reason to trip. I wasn't even thinking about Tasha. Do I wish it was her pussy that I was fucking? Yeah, but my mind was on Kaylin. I hadn't heard from him since I tried to kill his ass. What a lucky nigga! The surprise element was ruined by some nosy muthafucka. You gotta be careful doing dirty these days because it's always somebody not minding their own fuckin' business.

I glanced at my Patek Philippe. I had to meet up with Kendrick, so I wasn't planning on sticking around anyway. She was the one who wanted some dick. Shit, actually, I was running late. I jumped up, got dressed, and was out.

When I got into my ride, I saw my brother Kay get out of a yellow cab. Talking about thinking a nigga up. He came over to the passenger side and got in. "My little punk-ass brother, why are you riding in a cab way out here?"

"I had to see you." He leaned over, grabbed me, and hugged me. My brother got in the passenger side giving me a hug. I didn't know if this was the hug from Judas or not. I checked my hip for my hammer just in case. But I went with it. "I was just about to go holla at Kendrick." I stared into his eyes to see what he felt about Kendrick. I didn't know if he knew or not if Kendrick was in on my plot in Vegas.

He shrugged his shoulders, "I'm game. Plus I needed to holla at you about some money." We rode to the city choppin' it up. Kay was telling me about how his money was all tied up in the record company. And how he had to loan Trae some bread for his money issues. I was happy to hear my brother wanted to get back in the trenches. Even though I didn't trust him I still would welcome him back to the game with open arms. I know he didn't need any money from me. Trae neither. They both were stacked.

We ended up having dinner, just like old times. My ass had a little too much to drink. Combined with the weed I was high as hell. On the way back out to Mari's I had to piss and since Kaylin was knocked out, I pulled off the road right quick. I had to find a spot, since these honkies out here will lock you up for anything. I walked behind the building, pissing as if I would never stop. I never heard Kaylin's footsteps. This nigga had the gun pressed against the back of my head.

"So, this is how it ends." I turned slowly to face him. He cocked the hammer.

"Betrayal is worse than slaughter" he repeated the words off the headstone. Tears rolled down his face.

After I was done I looked him in his eyes, murder was the only thing I saw.

"You pussy!" I spat. "You a true bitch even in my last moments, I'll go to hell thinking of what a bitch of a brother you—"

My words were cut off with the blast, the .45's bark echoed into the night. That shit lifted me off my feet, knocking me against the wall and onto the ground. I struggled to breathe, holding my chest. He leaned down. I didn't know what he was doing. I hawked blood and spit right into his face. He put his hand over my mouth preventing me from breathing. I kicked and squirmed. My brother laughed.

"Now you see how me and my wife felt laying in that coffin. You are the bitch and you let miniscule situations cloud your judgment. You couldn't leave well enough alone, you just kept coming. Funny, I had this dream for some time now but I never knew how it would end. I can rest in peace, knowing that I am the one who sent you to hell. I love you big brother. Always did."

23

KAYLIN

I had taken Kyron's car to the chop shop where Bo was waiting on me. Once his body was discovered, all hell broke loose. Mari was the first to call me, and as soon as she could, she went over to my mother's house. Then, of course, Kendra and Kendrick were next, making a special trip, rushing over to my spot to interrogate me. My mother then sent a message for me to come over to see her as soon as possible. The three of us headed over there together.

Kendra, Kendrick, and I were in my mother's basement, and of course, all fingers were pointing at Trae. "Trae is locked up, so it couldn't have been him." I told them. I looked over at the twins, wearing my game face.

"That don't mean shit." Kendra's ass snapped, interrupting the thoughts of Kyron's and my last minutes together. My brother talked shit right up to his last breath.

"He's locked up, dummy! And as far as we know, Mari could have done it. Y'all sleeping on her; she knew about him and Tasha and all about that Vegas stunt."

"What Vegas stunt?" Kendra asked.

"Nah, Mari wouldn't have done that," Kendrick interrupted.

"What Vegas stunt?" Kendra wanted to know.

"Oh, this nigga didn't tell you?" I pointed over at Kendrick. I had his ass now. Kendra thought that her twin brother's shit didn't stink. "They all went to Vegas, including Mari, and Kyron gets with Tasha, drugs and rapes her. He ends up catching a case. A rape case."

"He what?" She looked at Kendrick with disgust.

"It wasn't like that," Kendrick lied.

"Yes, it was, Kendrick and you was in on that shit." I said. "But I'm through talking about it. Let yourselves out. I gotta go talk to my moms." I got up and left them sitting on the couch.

The only person who knew that I did the deed was Bo. He was Trae's first cousin and had come up with us, hustled and warred with us and I trusted him with my life. If anyone suspected it, that's all they had. I knew my secret would never leave his lips.

I went upstairs to see my moms. She was in the living room talking with the funeral director. She told me that she wanted to get it over as soon as possible, but I told her I was on top of that.

"Ma, I told you I would take care of everything."

She gave me the *stay in a child's place, shut up, I have company* look. "Excuse me, Mr. Holcomb. Then she turned to me and said, "This is Mr. Holcomb of Holcomb's Funeral Home. He was just leaving. But Mr. Holcomb, you remember my youngest son, Kaylin."

Mr. Holcomb stood up; he resembled George Jefferson. He may not have remembered me, but I remembered him. My father took my brother and me to his funeral home on several occasions. Mr. Holcomb would sit us down in his office and give us some ice cream, and my father and he would go to the next room and conduct business. My dad ran the streets and died in the streets.

"I do, Mama Santos." He held out his hand, and I shook it. "You might not remember me, but your daddy and I go way back. He used to bring you and your brother to the other funeral home over on 129th. I'ma make sure we have a good homecoming for your brother. I owe it to your father and your mother. Your brother, he's in these hands, which means good hands." He held both hands out, smiling from ear to ear.

"Thank you, Mr. Holcomb." I showed him to the door. "Has my mother paid you for your services yet?"

"Nooo! Your mother's money is no good with me. If I took money from your mother, your daddy would turn over in his grave."

"Give me your card," I told him. He went inside his vest pocket and came out with a business card.

"Call me anytime. I'm available around the clock."

"I appreciate it." I showed him out and went back inside to talk to my mother. She was in the kitchen cooking dinner.

"Ma, a free funeral? You know all he is going to do is throw that shit together. Is that what you want? I told you I would handle it."

"And you can. You can pick out everything except for his suit. I already let Mr. Holcomb know. Now, sit down. That girl Mari was by here." She let out a sigh. I braced myself. "She said that

281

Kyron raped Trae's wife. Kay, tell me why on earth would that girl say such a thing? What is the matter with her?"

"Ma, she's just angry with him, that's all."

"Who did this to your brother?"

"Mom, I wish I could tell you that. Kyron was not himself when he came home. He was stirring up a lot of trouble, making lots of enemies. It could have been anybody."

"You wish you could tell me? What does that mean? You know, but you can't tell me, or you don't know?"

"Mom, stop it."

"Well, tell me this. Do you think Trae did it because he wasn't able to finish him off at the hospital? And don't lie to me."

Damn. I had to choose my words and the way I said them carefully. "No, Mom. Trae wasn't trying to kill him; he wanted to scare him. He has enough trouble of his own. I've been meaning to tell you, he's in jail for two murders out there in California. So trust me when I tell you, he has his hands full. He doesn't even have a bond."

"Oh, my God!" She put the lid on the pot and grabbed her heart. "You boys . . . it seems like it's all catching up to you. I feared that it would happen like this. I honestly believed that I would never have to bury any of my three children. But I'm getting ready to bury my firstborn."

She grabbed a seat at the kitchen table, said a prayer, and then began to cry.

ANGEL

Kaylin had been running around with Mama Santos, getting everything together for Kyron's funeral. I saw it in him. He was numb throughout the whole thing, just going through the motions. He didn't even want to talk about it, which only made me think that he had something to do with his own brother's murder. I saw it in his demeanor.

The funeral was small and personal, with not more than twenty people. Nothing elaborate, and I was wondering where Kyron's friends were. Hell, he obviously didn't have any, because the few of us who were there were close family members. The twins, his sister Tamara, Mama Santos, Mari, her parents, and a gentleman who looked just like her. I was assuming that it was her brother.

The music coming from the organist was the only thing that was easing the tension and coldness in the air. Mama Santos had the pastor of her church, Reverend Mateo, deliver the eulogy. A few members from the church came out to pay their respects.

Kyron lay up there with a smirk on his face, wearing a pink silk tie and and gray pin-striped Armani suit. Mari stood over the gaudy burgundy casket with the gentlemen who could be her brother. The only people I saw shed a tear were her, Kendra, and Tamara. Hell, I only saw two flower arrangements. What a way to be sent home. No love at all.

After the funeral, I put in a day and a half at the office and then headed out to Cali. I needed some sunshine and a change of atmosphere. When I walked into the house, I was in for a big surprise. There sat all of my girls: Kyra, Tasha, and Jaz.

"Well, well, well!" I said as I set my luggage down. They all got up, and we engaged in a group hug.

"We honestly have to stop meeting like this," I told them.

"Meeting like what?" Kyra asked.

"Y'all know that lately ain't nothing going down in our lives but drama. Let's keep it real, now. And we can start with my drama." I kicked off my shoes, and everybody around me moaned and groaned. "What y'all trying to say? Y'all don't think I got drama?" I stood in the middle of the floor, with my hands on my hips. "We just buried Kyron."

"Girl, please. That ain't no drama. That's cause for celebration. Nobody cares about his crazy ass!" Jaz said as she brought the glass of wine to her mouth.

I looked over at Tasha, and she had a blank look on her face. "I agree. You need to do better than that," she said.

"Do you know that Kyron sent his goons after Kaylin? They took us to a graveyard way out in North Jersey somewhere, tossed us in it, and tried to bury us alive!"

"What?" There were gasps from everybody. All eyes were on me. I told them bitches I had drama.

"Umm-hmmm. If it wasn't for Lil' E being in that garage when they ran up on us, I would not be standing here right now. Y'all would be burying Kaylin and me, that is, if you would have found our bodies."

"You mean to say Kyron would do that to his own brother and his sister-in-law?" Tasha was obviously into her feelings. "That's low-down. But you can best believe that I am personally glad that the nigga is dead. If it wasn't for my respect for Mama Santos I would have went to the funeral and spit on his ass. I hate him!"

"I feel you. He did it. He tried to have us killed. Now that was a moment."

"That's fucked up!" Kyra said.

"Why does he hate his brother and Trae so much?" Tasha asked me.

"I don't know. Kaylin won't talk to me about it. But from the little bit I gathered from his sister Tamara, it was jealousy. Simple as that."

I looked around the room at everyone's face. We were all perplexed. Each one of us caught up in the thoughts of the many tragedies that had fallen into our lives. We had loved and lost. Everything we said we would not be we had become. The mood was becoming gloomier by the second. I walked over and plopped down next to Kyra. I needed the mood in the room to lighten up. That's why I was here. I needed to spread some good cheer.

"Look at your stomach, Kyra! You are glowing," I told her.

"Yes, I am very much pregnant. Thirteen weeks, to be exact." She smiled and rubbed her stomach.

"You look happy. Are you happy?" I wanted to know.

"Actually, I am."

I turned my attention to Jaz. "So, Ms. Thing, how are you and Faheem making out?"

"I might be moving back to Jersey," she announced. "I'm looking at the medical school at Robert Wood Johnson. Georgia is history. We are just about done packing. I've been trying to tell Faheem that he is overreacting and that we don't have to move, but he won't listen to me."

"Shit, the hell he is overreacting! You sleep on niggas if you want to. Trust me, I know. You see what just happened to us, and that was flesh and blood seeking to hurt us. So imagine what someone outside of family will do," I told her.

Our attention turned to the front door. Someone was banging hard. We all rushed to see who was banging as if they were the Po Po. When we got to the front door, we saw that's exactly who it was, the Po Po. I opened the door.

"Oh, shit," Jaz mumbled. "What done happened now?"

"Mrs. Tasha Macklin?"

"Yes? How can I help you?"

My name is Detective Clyde Allen. I'm with the L.A. County Police Department. Do you have a relative named Trina—"

"Yes, I do," she cut him off.

"Are you next of kin?"

"That's my sister, why?" Tasha grabbed her chest.

"We need you to come identify the body."

"Identify what? Why? What happened?" I could see her other hand begin to shake.

"Can you come with us now?" Mr. Allen asked her.

Tasha turned around and looked at all of us. Her eyes were tearing up fast, and her whole body was shaking. Even though we heard what they just said, she announced it again with her voice trembling. "It's Trina. Oh, God! They want me to identify her—" She started to say something, but then she fainted, sliding down the wall. We all rushed to her side.

The detective stood there, looking in through the screen door. "Do you need me to call an ambulance?" he asked.

"I don't know," I answered. Kyra had already rushed off to get a damp towel, and Jaz went for her cell phone. "I'm her attorney. Can you give me your card, and we'll get to the coroner's office as soon as we can? It's obvious that we can't leave right now."

He looked at me and then looked at Tasha. He went into his pocket and pulled out a business card. "Call me when you are on your way so I can meet you there. It doesn't matter what time it is. I'm hoping that Mrs. Macklin can answer a few questions."

"I will, and thank you for understanding."

After about a half hour, Tasha was okay and all riled up. She said later for the morgue. She wanted to go by Trina's apartment to do some investigating first. Kyra volunteered to stay home with the kids, and the rest of us piled into the truck and drove over to Trina's. When we arrived, it did appear that the neighborhood had had some excitement. The truck came to a stop, and Tasha dashed out. I was right on her heels.

"Excuse me, excuse me," she said to a young white girl who was carrying a skateboard. "What happened around here?"

"Tragedy. I never saw anything like it. They literally set the girl on fire. She was running through the parking lot, screaming and hollering. Here, look." She pulled out her iPhone, and we formed a circle around her, stretching our necks trying to get a good look.

I'll be damned if she hadn't caught some of the incident on her phone. She must have been upstairs, because the image was far away and aimed downward. And it was Trina. I could tell by her voice. The top part of her body was covered in flames. She was running and releasing blood-curdling screams. We all gasped. Tasha choked up and started crying.

You talking about karma? That was all that I could think about as I noticed that not one person tried to do anything to help Trina. People were running away, and some were just standing there, looking on in awe. Damn, that white chick wasn't the only one recording. I saw several phones raised up, obviously recording. This was going to be a hit on YouTube. Poor Trina kept burning until the fire department and an ambulance showed up.

"This will go viral, watch!" the white chick said.

The next thing we knew, Tasha had snatched the phone out of her hands, slammed it onto the ground, and started stomping on it.

"Hey! Hey!" The girl grabbed Tasha by her hair. "That's my

phone!" Then the poor girl was getting her ass whipped and didn't know why.

"That's my sister!" Tasha was screaming, crying out and kicking the girl. "My sister!"

"How was I supposed to know? That's my phone! I'ma sue your ass!" she yelled from the ground. Her skateboard was rolling away.

Tasha was shaking uncontrollably. We had to drag her to the truck and get out of there before the police came and charged us with assault. "They didn't have to do that! They didn't have to do her like that!" Tasha cried out.

Damn, this appeared to be the year of death for us. Death was all around us. And they say it comes in threes. I didn't see it stopping as I wondered who could have done this to Trina.

24

TRAE

The Los Angeles County Jail was the worst. I had to get out of there. It was like going from the Sheraton to a Motel 6. Tasha was being true to her word. She stopped coming to see me. Benny had been working night and day to get me moved. The only good news there was that it looked like I was going to beat the murder case with the chick, Sabeerah, from Jersey. My print in a burnt-down apartment? Bullshit. But for this new one, they were talking about having a speedy trial. Benny had a fit when I caught this one, but what the fuck was I supposed to do? Just so happened that Dirty Harry got caught bringing a cell phone to me, and he had some other shit on him, that wasn't mines. It could have been anybody's.

This first nigga was poppin' shit, saying my wife fucked it up for everybody. Then, when the nigga threatened to step to my wife, he crossed the line. We got into it, and when I finished with the nigga, he was no longer breathing. That shut all of them other muthafuckas up. All of this over a cell phone. But now this latest development had me stunned. There was another dude who stepped to me, supposedly sent by Li. He said he had a message for me, but I didn't give him the chance to deliver it. Li went back on his word. He put a number on my head right there in the county jail. So, now I was locked down 24/7, sleeping with one eye open, and it was driving me mad.

Time was moving slow as fuck in there for me. But from what I was told, outside it was a whole 'nother game. They buried Kyron, and word on the street was that I took him out. I'm mad that I didn't have the pleasure to do just that. As a matter of fact it depressed me. Kaylin went to Don Carlos, asking him to talk to Mr. Li, and just like I told them it would go down, it did. Mr. Li said he would assist me only if we put in some work for him. I'd been waiting for somebody to get word to me about what happened with that. The agreement put on the table was when they put in the work, I would walk outta here.

Politics and organized crime run this country. I hadn't heard anything about Charli. I didn't know if she was dead or alive. I did know that death had been all around us this year, more so than when I was out there hustlin'. However, nothing surprised me more than when I called home and they said that Trina, Tasha's sister, had been killed; somebody had burned that ass alive. That was some Hollywood shit that made me smile. It reminded me of the movie *New Jack City*. How in the end of the movie, Nino Brown got shot and fell over the banister. Ice-T smiled, put on his shades, and kept it moving. Even through all of the grief that Trina caused her sister, Tasha still took it real hard. The chick was so damn grimy, I was not surprised that she got taken out like that in style. I applauded the nigga that did it. He took some work off my hands.

"Macklin, visit! Let's goooo!"

"Did you say, 'Macklin, visit'?" I was hoping that I wasn't hearing things.

And then I heard it again. "Macklin, you got a visit! Let's go!"

The first cat was an actual officer. The second cat yelling out that I had a visit was an inmate. A certified nut. All he did all day was mimic the officers. "Pill call, chow time, visits!" The joint was an insane asylum, and I was beginning to feel the pressure.

I walked into the visiting area, and to my surprise, who did I see? Kendrick. I thought to myself, *What does this nigga want*? I grabbed a seat and sat down.

We glared at each other for a couple of minutes. I grabbed the phone off the receiver, and he grabbed his.

"What's up, man?" I asked him.

Finally, tears began to stream down his cheeks. "Why, Trae?"

I knew exactly what he was talking about. "I ain't have shit to do with it. I'm in here, nigga. But you know if I was out there, how it would have gone down. There would be no question. You know my work."

"We family, Trae." He looked at me teary-eyed.

I couldn't believe he said that, as I wondered what was going through his mind. I saw Kaylin standing in the cut. I guessed he was allowing Kendrick to say what he had to say. "You kiddin' me, right? Family don't fuck the next man's wife and then rape her."

"I ain't have nothing to do with that."

"Bullshit, Kendrick! You was right there, condoning the shit all along. So fuck Kyron, and fuck you. If I was out, I'd spit on the muthafucka's grave and take your fuckin' head off."

"Yeah, I know how you get down. That's why I handled shit. There is no need for war. I gave Kay my word. So to circumvent that, you did one of mines, and so I did one of yours."

I thought about what he was implying. *Trina.* I started to try to make this dumb nigga see, one more time that I didn't do Kyron, but I knew no matter what I said, he still was going to think I deaded the nigga.

"We even now. All scores are settled." He got up. I sat there numb, because I didn't know if this nigga was gonna come after me when the first opportunity presented itself. His mouth was saying one thing, but his eyes were saying another.

Kaylin banged on the glass. "Stay on your toes, boy! What's up with him?" He nodded toward Kendrick.

"Man, why you bring this nigga to see me?"

"He asked to come, plus we needed the extra muscle."

"You need to talk to him. He told you about Trina?"

"No. What about her?"

I let him think about it for a minute. When it dawned on Kay what I was talking about, he jumped up and went after him. Then Bo jumped into the seat. I let go of a huge smile. I hadn't seen my cousin in a long time. For Kay to have dug him up, and the smile that was glued to his face let me know that it was about to go down. Bo was called on when big things needed to be handled. Bo was a Macklin to the core. I sat up straight and gave him my undivided attention. "What rock did they pull you from out under?" I teased him.

"Yeah, nigga, it's me! 'Bout time y'all coming out of retirement. Y'all vacationing ass negroes! Don't worry about the rock, just know that I'm here. What's good with you, man? I miss your roguish ass."

"Y'all better be getting me the fuck outta here, that's what's good. I don't wear this jail shit well."

"Yeah, well, keep them deadly hands to yourself, then!" He chuckled. "But hell, nah. Fuck that! We Macklins go hard. Ain't shit changed."

"Why you hanging out with that nigga?" I was referring to Kaylin. I was still trying to piece together what they were up to.

"You already know, son. We about to make it do what it do once again. We did that for Li, and that was supposed to get you out, but we see you still here. He obviously ridin' on that slow bus. We went ham on that muthafucka, but you know Kay. Always gotta do things the right way, so we out here to see you, of course, and the big man." I knew he was referring to Don Carlos.

"Y'all saw him already?"

"Yeah, last night."

"What's up?"

"Maaaaaacklin! Time's up!" the officer yelled.

"The big man spoke to the gook. Li wants us to put more work in. That gook loved what we did. He want us permanently. But we got something for that ass!"

"Damn, how soon can I get outta here?"

"Hang tight, nigga! We on it."

Kaylin came back over to where I was. "Everything good, nigga. I got Kendrick. You just be sure to not drop the soap. We out."

"Fuck you, nigga," I said, and laughed as I placed the phone on the hook. As I walked back to my cell, I was actually excited. Them niggas, my niggas, were up to something big. It sounded like they were taking that piece of info I gave them on the Li organization and running with it.

Three days after them niggas came to see me, they moved me to another country-club spot, and Tasha was on her way to see me with the kids. I was amped up. We were all outside in the visiting area, waiting for the visits to come in, and the first group was processed into the yard, but there was no Tasha, Caliph, Kareem, or Shaheem. Then twenty minutes passed, and I grew antsier and antsier. I had yogurt and fruit cups waiting for the boys. Hell, that's all they had, everything else was chips, candy bars, and soda. The second group came in, and Tasha and the boys were the last ones on the line.

Tasha. What the fuck was up with her stomach?

"Daddy! Daddy! Daddy!" Caliph, Shaheem, and Kareem yelled and tackled me at the same time. My eyes were glued to her stomach as she sat down.

"Y'all sure are getting tall. Y'all taking care of your mother?"

"Yes, Daddy," the twins answered.

Caliph simply nodded his head. Then he asked, "Are you coming home today? Mommy said you was coming home."

"I'll be there. Y'all want to play on the swings? Or finger paint?" I was in shock looking at Tasha.

"Both," they all yelled out. I was glad that this spot had all sorts of activities for the kids. The playground had swings, sliding boards, a merry-go-round and a netted tent with the plastic balls. They had outside volunteers to come in and set up a table for arts and crafts and a puppet show. This was almost like being home.

I needed to get them situated and then get back to Tasha. I had to find out what the fuck was up with her. "Get on the swings first. Your mom and I will be over there in a few minutes."

"Yaaayyyy!" They all squealed and took off running.

I couldn't stop staring at Tasha. She got up and came over to me. I couldn't open my mouth to say shit.

She grabbed my hand and placed it on her belly. "Hey, baby."

"Tasha, are you going to tell me what the fuck happened?" I was trying to brace myself for the worst. I was, like, I knew this nigga didn't think for one minute that he was going to have the last laugh from the grave.

"What do you mean, what happened? I'm pregnant, silly. It's a girl. We got us a baby girl!"

"Who is us, Tasha?" I swear I couldn't handle this bullshit. Not again.

"You and me, silly. I had the DNA test, Trae, and it's your baby."

I breathed a sigh of relief.

After Tasha and the kids left, I sat alone with my thoughts. I was happy about Tasha being pregnant with a girl. Hearing that made everything worth it. Wow! A little princess. Wait until my mom heard this. I couldn't help but smile, something that I didn't get to do often.

My thoughts drifted to Kyron and what I had done to him.

I was a man. A black man in a country that was still ruled by white men. In America, even though we had a black president, I had to be my own man. All I really had in this world was my word and what I stood for as a man. What Kyron did went against my manhood. I knew I might have seemed crazy with how I handled the situation, but a man has to do what a man has to to do. I had to defend my woman's honor and my manhood. That's right. You didn't come out of pocket at me and think I was going to roll over and die. I did what men do. I fought for what was mines.

KAYLIN

Over the next couple of weeks, I managed to put everything in motion. The work Bo and I put in for the Li organization added at least six months to our already-plush financial cushions. I saw exactly how Trae got sucked into the organization. I hated to admit it, but I liked the way they got down. They had systems in place. There was no rah-rah bullshit. Everyone knew his role, from the clients all the way up to the top of the ladder.

Their problem was dealing with black people. Our people didn't trust them, and they acted as if we were beneath them. Li needed to give his organization diversity training, because they were throwing a lot of money away. And Li was not allowing just any black man into the organization. He needed Trae, but his daughter getting fucked up had him thinking that he would rather take a loss. So he used me to fill in for Trae, and now he wanted me to stay on board, but that wasn't happening.

For our next order of business, I brought Tasha and the kids back to New York with me. I needed to make sure I had them all close by until Trae was released. I wasn't trusting Li. He was not a man of his word and we needed to make this final move. As luck would have it, Faheem and Jaz also came back to the East Coast. They found a house in Jersey out in Little Falls. Jaz had her sights on attending Robert Wood Johnson Medical School. Faheem was recovering well, and having all of us back together out East, it seemed as if the family was getting stronger. Just about all of the little problems went away, and now I was about to handle the biggest one.

"You know I love you, right?" I said to Angel as we looked into each other's eyes.

"Yes. And I think you just got me pregnant," she said, looking at me like I stole something precious.

"I hope so. And don't be talking shit, either. You heard the reverend, he said, 'honor and obey.'" I kissed her lips and then her stomach before I got up.

"Whatever," she said as she threw the pillow at me.

I went into the bathroom, hopped into the shower, and let the hot, steamy water clear my mind. I then went over my plan one more time carefully, examining each detail. When I emerged, Angel was fast asleep. I got dressed and walked over to her, leaned in, and kissed her forehead. She let out a slight moan and then a light snore. I smiled, walked over to my spot, grabbed my straps, and headed out.

Once I got off the plane, I met up with Rick. I gave him the cash I had for him, a tape and the exact address of where I was meeting Mr. Li. I collected the package he had for me, which was a Glock 40 and then I moved to my designated location. As I stood enjoying the crisp California air, I thought about how far we had come. Trae and I had been to hell and back. We were blessed to get out of the streets for the most part and settle down, and we were looking forward to enjoying life. We had women who loved us, the type that every thug needed. We believed that our matrimony would be lived out happily ever after. However, as fate would have it, there was no justice for a thug.

When the limo pulled up, I took a deep breath and walked up to the curb. There was no turning back. Two Asian gentlemen jumped out, and I was patted down. Once my Glock was removed, I was directed to the backseat. We rode in silence for about thirty minutes. When we pulled up to Mr. Li's office, I braced myself for the work at hand but couldn't help but marvel at the sight before me. It looked to be about eight office buildings, six stories high. The outside was ultramodern, complete with precise, landscaped layouts, glass and marble exteriors, beautiful atrium gardens, fountains, waterfalls surrounded by marble and granite statues. It was not a game. All of this belonged to Li, Hammerstein, and Burke.

I followed my escorts inside the softly lit foyer and was intrigued once again. The walls of the plush leather waiting area displayed artwork that I was sure started at a mil. I was led onto the round glass elevator that took us up to the top floor. When the glass doors slid open, we made our way down the hall to a glass conference room. There were guests already in place mingling. No one came over and introduced himself to me, so I stood in a corner watching everyone interact. The room was filled with men of Asian descent. Each of them appeared the same: calm, cool, and calculating. I could tell that these men were not his workers but his peers. There wasn't a woman in sight.

"Mr. Santos."

I turned toward the direction of the voice. "Mr. Li," I said as I moved toward him. When I got within five feet, I stopped and bowed.

He moved toward me and shook my hand. "Please, I want you to mingle a little bit. Why are you standing here alone?"

"If I may, I would like to speak to you in private," I requested.

"Yes." He turned to his guests and said, "Gentlemen, please continue to make yourselves at home. I shall return with our guest of honor." He motioned for me to come with him, and we exited the room.

Guest of honor?

Once in his private office, I marveled at the cases of swords and expensive jade vases and paintings. "Those are ancient artifacts and have been in my family for generations." He walked over and sat behind his big desk and motioned for me to sit in one of the chairs in front of the desk. "So, Mr. Santos, how may I assist you?"

"We did your work, and you said that you were very satisfied."

"Indeed, I am. I was very impressed. So much so that you are my guest of honor. And again, I want you to remain on board with us. Have you thought about my offer?"

"That's what I need to talk to you about. I'm honored that you even would consider me. But I have to decline. My allegiance is with Don Carlos. He has become like a second father to me. But I came to humbly request that you release my partner, Trae Macklin, of all business ties that he has with your organization. I give you my word that Mr. Macklin is leaving the business for good. He's agreed to leave town and have no future dealings with you or any members of your organization. We are requesting a clean slate and no more ties. With all due respect, Mr. Li, I need you to be a man of your word and let my partner go, free and clear, honoring your word that no harm will come to him or his family."

He paused, took a deep breath, then reached forward and took a cigar from the box directly across from him. "That I cannot do. Not yet," he said, lighting it and taking a deep pull. "However, it surprises me that you would think that it would be that easy to get out of a business that we have put our sweat and blood into . . . literally."

"You said that your honor was all that you had. Yet you don't stand by your word? I'm confused."

"I respect you, Mr. Santos. You are not like Mr. Macklin. You are led by your mind and your spirit. But Mr. Macklin, much like my daughter, can be led by carnal desires."

"What does carnal desire have to do with this? You said if we completed the job for you, my partner would be released. We delivered. And then you asked us to do it again. We did."

"Again, Mr. Santos, I'm amazed that you believe that leaving this lifestyle would be as simple as a verbal request. One would say that if it took blood to enter this business, it will take blood to exit." Those words rolled off his tongue effortlessly, and then he took another pull of his cigar.

"A wise man once said your honor is all that you have. Were those not your words, Mr. Li? Do you not stand by that statement? Are you not a man of your word?"

"Don't lecture me about keeping my word. Did Mr. Macklin keep his word when I told him to stay away from my daughter? Where was the honor in having a man come into your house, do business, and disrespect the head of the household? I've had men killed for lesser transgressions. Your partner should be thanking me for allowing him to see the light of day, Mr. Santos. Wouldn't you agree? Think about it."

I was trying hard to keep a level head. This muthafucka was really pressing his luck. He was going back on his word as if it was nothing and acting as if we were a bunch of pussy-ass muthafuckas. "Mr. Li, man to man, what would you do if you were constantly served pussy on a plate crafted of fine china that you didn't order? Wouldn't you agree that eventually you're going to eat it?"

He chuckled. "Do you think insulting me will help your friend, Mr. Santos?"

"What? You can dish it, but you can't take it? You see, men

like you will milk a nigga until you are done with him and then dispose of the carcass. But you underestimated these niggas. However, I was simply trying to prove a point, especially since we seem to be mixing business with pleasure."

"If that's all you are trying to do, then I don't think there is anything else for us to discuss." As soon as those words left his mouth, the two guards pounced on me and began whipping my ass. I was barely holding my own. When the tallest one pulled out a machete, I was like, *oh shit*.

"Mr. Li, I got something that you want to see!" I yelled out. "Give me one minute."

He simply raised his hand and the two goons let me fall to the floor. It took a minute for me to get up. I stood up wobbling and said, "I want to make you a deal. You like our work, right?" I asked as I pulled out my cell phone.

Mr. Li sat back in his chair with a smirk on his face, waiting to hear what I was about to propose. "This should be entertaining. You people are good at putting on a show."

I set the phone on the table, pulled up a file, and pressed play. I sat down. Mr. Li looked down at the video that was now in progress. His eyes widened, and sweat began to form on his brow. I could see him fidget in his chair. He would have a heart attack if he knew that Trae got this intel from his very own daughter. I was only showing him one meeting of him discussing the takeover of the banking system. I fast forwarded and showed him a meeting of them walking through the plant where they were making the new dope. Once I knew that he got my point, I turned it off.

"That doesn't prove anything."

"I have several meetings in their entirety. What would the government think about you rigging their banking system and partnering with North Korea and Iran?" That shit was over my head. But I had it. And I knew what it was worth.

"You are playing a dangerous game, Mr. Santos. Even though you have nothing."

"And what about this?" I took out a notepad, opened it, and slid it over to him.

When he looked at it and realized what it was, he smashed his fist on the table. His office door came open, and in stepped two of his bodyguards. *Was I going to die right here for getting caught up in Trae's bullshit?* "Where did you get that? That formula belongs to me!"

I pulled the notepad back and placed it inside my jacket. It was do or die at this point. "Mr. Li, you have plenty of workers, business associates, whatever you want to call them. You don't need Trae. So here's my offer. Free my partner, and make a deposit of forty million into this account. The twenty you promised Trae if he put in three years. And twenty for me." I slid a piece of paper across the desk to him. "I gotta give it to you. A drug more addictive than crack cocaine? I don't want this to see the light of day. Leave us the fuck alone. I want both of our families' names to be free and clear. I want us to be untouchable. I see that your word ain't shit, so there are nine of these, in nine different places in the world. The people who have them, all they need is to not hear from me on a certain day at a certain time, and this formula will go viral. Everyone will have it, and you will have so much competition you would have sacrificed all of the research and development time and dollars you put into this. But more important is the video of your meeting. That shit there will get you kicked out of this land of opportunity, if not killed." I glared at him. "Do we have a deal?" I sat waiting for his response.

Mr. Li jumped out of his chair, slammed his fist onto his desk, and yelled, "You want to go to war with me? You are nothing! You think you can come into my house, shut down my operation, and get away with it? You fucking porch monkey! Are you ready to go to war with me?" The veins were popping around his neck, and he was damn near foaming at the mouth, looking at me through glossy eyes. I remained seated and calm, but my heart was pounding. The two guards were posted on each side of me, waiting on the order to finish me off.

"Do we have a deal?"

I asked him again.

"How did Mr. Macklin get that?" He began pacing the floor.

"I don't know. He wouldn't tell me. He said he would only reveal that if he needed to."

Mr. Li walked back and forth in silence for several minutes. I waited. Finally, he said, "I have some stipulations of my own. You have forty-eight hours to leave the state. I don't want you back here, and if I hear anything about you in my backyard, the deal is off. Whatever business we had is done and forgotten. Mr. Santos and Mr. Macklin, you no longer exist."

"I have no problem with that."

"Good." He reached for his phone and made two quick calls, speaking in his native tongue. When he was done, he carefully placed the phone on the receiver. "You have what you wanted. I can only hope that you are a man of your word," he said, now humble and uncertain. "I will have your head in the next life."

I rose to my feet, grabbed my phone, and headed for the door.

"Maybe. Maybe not. But until then, *honor thy thug*, muthafucka."

I was out.

ACKNOWLEDGMENTS

All praise is forever due to the Creator. Book #12!! Who would have thunk it! Yah Yah, love you much. Don't know what I'd do without you. The Staff. Never seen such dedicated folks ever. Love you all. You know who you are, Hasana (wahidaclark. org), Sherry, Brenda, Jennifer, Sabir, Jabaar, Kisha, Hadiyah, Lindsey. My fabulous Street Team. You guys are in a league of your own. Slim and Baby, thank you for allowing me to do me and opening new doors. Cash Money Content Staff, Vernon Brown, Marc Gerald, Molly Derse (the hardest working little lady in publishing), Donna Torrence, Dawnalisa Johnson, Kia Selby, Vickie Charles. To my Editorial Team, you guys Rock!! You guys make my job very challenging and you push me to the limit! We got another New York Times Best Seller on our hands! Al-Nisa Bracey, Intelligent Allah, Maxine Thompson (the backstory police) ☺, Treena Burnette, Erick Gray. Keisha Caldwell, you really, really stepped it up on this project. I am so proud of you. Nuance Art, you are awesome!! I am so proud of you! The cover to this one is superior. Thank you for being my right hand man and traveling partner!!!! Omar of the NYPD, thanks for the input on my murder scene. 'Preciate it. Oh, can't forget my agent, the pitbull in a skirt, Claudia Menza. The WCP authors, you guys rock. Stay on your grind and remember, books don't sell by themselves.

This one goes out to my readers!!!!! I aim to please!! Let's goooooo!

2013 is the year for the Official Queen of Street Literature! Watch for me!

Follow me on twitter @wahidaclark
honorthythug.com
wclarkpublishing.com

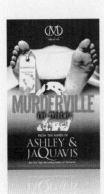

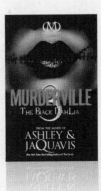

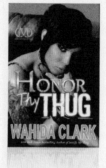

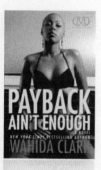